A House of Light and Stone

E.J. Runyon

Inspired Quill Publishing

Published by Inspired Quill: September 2014

First Edition

Portions of two chapters within this novel, in a slightly different form, have appeared previously in another publication as noted: "Secrets of the Days and Nights" And "Dead for a While", both from the short story collection, *Claiming One*, Inspired Quill, 2012

Contact the author through their website: www.ej-runyon.com

Chief Editor: Sara-Jayne Slack

Cover Design by: Venetia Jackson

Paperback ISBN: 978-1-908600-40-0
eBook ISBN: 978-1-908600-41-7
Print Edition
Printed in the United Kingdom
1 2 3 4 5 6 7 8 9 10

Inspired Quill Publishing, UK
Business Reg. No. 7592847
http://www.inspired-quill.com

Dedication

For NCG, who gave me all the art in the world.

For ITV, who didn't stop me from taking it.

In Memory

P.G. and S.C

"I do not tolerate a world emptied of you…. In the dark, I have pored over the loss of you like pale gold."

– Catherynne M. Valente, *Deathless*

Acknowledgements

Grateful does not begin to express my appreciation to Joni Hockert-Waite and Jeff Waite of Halifax, Nova Scotia who, in 2003, offered me a space to write and a room to sleep in while this novel was just getting underway.

Without their patronage and deep friendship this book would not shine as brightly as it does in my heart.

Also, a thank you to the families of my youth for sense memories in bringing the children in this novel to life: Maybelline, Tammy, Wendy, and Danny-Ray, who lived down the street in East L.A.

Chapters

Secrets of the Days
and Nights

THAT CHRISTMAS WHEN I was still ten, there was more than just the big red book from Mr. St. John for me under the tree. Mama gave me a collection of the Brothers Grimm Fairy Tales. And one big, shiny white book about myths for children, by a guy whose last name was Kingsley. That was the best of the two. The myths.

Barbie got a sewing kit in a round blue basket, with a pincushion in the shape of a tomato. And a new pink brush-and-comb set. She wouldn't let me touch it, hissing, "For blonde hair only. *Don't* even think about using it."

Chance got a magician's cape with a top hat and a play wand. Mama was real good with presents when Christmas came around.

Mama invited Mr. St. John, our social worker, this Christmas. He gave us a slim book for the whole family, called The Prophet. Mama was touched. You could see it in her face. My big brother Artie opened that gift up, after Mama read the tag and handed it to him. We all reached for it but he held it up over our heads yelling, "Hold it. I'm doing this. *Pero primero siéntense.* Siddown."

So all us kids sat down in the wrappings and ribbons and then Artie went through the table of contents, reading the chapter titles and whose name Mr. St. John had written next to them. I felt very proud hearing Artie say my name, "On Self-Knowledge. *Duffy.*" Because then he turned to the page and read out from the chapter, "Your hearts know in silence the secrets of the days and the nights…" Justine and Artie both nodded at that. They're the oldest of us five, so I figured maybe later I'd ask them what it was supposed to mean.

Mama's chapter was 'Reason and Passion.' I found that out after, when I got the book to hold and flip through. Artie must have missed it, 'cause he hadn't read that out loud. The drawings were nice, kind of fluffy, but only in one color.

"Duffy. Coffee." Mama said, and I ran to the kitchen to put a pan of water on to boil. Coffee was one of my jobs. You have to use matches to get the burner going. And you have to be sure to blow out the match, then run it under water from the sink, and then you still can't just drop it into the trash. Just in case. So there's lots of steps. But most of the time I was good at it.

I ran back to the Christmas, and Mr. St. John and Mama were on the sofa, laughing over something. Her eyes were bright, and I was glad it was a nice morning with nothing going wrong. Everybody was smiling. Chance kept granting wishes to the girls. "Wishes for ladies!" he called, tossing the cape back over one shoulder. "I got wishes for ladies here." The top hat was too big for his five-year-old head, and only his ears kept it from falling onto his nose.

I scooped up The Prophet and brought it over to Mama. "Mama, here's you," I said, holding out the book to show her the chapter in the list.

While she was reading the title from my hands, Mr. St. John said, "You two have the nicest dark hair." Mama liked that compliment. With Mr. St. John just back from the Peace Corps she thought he'd be a good person for Artie to be around.

Mama said, "Let's see the chapter," and I flipped to it. Holding the book out like a waiter at a table with a steak on a plate. Like they do in the movies. She was still smiling at his comment, and I added, "But Mama's has the coppery red in it."

She couldn't have gotten too far in reading when she reached up and laid her hand on my shoulder; her thumb didn't move much, but the fingers, unseen by Mr. St. John, with her long red nails, they dug into the back of my shoulder. I straightened up. The burning was hard, but I didn't bend at the knees. Didn't cry out. I saw I'd done something wrong, maybe I showed off. So I closed the book and held it on the side she didn't have a grip on. I pulled the book away, unhurried, till it was behind my back. And still she didn't let go.

"Thank you, m'hijita," she said in a low voice. Then she released me and folded her hands in her lap, turning back to Mr. St. John being nice to her.

"Aannnny wish you want…" Chance cried out.

BARBIE YELLED FROM the kitchen, "The coffee water's boiled off again!" And then my knees did tremble. If Mama got mad the Christmas was ruined. But Justine jumped right up, saying, "I got it, Mama." And Mr. St. John, he stood up, too, straight and tall like a hero, "I need some gum. Duff—want to walk with me to the corner store?" And like Cary Grant, he grabbed up his coat and me, and we stepped to the front door.

And just that fast I was outside and safe.

HE DIDN'T NEED me to get any gum, but I was glad for the rescue just the same. The Union Pacific train whistle sounded low and long a few blocks away and I thought of the hobos and the glue sniffers who hung around the tracks. Artie warned us about staying away from them. I figured if Mr. St. John could have a talk with them, maybe they'd all go join the Peace Corps too, so Chance and I could go and find bottles along the tracks to sell. That might make Mama happy, us helping out by bringing her a loaf of bread or a quarter worth of sandwich meat.

Coming out of the corner store, Mr. St. John walked on the outside of the curb, like I was a lady. I thought of something ladylike to say, because I wanted the Peace Corps stuff to rub off on me, too. "Thank you for the book, Mr. St. John."

"Oh, you're welcome, Duff. I'm sure you're going to get a lot from it as time goes by." He smiled down at me from way up high. His sky-blue eyes were still strange to see, here in this neighborhood. Here we were all mostly Mexican. Even the other kids in my family, half-white, all but me, but they didn't have eyes as blue as that.

"Tell me something I don't know?" I asked. It was a game we played whenever he visited. He was the only one who wasn't mad that I'd been skipped up two grades; that was something kids in East L.A. weren't supposed to do.

"Hummm. Look at your hand, Duff. You see these lines?" he asked, pointing to his own hand. "Here? This one and this and this one?"

I looked at mine. "Uh-huh."

"They're very important. That top one's your heart line. That one's your head line." He reached and ran his nail along that second line and my fingers curled. I giggled. He went back to his own palm. "This last one here's your life line; look, see how long and deep that one is? Know why?"

I looked at the deep brown line running off my palm and into my wrist. "'Cause I'm Mexican?"

"Close," he said. "It's because you've got an abundance of energy. You'll be very determined to reach any goal you're questing after."

"—like a lucky charm?" It was a really deep line.

"Sure. That line says you have what it takes to get any-where you aspire to."

Like a lucky charm. Right there in my hand. I'd never drop it. And no one could come take it away.

"Can I ask you something, Mr. St. John?"

"Sure, Duff." We walked slow, and it was nice to not be hurrying.

"When you said to reach any goal I'm questing after. You mean like Theseus and the Minotaur? Through a labyrinth?"

"Sure. That's right, like a Quest. You accept this chal-lenge and you'll be rewarded at the end."

"What challenge?" I asked.

"The one from your chapter in The Prophet; 'On Self-Knowledge.'"

"What'll I get?"

"What do you want, Duff?"

I thought a moment while I concentrated on not stepping on any of the sidewalk cracks. My own Quest, boy!

"To be somebody," I decided.

"You are someone. You're Duffy Chavez. The girl with the lovely dark hair." He swung my arm all playful when he said it, and spun me around like we were headed back to the store, but I stopped walking and got serious in my eyes, so he knew I wasn't goofing around. I needed to be clear. I wanted him to understand. I looked back behind me to my house and then real low I told him: "No, I mean to *be* somebody, to not be invisible."

"Ah." He nodded. "Well, yes. I believe that's a fitting reward."

He didn't make us start walking on again. He put his hand on my shoulder. It really hurt from when Mama had grabbed me.

I waited for the special words of the Challenge, like in the myths. But he was looking far off down our street. Way beyond the brown of Mama's front door. And finally I asked,

"If I accept your challenge can I have that as a prize? Can I end up being somebody?" I looked up into his face.

"Yes, Honey," he said. "With self-knowledge you can definitely be somebody."

"Should I kneel or something?"

He smiled down at me, "No, this is 1965. The New Frontier and all. Very advanced. How about we shake on it?" And he took his hand from my shoulder and held it out to me. I liked it better on my shoulder. Even through the hurt.

"Okay, Mr. St. John. I accept this challenge." I shook his hand real hard.

THAT MORNING AFTER Christmas, when the rest of the house was sleeping, I opened up the Writer's book he'd given me and on that inside page I wrote: "Duffy Pilar Chavez, Age 11, 1966." Even though it was still 1965, and I was going to stay age ten until July came again. And even though "Duffy," a nickname, was my sister's way of saying DeFoe when we'd been babies and either one's a silly name for a girl to have, anyway.

IT WAS THE beginning of January when we heard the news that Mama had found us a new house and we couldn't stay here on Hockert Street any more. She told us over dinner. All five of us at the table and her at the kitchen doorway, standing like she was getting ready to run if we took the news bad. Artie and Justine and Barbie, all blonde and older than me, Chance, the baby, and blonde too. Then me, just Duffy, with the brownest eyes and as jet-black hair as you could get. All looking and waiting for Mama to say more.

She'd made us flank steak tacos with all the toppings in pretty little colored bowls, set out up and down the table, and a big casserole dish of Spanish rice, and some zucchini with melted jack cheese on it for the vegetable. And we had red Kool-Aid, too: Chance's favorite dinner. Mama always made what he liked best, her baby boy. Although Artie, being the oldest of us all, was the champion of eating the most tacos.

"It's a bigger place, a nicer neighborhood." Mama's cough broke into her words, "—no trains." She covered her mouth with the crook of her elbow, then breathed in big to keep talking. "—and I think it's a good move." None of us answered. Mama reached up with the heel of her palm, cigarette pointed up to the ceiling between two fingers, and wiped back a curl off her forehead.

Because Justine was the oldest girl I figured she'd be the first to say something. But no one spoke up. Barbie started in softly tapping the table leg with her foot, till each tap grew into a kick, her blonde bangs jumping. Tick, tick, tock, tock, whap, whap, the noise went, till her short pageboy haircut was doing the same jump around her ears, the noise growing from mild to mean. Justine let out a breath, and Chance asked if anyone was going to eat the last taco.

I reached over to put it on his plate. Justine finally said, "Okay Mama, we'll start packing after dinner." Mama took another drag from her cigarette, ran her finger around the top of her cup, started to say one more thing, then stopped herself; she turned and left us to eat.

After doing the dinner dishes and sweeping the kitchen, we met in the back bedroom, the one with the bunk beds and my rollaway cot. Artie stood us in a row, tall to small, and handed us each two dimes. "If it's a trick and we're gonna be picked up for foster homes again, you keep these dimes," he said. "There's an extra in case you lose one. If they take these away from you, just find some bottles to sell and hide that dime somewheres they won't find. No one's gonna do us like the last time."

We all nodded, except Chance, who'd been born while we were all away those five years. He didn't really know about how it was, except for my stories. He just held his palm up, moving it so his dimes caught light and threw it up onto the ceiling, switching from foot to foot. Artie rested his hand on Chance's shoulder, and then Chance looked up at us, finally listening.

"Anybody tries anything this time, and we'll run to a phone booth and call the cops. Just dial 0 and a lady will help. Got it?" All of us nodded; if the worst came this time, we'd be ready—we had dimes, we wouldn't let it happen again, we had a plan, we'd made a pact.

AFTER THAT WE walked back into the living room and Artie asked if we should take all our stuff or not. Mama frowned at us, a strange look in her eyes—like she'd been fooled by the question. "Of course. We're not leaving anything. Pack it all."

But she might've been lying, and we needed to know for reals. The Foster Homes were still in our minds and she really didn't see what a brave thing it was for Artie to step up and ask.

BUT MR. ST. John, he didn't come the next day with the others to take us away in separate black cars. Like those times before. That was the part I hated the most, seeing Justine kneeling and looking back at me while I did the same from a car going the other way. Me alone in another car riding farther and farther away from the rest.

MAMA WASN'T FOOLING; we really were moving—all of us—to a newer, bigger house; she was taking all of us with her. Even me. The one who got Mama mad all the time. Sometimes, I thought if we were Indian that would be what the tribe would call me: The Mad-Getter.

When we had just moved back in with Mama she would blow up some times. Like a sudden monster you forgot to think about in a TV show. Then she'd line us all up for a punishment—even when only one of us had done something wrong. Like playing so hard something would get broke. "Which one of you idiots is going to be first?" she'd ask.

And I'd always wait a breath; send a word from my mind to the guilty one. But they never moved from the line. So then I'd step forward. Just to be done with it. She hated me doing it that way. Maybe it made her feel bad that we were all idiots all the time. Maybe it was that she liked, really liked, to fight. And I failed her. 'Cause she would get madder and yell, "Dammit—fight with me!" But I couldn't.

So we packed the house up. And we didn't complain or whine, like I think Mama thought we would. She kept walking from room to room, looking in at us, something like confusion in her eyes. With me, when our eyes met we stayed that way for a moment, there was that disappointed look—then she just turned away and I didn't look again.

Mama told us we just needed a truck for the boxes and the washing machine. The furniture was being moved for us. She was nervous when the furniture company came and took all the beds and chests and lamps and the sofa and chairs.

But we'd been moved lots of times before, and this was nothing new. Like Artie always joked, we'd been born into captivity. She was the only one who wasn't used to it. Her and baby Chance.

THE MORNING AFTER the guys in the 1st Street Furniture truck took everything, Mama yelled, "Duffy, come get these milk bottles!" I'd just been thinking how great it was that the store we got the sofa and beds from was kind enough to take our stuff to the next house too, their store's jingle circling and circling under my breath.

We were eating breakfast standing at the counters in the kitchen and Mama waited for me at the front door. She wasn't in a good mood. She'd been fighting with Justine all morning, there was nowhere to sit, and now she was starting in on Artie. She slammed the front door closed as I came near, and she walked back into the kitchen. Yelling more.

I pulled two of the half-gallon bottles from the wood and metal milk crate, and walked back to the kitchen with each of them pulling on my arm sockets. There'd be three other trips to get them all.

"What's this gonna cost me, buster?" she was asking Artie. She'd set to work on making the lunches. Five of them. The boys got a full baloney and cheese sandwich and a full peanut butter-and-jelly one, too. Us girls got the lunchmeat and cheese, but only a half of the peanut butter and jelly. Chance was standing on an old milk crate at the counter, waiting to drop in the apples, one to each lunch bag. The voice on the radio sang 'Trece Treinta! K-W-K-W!' and then the man said, "Ahora, más."

On the last trip through the living room with the last of the milk my fingers gave out, and one of the bottles slipped from my grip and shattered on the wood floor. I froze but couldn't stop myself; I started crying, thinking of the beating that was coming next.

Mama came out and held the other kids back with her outstretched arm, "Artie get a mop. Chance stay out of here, you're barefoot."

I looked up at her; she looked like she wanted to cry, too. "It's okay. Just stand still," and she wasn't mad.

I'd been trying so hard. She reached in and plucked me from the flood and she kept repeating, "It's okay. Only milk. Don't cry." And while Artie mopped and swept up the glass, she leaned against the wall and slid down to sitting with me in her arms, against the wall and out of the huge milk puddle. She held me and the surviving bottle in her lap, and stroked my hair, and softly, in Spanish, she kept saying, "No *estoy ojado.*" It's okay.

THAT NIGHT BEFORE the moving day we spent sleeping on the floor, using clothes and sheets to make lumpy pallets. I told Chance that this was how cowboys slept—out on the range, under the stars. The blue shadows of the empty room and the boxes piled high like far-off mesas helped the story as I whispered it to him. "The cowboys, they get to sing to the cattle, low and soft 'cause it's night and they don't want to wake up any coyotes."

I went on and on about cactus and rattlers and the moon on the hills in the distance, till I could hear his breathing slowing down for sleep. I rolled over and scrunched even closer to him to keep warm. He lifted his head and whispered in my ear, "Duffy, can we be cowboys when we get big?"

"I thought you wanted to dance on the TV."

"Can't we do both?"

ME AND CHANCE sat in the back of a truck, stuffed in between the boxes and the washing machine. Artie whistled as he tied a tarp, flat, over us, wrapping the ropes tight, high up against the truck's fence sides; turning the sky to a circus tent. Though we could see out the sides still. He wiggled his fingers to us and patted the truck's slat-sides. The girls, Barbie and Justine, were up in the cab next to Mama, and then Artie got to driving—tall behind the wheel, even though he was only just past fifteen by a month or two.

The streets slipped past us, and I watched them go from out the back of the truck slats. There was the liquor store Mama sent me running to, to get her cigarettes. The Amigos' Burger where she'd meet us after work each payday, to treat us to hot dogs and soda, all of us each getting to choose anything we wanted from the menu board. It was all getting away—the school, the playground. All of it.

I tried to make each place a story in my brain. Something to hold and remember for my New Year journal. Something to retell Chance late at night. Something saved, because Artie was going to be on the freeway soon headed someplace only he and Mama knew how to get to, going so fast I knew we'd never see any of this again.

"Once, on Hockert Street, I met Mama for the first time," I told Chance. "I was little, as small as you are now."

He hunched his shoulders down and leaned his head in close, to hear me over the rush of the freeway noise. "Were you in kinnergarden like me?"

"No, I got to skip that, you gonna listen? Well, Mama, she was the most beautiful lady I'd ever seen up close. Like a movie star. Like Sophia Loren."

Chance added, "An' she wore a red dress with a big

shiny black leather belt."

"And big black, round earrings, too," I said. "There on the front porch, with the four of us waiting and inside a baby was crying. She took me aside and told me, 'If you're good and you help me with all the others, I'll let you in and you can stay.'"

"An' you peeked in the door to see the noise and saw me asleep, barely a baby, and that's why you're my guardian angel." He nodded. This was one of the "How I Met You" stories I'd told Chance over and over again. He knew most of them by heart. You have to do that coming from Foster Homes. No one else knows if I cried as a baby, or if I was sweet or good, no one ever will. I wanted for Chance to have things different. And from now on I'd have to add the Hockert Street stories to them, too.

The freeway's wind was rushing over our curved backs now, hitting us under the tarp-sky. The force of it keeping us low, wrapped into ourselves: a punishment. And then it came to me all at once, the secret of the days and nights. A new place wasn't just new to whoever moved there. Me and Chance, we were gonna be new too.

The back of my neck tingled with the thought and suddenly that freeway wind wasn't hurting me anymore. It was washing all of my life away. Cleaning me up to any new person I wanted to be once we got to whatever new street Mama had for us. I could pick out the best of me and only be that. I could win the challenge and never drop a bottle of milk again in my whole new life. I could teach Chance to do the same.

I turned my head from the smell of gas around us to his ear, and raised my voice loud over the noise of freeway.

"Once, when we were locked out and it was getting dark, and Mama was still at her job, Artie and Justine were nowhere to be found—"

"An' my stomach was hurting 'cause I was hungry—" Chance added.

"—an' I found a big box and stood on it, I lifted you up on my shoulders, up against the house. Even though your feet wobbled, and you were a-scared and shaking, you were brave. You crawled through the little window up over the bunk beds in the back room. You let us in and saved the day." I never told Chance the part about me not wanting to jump up on the box and climb through the window myself with him below watching: a-scared to do it because he'd see under my dress, that I had dirty underwears on and maybe he'd laugh at me. I was new now; I could change my stories like I wanted. My underwear secret I'd save for the journal.

Chance grinned down into his knees, remembering how he'd saved the day. "We ate the rice from the refrig-alater."

So, I said, "And the moral is, even the smallest have gifts to share."

En Mi Vida Loca

OUR TRUCK TURNED. We began going down a steep hill; so steep that Chance and I were leaning back, nearly crushed by the boxes that slid up against us with the gravity of the hill. Then we turned another corner, so we both got pushed in the other direction. Finally, we came to a stop. We breathed better again once Artie pulled the tarp aside.

The sign on the corner we'd just passed read Elliott Street, and I thought that was good: so many repeating letters, Chance could learn that easy.

With the tarp pulled off we stood to see the new place we were at. Chance and I waited for Mama to come out of the truck, to see which house she walked up to. The one we'd parked in front of, that couldn't be it, that house was giant. Nearly twice as wide as our Hockert Street house. We stood there in front of the brilliant white stucco one, Chance hopping and squirming like he really had to go, after all that pushing and crushing. Around the two arched windows sitting on both sides of a big red door was a cheerful red trim, and the roof was Spanish tile.

Climbing up and along the wall between the driveway and the next house, dazzling red, pink, and magenta flowers grew on tangled green vines. Flowers the colors of party dresses—right there in that pretty front yard. I turned from it, looking across the street. To find the house I thought would be ours.

But it *was* the big white stucco one she walked towards, with a ring of keys in her hand. Mama didn't look to the left or the right, just marched right up to the red door, as though she wasn't uncomfortable about its size or brightness, like I felt.

"*Venga*," she called. And we all followed her up the walk.

Inside, I stood at one living room wall, and then, walking as big as I could across the floor and on through the door to the front bedroom, I counted as I went. I got up to twenty-five steps before I hit the wall in there. Both the living room and the front bedroom had those arched windows I'd seen from the sidewalk, facing all that grass out there on the front lawn, so big that with my arms stretched wide I couldn't touch both sills at the same time.

This house counted one more bedroom than the old house, each of them big as our old back bedroom. I was sure Mama could fit a dresser and bunk beds and a cot in any of them.

There was also an extra room between the kitchen and living room: a dining room, Mama said. "Just like on TV," Barbie sighed. We heard the toilet flush, then Chance came running in, sliding on the wooden floors.

"Mama, I counted, there's seven rooms here—one for each of us plus the bathroom left over!" Mama touched his head, but just kept walking right through to the kitchen. "Duffy, will you choose a room with me?" he begged, pulling at my shirt, "Please?"

"Sure, later." I said; my hands were busy now, Justine had brought in a few boxes. And I followed Mama into the kitchen with one.

She stood at the sink with a box of towels and table-cloths and stared out the window to the backyard. That was bigger, too. And there was a garage out there. And a tree. It didn't have any leaves, but it looked real good for climbing.

My box of loose cups and dishes slipped from my arms, landing heavy on the linoleum. Mama turned; just that quick, she slapped me. I blinked plenty to clear the spots but I didn't cry. That's what you get for being clumsy. She faced that backyard again. Just stood there, still as a statue of Mary, looking out the window, not noticing the racket the others were making through the echoing rooms.

"There's a fruit tree out here," she said, but not to me. "The windows in the front?" She turned then.

"Uh-huh."

"They're called picture windows."

I stopped checking in the box for anything broken, then looked over my shoulder to the living room. "How come?"

She was back to gazing out at the yard and its fruit tree. Her voice aimed at the window over the sink, still talking just for herself. "They edge the view, like a picture frame does—hence, picture windows."

"Oh," I said, "Neat!" thinking of the lawn, the flowers on the green vines. "Picture windows."

Chance yelled from somewhere farther back in the house, and us girls and Mama went running, thinking he'd hurt himself. But he was just there swinging on a door that led out to the yard from the bedroom at the back end of the hallway.

In this way-back bedroom, I leaned against one of the walls, feeling the same bumpy white that the outside wall had. Mama said, "It's an add-on." That made Barbie think of leftovers and she said so, moving on to the next room ahead of everybody else. But most of us in there stayed, still exploring.

You had to step down into this room. It made me feel like the rest of the house wasn't attached to it. I kind of liked that thought, being back here, even if it might be with the boys. I could make believe I lived all alone. My own place. Maybe it was part of the Quest.

The middle bedroom was smaller; Barbie kept stroking the bright yellow flowers on the wallpaper. The walls seemed to glow, Mama said, "Because of the southern exposure." And I saved the words to ask about later, it sounded so sweet. Gentle. Barbie opened the closet door, then the other door that turned out to lead direct to the bathroom. "Yeah!" she said, like the room was already hers. Kind of funny, because all of us were just looking in, not stepping into this one, so maybe it already was.

The front bedroom had no wallpaper, but there was the other picture window. So it was just as sunny; Mama said it would be the last to get the sunset in the afternoons. And we nodded, like, *what a good thing,* since she seemed to think so. You couldn't get into the bath from this one like you could from Barbie's, but Justine told Mama, "That's good for privacy."

I thought with the privacy, Mama would want this room, that Barbie and Justine would share the pretty yellow one. And the boys and me would go in the back, like at the other house.

But Barbie started whining. "How come I never get what I want?" And that was such a big fat lie that no one even bothered rolling their eyes. "It's because I'm in the middle. You hate me."

Then Chance piped in, "I hate yellow. I don't want that other room."

Justine just crossed her arms, glaring. "If she gets a room, I do too."

Sometimes I felt as embarrassed by Justine being all girly and bossy and unfair, as I do all the time with Barbie. And this was one of the times, 'cause they made Mama say, "Well, the way I'm in and out at the jobs I might as well stay on the sofa. It's closer to fall on when I feel like collapsing. Okay, you all work it out for yourselves. But, I'll get my pound of flesh out of this, girls." She pointed, first at Justine then Barbie, "…*en pueden estar seguro de ésto*." And she left it to them to decide.

BARBIE CAME IN with our kitchen radio and plugged it in. Mexican music filled the living room. "*Lo Siento Mi Vida*," was the song someone sang, my sorry life. Mama reached around her and hugged Barbie tight. "Smart move, precious."

Artie's voice came in through the door, echoing into the wide rooms from where he waited out at the curb, yelling from the back of the truck for us monkeys to come get some of these boxes. And all us kids went running. He stood there handing stuff down to us, one after another, us like a line of ants working hard to get it all done before the sun went down there on Elliott Street.

Once Artie wrestled the washing machine down he got back into the truck cab. "Arturo," Mama said, giving him the coins she'd pulled from her jeans, making the sign of the cross on his forehead. She told him which bus he'd need to catch to get back here. "From there you walk down under the bridge, then up, and left here."

Artie nodded and nodded. "Got it." Then he whistled as he jerked the truck into gear, driving it away like a grown-up. We all stood there at the curb a second, next to the washing machine, watching him go till the truck turned to make it up that hill.

Mama bumped the washer with her hip, eyeing us girls. "Push it as far as you can down the driveway—he can bring it in after the truck's dropped off."

"When's the furniture coming, Mama?" Chance asked.

"Never. Now get to work," Mama said, rubbing her forehead as she walked back up to the front door.

Chance laughed, then I did, soon the girls joined in, laughing at Mama's joke while we worked to get the washing machine up the driveway. 'This is Boyle Heights, see?', 'Man! Look how far we hiked from Hockert Street.' Hee-hee. 'So we'll camp out up on this mountain from now on!' and 'Look, I'm a cowboy, snoozing on my saddle!' Ha-ha-ha.

EVEN THOUGH I'M ten and look like eight at the most, Barbie is eleven, and Justine is thirteen, all of us are pretty short, but together we're way more stronger than we look. The three of us managed to get the washing machine up the stairs and in through the back door. Then down the hallway to the little space with the laundry sink, near the kitchen. We hooked it up, then stood back, feeling proud. Grinning.

ONCE THE BOXES were all indoors, Mama sat on the living room floor opening one after the other to see what we'd packed. Telling us, "Bathroom. Girl's room. Kitchen. This stays here. The front closet. Artie's room." Then each of us girls began pushing or pulling the boxes into the rooms she'd called out. Mama sang along to the radio, throwing her head back, crooning with the singers, long and low. Her dark hair, swaying against her neck to the music. The song Chance liked best was *"Besame, querido," kiss me darling;* Chance danced next to her, cha-cha-cha-ing like he was a grown-up lady on TV, his hand up flat to his middle, eyes half shut, head to the side and hips wiggling. Mama smiling and smiling.

We still hadn't settled for sure who'd be in each bedroom. The furniture wasn't here yet. But with the music up loud, Mama singing, Artie heading back, and shadows growing on the walls through the big picture windows, it seemed okay not to know as the sun finally set.

MAMA'S MOOD STAYED good the next morning. She leaned against the kitchen counter waiting for her coffee, reading the job ads from the paper, circling things here and there. I put her coffee cup near her elbow, stretching to read some of them she'd marked. "What's a Girl Friday?"

"Long or short of it?" she asked, puffing on her cigarette.

I jumped up on the counter for a sit. I always asked for long, it kept her talking to me more. But she waited, staring; I wondered if this would be a sad story.

"*Qué* ..." she shrugged. "Okay, this guy, DeFoe, wrote a book called Robinson Crusoe—"

"What's a Crusoe?"

"Ay! You wanna know or not, *mocosa*?" Snot, which was one of her favorites when she liked me.

"Sorry, but wait, real quick. DeFoe? Like my name? How old were you when you read this?"

"I didn't. Someone I knew read it aloud. A…friend, back in college. Read it to us all summer long one year. Just before Artie was born. A while back—*en mi vida loca*—" she trailed off; frowned again into her coffee. She shook her head.

"So, the full title is, like, fifteen words long or something, and in the story the guy—" she stopped to take a sip, and a long, long breath. "—this Robinson Crusoe fellow, he's stranded on this desert island alone and bereft, until he chances on this footprint in the sand. Realizes that he's not alone on his little island, joyous 'cause he meets a native there. And he calls the native Friday; 'cause that's the day he meets him."

The corner of her eyes had turned up talking to me, and I let out my breath. It wasn't that sad after all. She continued telling me all about Friday and the Crusoe, in between making circles on the ads, and drags off her second cigarette. And I thought—that would be a great book to read next, no matter how long the title was.

"Hey, Mama, one more question?" I raised my hand, like in school.

"Okay, one." She nodded, circling another ad.

"If you didn't name me DeFoe, but instead named me for the day you met me what day would I be called?"

"I have no idea. You know your daddy named you—not me. Silly stunt at that. You wanna hear more of this or ask stupid questions of me?"

I risked it, "Stupi—"

She laughed and reached to pinch my cheek, like she does every once in a while when she's feeling really, really good. I squirmed and giggled, knowing what was coming:

"*Ay, m'hijita,*" she said in a love voice, her eyes crinkled up, "you're sooo ugly."

ONCE I FOUND the box that the cleanser and sponges were in, I went to work in the bathroom. In the living room, Chance dragged a milk crate into the corner and Barbie sat Roy's little TV on it. Roy was Mama's newest boyfriend.

Mama said we'd deal with the windows soon enough— for now we'd hang sheets on the two front ones. So that's what we did.

Barbie had opened most of the boxes in the kitchen, and she sat on the floor pointing to drawers and cupboards for where the stuff went that Chance held up for her to see. Then each of us girls started unpacking boxes we'd dragged into the rooms the day before.

From the front door Mama called out, "Wish me luck— be good or else." And we heard it slam.

Barbie right away switched the radio from the Spanish station to KRLA, then turned the volume up even louder. And from all the rooms you could hear us all singing along to the new song. Chance ran from room to room begging to help, but I was the only one who said, "Yeah, sure, you can do this." And gave him the job of finding all the shoes, putting them in a corner. We left Artie's boxes for him to do 'cause sometimes he could be picky about us touching his stuff.

Barbie started in giggling. When she kept it up, higher and higher, me and Chance came out of the back room to see what was so funny—Justine was singing *Unchained Melody* to the front door like it was a guy standing here.

Begging and pleading, her hands on her heart, beseeching it. Like a singer on a TV show.

ALL OF US were feeling pretty happy in this new big house. Nobody fought for most of the whole day. Mama was out looking for work, and maybe that's where Artie was off doing as well. The music was loud like we liked it when there was work to do. Justine turned on the floor heater so the place was toasty. Chance stopped his work and sat on the floor to pull his socks off; it was that warm.

"Duffy, what'll I do when all the shoes are here?" he asked, wiggling his toes.

I kneeled back onto my rear, looking at his pile of shoes so far—most of them didn't fit either of us anymore; I could see that from my side of the room. There were tennies with big holes in the toes, the scuffed-up, white church shoes I wore up till last year when the sole started flapping away from the top.

"Wait till I'm done with this pallet, okay?"

"What else can I do?" he asked, forgetting the shoes that quick.

"Shoes first," I told him, pointing back to the pile. "I'll save all the pillow cases for you to do. Okay?" He nodded, looking around at all the stuff on the floor, then pounced on another shoe for the collection. "You sure are good at that," I told him. "If you keep this up and I get any money maybe I can buy you a present for the good job you always do.

What would you wish for?"

"I have no idea," he said to the pile of stuff—concentrating on his next shoe find. "You know what I like better'n me. What should I want? A toy or a book?"

I knew I'd want to give him a book so I said, "Toy."

I'd learned that from Mama. Gifts are what someone wants not what you want to give them.

Maybe I'd get him a toy *and* a book.

"DOES THIS FIT us?" I asked for the fifteenth time, "No!" Chance yelled. "Into the Goodwill box!" This one I tossed over my shoulder and it just missed going in. So Chance jumped for it, then scrambled back to his pallet to wait for the next one.

"Does *this* fit us?" I asked. Not even straightening up all the way, my hand on my bent knee. My chest was hurting. I don't have good blood in my veins.

"No!" Chance yelled, already on his knees to scramble—since my aim's really rotten from the front or behind. I tossed it; he scrambled, yelling again, "*In*to the Box!"

"MAMA AND ARTIE'RE back!" Barbie yelled from the kitchen. Chance ran off like a shot. I tossed the rest of the old shoes into the Goodwill box, pushing it into the corner where the pile of shoes had started.

Chance dragged Mama down the hallway to come see the work we'd done with the shoes. Artie came back with them too.

I told him real quick, "We left your boxes alone—but I made you a better pallet."

"See, Mama? I got up all the shoes and we made a

Goodwill box."

"What'd you think?" I sat down on my own pallet. "Mama, Chance thought up the Goodwill box all by himself."

"Nah. We thought it together, Duff."

She was thinking other things, 'cause her eyes weren't looking around at the cleaned-up space. But she said, "Good—less for me to get to later." And that felt like hearing she was happy.

Chance and me smiled at each other.

"We'll push the box into the hall for Barbie and Justine," I offered.

She took a second to hug Chance. "Good job, *m'hijo*."

Chance got right on shoving the box to the step, up into the rest of the house. And Artie lifted it up for Chance to push it farther down the hall. Then it was just me in the room.

FROM UNDER THE pillow on my pallet, I pulled out my Journal, opening it to its first blank page. I leaned back against the wall to think, but the bumpy stucco against my spine made me change my mind—so I rolled onto my stomach instead. Writing alone in a nice clean room: the feeling was wonderful. The only thing that could make it better, I thought, was a big-headed cat sitting near me. All furry and purring.

I stared at the page for a very long time; I closed the book, lowering my chin down onto it. I didn't want to ruin it. I didn't know for sure if I could do it right or not. There seemed like a lot of poetry in my head. Stories came to me all the time—but were they good enough for a book? I just didn't know for sure yet.

ARTIE CAME BACK in singing to *Mr. Tambourine Man* from the radio. So I tucked the Journal back under my pillow, asking if we could explore the garage together today.

"Sorry, Muskrat, I gotta go somewhere with Mama. Maybe later."

"What'd you gotta do?" I sat up. "Can I help?"

"Nah. It's men's work, Duff."

I showed him my muscle. Stood to do a handstand that lasted for nine counts before I fell sideways. "I'm strong; I can lend a hand. C'mon Artie, lemme help." But he dumped out one of his boxes, ignoring my second handstand try. He dumped another box, then a third, then he pulled a white shirt out of the pile. It had a necktie already around its collar.

"You wanna help? How 'bout ironing this for me?" But I shrank back from it.

"You better ask Barbie," I said, real small.

And he took a second to look from the limp shirt to me before he turned red, mumbling, "Sorry Muskrat, I forgot."

But still, it felt like he didn't care. Like he'd forgotten all about the brown crescent on my back, from Mama and the Iron. Me being underfoot that time I was still new to her. I wanted to be strong so I offered, "I'll set up the board and sprinkle the shirt for you." But he was already headed out of the room, singing about waves and forgetting.

I STAYED BEHIND in the bedroom, ashamed for not being strong. I knelt to shove all Artie's stuff back onto his boxes. The song on the radio changed. And I tried another handstand; I got to the count of twelve before I fell over.

Beauty and Grace

"**D**UFFY! GO TO the store and get…" Mama yelled from somewhere in the house. Justine and me were in the middle bedroom, pins and thread in our mouths. Cutting sheets to make curtains. Mama'd sent Artie out for packets of dye for the sheets, different colors for each room. "Presentation is everything," she'd told us. Justine and Barbie did the dyeing. And now we were cutting and hemming them for each window size. I dropped the sheet I was pinning and ran. All of these rooms were so large I hoped there'd never be a time I'd get a punishment for not hearing her calling me. I ran to the other bedroom first, then I spun off the hallway wall, into the living room.

Mama had her purse out. "I gotta get ready for Roy—I don't need this now. You come when I call you, dammit. Milk, bread, margarine, sugar, Chesterfields. Oh hell—" she stopped. "¡*Mierda!*—they don't know you." Under her breath she added, "¿*Por qué estas cosas siempre me pasan a mí?*" I wanted to say it wouldn't be a trouble if she went with me the first time. But I didn't. I stood still, waited for her to make up her mind: to let me go back to the curtains or send me to the store.

"Okay, forget the cigarettes. Just get everything else." She handed over a few dollar bills.

"Mama?"

"What?"

"Where's the store?"

It was wrong to ask because she grabbed me by the back of the neck and squeezed. She walked me out our front door, onto the porch. From there out to the curb. Using all of me as a pointer she aimed my head down the block to the opposite corner, four houses down, across from our side of Elliott Street.

My face grew hot when I saw the sign with the blue writing from there: JOHNNIE'S MARKET—FRUTAS Y VEDURAS FRESCAS. What a stupid. How did I miss that?

"*Alli está. Idiota.*" Yes, I was, 'cause there it was.

She let me loose and I started running, Milk, bread, sugar, margarine, milk, bread, sugar, margarine. I didn't even glance to both sides as I flew across the street. Four things. Four things. Then I was at the little market.

A shiny metal sign for soda hung from the bottom part of the wooden screen door. As I reached to yank it, it opened on its own. I ran right into a blonde girl coming out at the same time. We bumped so hard when we hit my neck snapped back. The dollars fell from my fist. I didn't fall. The blonde girl made a sharp *Ooof* sound over the banging of the screened door, but she didn't fall either.

When we both reached down for the dropped dollars— *CRACK*—our heads clunked. That brought us both down. Fast. Her, to her knees, and me, back on my rear. The cupcake she carried landed under me as I sat with a thump, my hands out behind to catch me.

"Ahh!"

"Owww!"

"You okay—"

"—uh—sorry."

"Here, lemme—"

"No—I got it." We scrambled for the money; getting back to our feet. "You okay?" I asked, before I saw the cupcake mess under me.

"Oh, Man! I'm sooo sorry," I apologized. "I clobbered your Hostess!"

"—and you sat on it, too." We both laughed, while we held our heads and moaned. She was blonde. I saw we could've been related; we had the same look at the eyes and chin. She seemed friendly.

For my Quest, I'd started watching other girls to see what it took to be a real one. So I'd have an idea of how to do it, once I'd met the challenge.

"Bird food," she added, making it harder to keep the pounding head pain away.

"Doggie surprise," I said, looking down at the messy sidewalk. I shook my head, wise-cracking, "You can't kiss *that* up to God."

She nodded, making the sign of the cross. "That shows you; ten cents."

"I can buy you another one."

"Nah, I mean, I should've put that ten cents in the collection last Sunday. Like I was s'posed to. I'm Becca," she added, tilting her head in the sunshine. "Who're you?" She smiled at me.

I thought, Yeah, I'd like to be this girl. She's nice. She reached for my free hand, inspecting the bloody scrape on the heel of my palm. "Ooo—my mom can Mercurochrome this if you want."

I snapped out of the laughing. Mama! I'd better be quick.

"I'm Duffy," I said. "But I gotta go, my Mom—wants some stuff. I'm really sorry about your cupcake—you wanna come in an' get another one?" I talked fast as I scooted past her to the door; if she wanted one she'd have to come into the market.

"Nah, My mom o—" But I stepped inside already, getting my eyes adjusted to the dimness in the store. From outside she called, "Bye!"

THE DOOR'D MADE a little bell noise. I'd been in lots of markets for Mama. This was a nicer one than some. You could tell they had a neat and full store here. The aisles were wider than most: uncluttered. The floors swept clean and the smells weren't old. A lady's voice called from another aisle, "If you don't see it just ask." And I walked up and down till I found her, pouring rice into a bin from a big bag. She looked like her market, blonde and tidy. Probably she smelled good, too.

Everything in her market was easy to find; I just wanted to say hi and let her know Mama might send me in with a note about buying Chesterfields. The Lady looked up at me and straightened. Her metal scoop she held dropped, spilling rice onto her feet, then she jumped back. She cussed light and dainty in what sounded like French, under her breath. I stooped to help, but she said, "Thanks, dear. I'll manage."

But one of the things I already Self-Knew was that I like to help. So I hunkered down and began pushing the scattered rice into one space. I had a nice pile going when she came back with a broom and dustpan. She sang along to her radio, not upset at me about me making her spill the rice at all.

She kept looking at me, out of the corner of her eye. I wondered if my practicing to be a real girl was working already; maybe she liked the girl she saw. Maybe the Quest was working. Maybe this would be easier than expected.

SHE RANG EVERYTHING up, taking my dollars. Telling me her name: *Mrs. Bettencourt.* A photo hung from the side of her register. I saw it and thought—*what am I doing in this picture?* In the dimness of the market, I saw it was a tall, laughing man who looked just like me. I leaned in to see better. Behind him stood a big brick building with concrete arches set in high doorways. He posed half-in half-out of the shade of some big tree. Standing with two girls: a blonde one laughing toward the camera, her arm bent up high on his shoulder, and the other one, darker, pregnant, leaning with her books against him, cradled in the crook of his arm. Her face against his chest. *Maybe that was France, there in the picture*, I thought.

"*UCLA*," she said, handing me change. Because she could see me looking at the picture. *Sure sounds like French.* She waited, watching me, a smile on her face.

"Oh." I nodded; I thought about curtsying, then decided, *nah.*

I hurried away from the register to the door, practicing in my head what I'd say about taking so long.

Practicing how many steps it would take to not turn my back to Mama. How many steps to get my shorts into the washer. Without her seeing my behind and the cupcake smear. Practicing to not be the Mad-Getter today. I pushed the door open with my elbow, spinning to face the street again, to start running.

There she stood, waiting. The girl, Becca. I smiled, ducked my head, running past fast with my bag, "See ya!"

WHEN I GOT to my porch, I stopped to look back. There she was, still watching me. And the Market Lady stood at her screened door, doing the same. I took fifteen cents of the market change; putting each coin in a different pocket. A song came to me, maybe I'd heard it in the Market, the words were right there in my head, carrying me all the way into the kitchen.

I didn't need to explain anything to Mama, in front of the bathroom mirror. I handed her the change while she leaned up close, making up her face for Roy. She murmured, "You never should spend too much time looking at yourself in the mirror, Duffy. Never." Then she seemed to notice me and asked, "What do you have to be grinning at?"

THE FURNITURE STILL hadn't come yet. We'd been at the new house for three days now. And everyone was afraid to say anything out loud about it. Dinner that night was Chile Colorado: little hunks of stewing beef Mama'd cooked all afternoon in homemade tomato sauce and onions, with big spoonfuls of her red chile spices from a jar of homemade and plenty of garlic salt. When I grew up I'd feed people just like she did. You could smell it way out on the sidewalk where we played until dinner. Mama always cooked like a priest was coming for a meal.

Finally, Barbie complained about having to eat standing up. And before Mama could reach over to hit her, Artie said, "Shut up and finish. We're getting new furniture."

"What about the truck?" Chance asked from the floor, "What about the old furniture?" he sat with his knees together, his little legs spread out left and right behind him. Artie looked at Mama a second longer. Then, he told Chance, "That truck got in a crash, Chance. It's all broken now."

"Even my bunk bed?" he asked, putting his plate down. "And the kitchen table?"

"Yeah, all of it. I, um, saw it from the freeway when I took the littler truck back to the yard."

"*When* are we getting new furniture, Artie?"

"Later in the month. Okay?"

Chance thought about this. "Okay," he said, picking his plate back up from the floor.

We all smiled, but no one else asked anything more. For the rest of dinner I tried making jokes to keep Chance laughing. I kept my eyes down. So I wouldn't catch Artie's. Or see Mama's face.

Lucky there was only the one light from the ceiling to see by.

THERE WAS STILL the backyard to explore. So me and Chance packed up some peanut butter-and-jam sandwiches, setting out the next morning. The grass back there reached a lot taller than in the front lawn. Chance was wearing one of Barbie's old Easter bonnets for a safari helmet. I'd found him a wooden hanger to use for a machete in case of vines. I brought along a can of baking powder-snake repellent in case that fruit tree was found to be home to a boa constrictor. Who knew what waited out in the weeds at the far fence?

Right from the start we found a nice pile of rocks, marble sized, then a bit bigger. Chance said, "Wouldn't it be great to make a rock garden for Mama to come see?"

He dropped his machete and we squatted down and got right to work, but after a short time the backs of my knees began to tingle. I had to stand up because the pinpricks were starting to bug me. Chance kept at it, he duck-walked around, his knees higher than his rear; he surveyed the garden from all sides. Piling rocks together for fountains and benches. Stacking them up for statues and things where I directed they'd look best.

I noticed a barbecue leaning up against the side of the garage. We'd never had a barbecue at any of the houses I'd ever lived at. So I shaded my eyes, put my hand on my hip, and I pointed, yelling, "Eureka! Bring the pick axes and sifting trays, men!"

"I love archie-ollie-gee!" Chance crowed, as we bounded across the savannah to the new dig.

It only had two of its legs. I jiggled the wooden handle on its lid to see if it was broke or not. "Caution, Professor." I shielded my eyes against shooting X-rays or angry bats. And because Chance'd left his machete back at the rock garden, he took two, not one, hops backwards for safety.

We peered into the barbecue and saw a rack like the kind in our oven. "Hummm, from the looks of things, Professor, this is either ashes from a burial mound or a site for burnt offerings from the tribe." Chance looked puzzled so I added, "Sacrifices by fire, probably meat."

He nodded, scratching under his helmet, making the last pink daisy wobble. Then I felt it and yelled for real, "*¡Ay, Chinga!* Something's on me!" We both screamed. I dropped the lid. We ran for the back porch.

At Base Camp we fortified ourselves with the nutrition of the peanut butter sandwiches. Then, we stood to machete our way back out to the far fence in search of the legendary Waterfall of Death. Back up river again, we got indoors in plenty of time for the Professor's nap.

Two, then three Mondays passed since we'd moved. I was on my pallet in the way back bedroom with Chance and Artie. Barbie'd claimed the yellow bedroom near the bathroom. And Justine slept in the front one with the picture window. Mama was sleeping in the living room, and we were all still on the floors.

I thought about Mr. St. John and my Quest. About Self-Knowledge. About the number of days I'd been out of school. Too many. Mama was still pretty tired all the time. And not having a soft place to sleep made her plenty grumpy. But, *a Quest is never easy*, I told myself. So I decided I'd be brave.

After breakfast I went into the living room to see if Mama was up. She was. So I knelt to ask, "Mama, when can I start school again?"

She lay there under her covers with a cigarette raised in one hand and the other arm across her eyes. She didn't move. Her smoke rose and twirled against the light from the window. Then, like a little girl talking, she let out a small whisper, "All I'm looking for is some Beauty and Grace. Is that too much to ask for in this life?" I knew she wasn't talking to me, so I just waited. I watched the smoke dancing. Even though it hurt to be kneeling that long.

She puffed on her cigarette again, her arm still over her eyes. She coughed. "Maybe next week," she said finally. "I'm looking for more work all this week."

"Could Justine take me? To sign me up? I don't want to lose any more days."

"What did I just say?"

She'd asked for Beauty and Grace. "Yes, Ma'am."

I LIKED THIS corner Market. I liked knowing how much everything cost. And being strong enough to carry two bags home without stopping to put them down. I like working hard at contributing to Mama getting her Beauty and Grace. It made me proud when Mrs. Bettencourt, the lady with the photo of France at her register, let me bring in Mama's monthly blue check, with the tiny squares stamped out. To cash and to buy money orders for bills. She just took a look at the name, smiled at me, saying, "Here you go, Miss Michealson," like it was *my* check. Her counting out the bills in twenties and tens into my hand. I told her I was Miss Chavez. And she nodded, "Ahh—well, yes, of course."

She told me her daughter was over at catechism, but, "Next time there's time in your schedule, maybe you could come over and play." She teased in such a nice way; I even told Justine about her. Between Mrs. Bettencourt's daughter and the girl I'd run into I might make some friends. I thought if I kept that to myself I'd be practicing my own type of Grace. And all the running back and forth to her store might make me the fastest runner in the sixth. If I ever started school here.

ONE SATURDAY, AFTER Mama left for her newest job, the three of us, Barbie, Chance, and me, were still watching cartoons on Roy's little TV that he'd lent us. There was a knock on the front door. Barbie got up, going to the window to see who knocked. She peeked out, then yelled, "There's a girl out here." This meant it wasn't someone she knew so she wouldn't be opening the door.

Chance jumped out from his blanket and skidded across the wood floor in his socks, "I'll get it!" He bammed into the wall, turning on the overhead light. Then he opened the door, forgetting he was still in his underwear and tee-shirt. The sun streamed in all around his silhouette, in through the space between his thin little legs. He looked down and dropped; crawling behind the open door like a baby. "Duffy!" he cried.

Barbie was back down, wrapping herself up in the blankets we'd brought from the bedrooms. The door opened even wider 'cause Chance had a hold of the doorknob; scooched against the wall.

So I stood and went, pulling him up behind me, like his shield. I said, "Be right with you." Then I sidestepped with him behind me into the front bedroom, shoving him in, giggling, closing the door behind me.

It was Becca, with the cupcake from in front of the corner market. She stood looking in at the empty living room and through to the empty dining room, on to the kitchen beyond. Looking at Barbie in the heap of blankets, at the little TV on the wooden milk crate.

I stepped out onto the porch, shielding my eyebrows—

the sunshine always made them hurt. It was very bright out there, but cold. My shorts were too thin, but I didn't want to keep her waiting on the porch for me to change. Becca had on jeans and a sweater.

"My mom's not home so I can't let you in," I apologized.

"That's okay," she said. "Can you come out?"

"Ummm—" I thought about it. Barbie would tell for sure. I just knew it. I looked to the flowers on the driveway wall and nodded, smiling. "We can go in the backyard. You can be there, just not inside."

"Great." She smiled too. Again I saw my own cheeks and eyes there in her grinning face.

She could be Barbie or Justine's sister, I thought; they all have that nice wavy blonde hair, like Chance and Artie, too. *It's just me with these black curls.*

We jumped off the side of the porch, race-walking down the path to the gate that led to the backyard. Both of us shivering from the cold.

"So, your furniture's still in storage? Will it be coming later from someplace?"

How kind. "Yeah," I said. From someplace.

I SWEPT MY hand out, arcing, to the big backyard, like a tour guide. "—and here we have the queen's eastern garden." She laughed, stepping into the yard ahead of me. It was like right away she wanted to play the game. Like she'd known me for a long time. The sky seemed the bluest kind of Morning Blue. I showed her Chance's rock garden. I wanted to keep her interested. Maybe she'd end up being my friend. I wished I'd come out with a sweater.

"Once I introduce you to my mom then I can let you come in anytime you come over," I promised. "She just needs to meet you first."

"That's okay," she said again. "I know how moms are."

"You have any brothers or sisters?"

"Nope, it's just me and my Mom."

I felt so happy that she was here talking that I did a handstand right there on the grass. Then popped back up on my feet—smiling at her.

"Neat!" She reached for my top and pulled it up, "What's this from?"

Her finger traced a light line on the small of my back, her finger going along another scar from a long time ago. When I was smaller, and not so good at paying strict attention to things.

"That's from a way long time ago. I can't remember from what," I said, whapping at the tree branch closest to me.

"Wow—it must have hurt pretty bad, it's still kinda angry looking." I thought to explain. About Foster Homes. "Yeah, well, I heal really bad, too." I said. "D'ja get that cupcake situation fixed?" I cracked wise, to change the subject, kneeling down under the fruit tree in the grass.

It was still a little wet. *Maybe*, I thought, *I should go get a blanket from inside.*

Becca shrugged, "Nah, it was a complete wipeout."

"Do you live near here?" I asked.

She waved behind her to the street. "I live over Johnnie's, y'know, the market?"

"I didn't know there was houses up there."

"Oh, yeah, we've been there since I was little. My bedroom's right over the street. I can see all the way to the bottom of the hill from my window. And from Elliott Street over to the Third Street bridge, too." She was still standing, looking all around at the yard here. "You can see the Sears building from up there. That high of a bedroom's like being up in the bow of a sailing ship or something. I get a streetlamp for a night light, right next to my bed."

"The Market people live somewheres else?"

She stopped her looking then, laughing, "*We're* the Market people. My mom owns the Market."

"That must be so cool." *Run down stairs for groceries*, I thought: what a deal.

"It's okay. But it's just an apartment. I don't have a yard like this."

I nearly said, *neither do we*, until I looked around too, realizing—we do now.

What You Can Give

"**M**Y MOM NOTICED that you're in and out of the Market all the time. She thought you'd like it if I came over and introduced myself."

"I like running, so I guess my mom sends me the most."

"I'm in sixth; what grade are you, fourth or fifth?" asked Becca.

"Nah, I'm sixth too, I mean—when I get registered." I pulled at some of the grass under my hand. "My mom's real busy since we moved. And she hasn't had time to take us yet."

"You're sixth?" She pulled me up and stood us back-to-back to measure. When Becca grabbed my hand I felt my stomach grab with it, she yanked me standing so quick. A weird feeling, not scary, but not normal either. When people get too close you can get hurt before you know it. Parts of her back were up against mine. And I moved aside right away. She said, "Man, you're small for sixth; I'd never find you on the playground."

I told her, "I guess I could walk around with a red balloon." Then I added, "I was skipped, they wanted to move me up farther, but my mom said no. So me and my sister,

Barbie, we're both in sixth, but she's eleven, like you should be. Is the school far from here?"

"I'm twelve and in sixth." She was back to looking at the yard, like it was candy. "About five blocks, up and down the hill, but not so far, unless it's too cold in the morning— then it's like miles and miles. You can see your breath when you walk. I use that time for practicing smoking." She faked puffing and exhaling, like a lady in a movie. Then she reached overhead, to whap at a branch above like I'd done. "So you must be real smart, huh?"

I ignored that. "Yeecch. I hate cigarettes." I made a face, and tried to whap at her branch, too, but missed, "and coffee, too."

"You drink *coffee?*" she asked, her eyes wide, "*That'll* stunt your growth!" And we were both off laughing again, one hundred percent happy. Like on the sidewalk in front of her mom's Market.

CHANCE CAME OUT, wanting to listen to Becca but I told him, "First go get shoes on, or no deal." So he ran back in on his tiptoes, through the high damp grass.

Becca told me our tree was a Plum and all summer you could pick fruit from it. "Great for making jam," she said. I figured that was good news to pass on to Barbie.

"We all like plums. But I think only Chance could climb this. It looks pretty thin, up close."

We both looked up into the bare branches; I dropped down to my knees and sat back on my feet.

"Do you have a lot of friends at school?"

"Some," she said, taking a seat next to me, her back on the tree's trunk. "I'm not one of the smarter kids and not one of the dumber ones so I fit in with just about anybody."

Maybe she said that because I told her I was skipped.

Sandwiches, I thought, maybe I could make her a sandwich. Then it dawned on me how much she kept smiling while looking around the yard, so I asked, "Wanna explore?"

And she said, "Yeah!"

We waited for Chance. "You must be the first girl I've ever seen who wants to have her baby brother to tag along."

It sounded like she didn't, so I asked right out, "Would you rather play with him or go home?"

But she said, "No, I think he's a cutie." When he came back out I let her be the expedition chief. As reward, for the Grace of accepting Chance. I was the native guide.

We made Chance be the native bearer, and we moved with extreme caution farther and farther from the house, "Into the depths of the unknown," I narrated, as we rounded the corner behind the garage.

"This is wide enough to store your bikes back here," said Becca.

And I thought, *Yeah, right. Once we swipe a few and repaint 'em.*

But then I pinched my leg, reminding myself about the Quest.

I took a chance, asking, "Do you think we can walk to school together some time? Maybe at school you can you introduce me to kids?"

Becca stopped measuring the space for bikes, she turned, giving me the broadest smile and said, "Sure. We can do that." You could see how much she looked like her mom right then.

I told her about the school I used to go to, how far it

was from our house and how close to the railroad tracks we had to walk to get there.

She got especially interested about the hobos I told her about; how they lived in the empty boxcars. So I came up with a lot about them for her while we came back around the garage and went to sit under the tree to just talk.

"Once they chased me!" Chance butted in. The sun was getting higher and stronger.

"They never did," I told her when her eyes got wide. "Really, he's just telling stories."

"They mighta," he told her, nodding to make her believe, "They coulda."

She reached over, rubbed his head. "Bet'cha you'd be real brave if they did, huh, Chance?"

"Mama used to make them sandwiches and give 'em apples when they came to our house," he told her.

"Charity is what you can give, not how much you can give," I quoted. "That's what she says."

"I'd be afraid," Becca shrugged.

Chance got up on his knees; he came up to Becca's side. "Can I touch your hair?"

And she nodded. "Sure."

She did have really nice thick, blonde hair, and it wasn't a pageboy cut like Barbie's, up to her ears. Chance couldn't get enough of it, till I finally took his hand back scolding, "Enough."

"I like yours more," she said. "Curls are so neat, not to mention being lucky with having it so black and so long. Having hair that long must be so nice when you're dressed up to go out somewhere. You can do such classy things with it. Like movie stars. Y' know?"

And God bless Chance, he hardly laughed at all.

CHANCE ASKED, "YOU know any cuss words, Becca?"

"A few," she smiled, "but I'm not gonna teach any to you. So don't hold your breath."

"Know any in Spanish?" he tried.

But I told him, "*Cuidado.* You're cruisin' for a bruisin', Mister-man."

And Becca thought that was the silliest thing she'd ever heard. That set us off; we all ended up laughing over new ones we tried making up. Chance thought up, *You'll be foundin' a poundin'* And for a bit I thought I'd faint, I was laughing so hard.

"Hey!" Chance yelled, "your nails are painted! Get a load of this, Duff!"

Barbie and Justine were the only other girls I personally knew who'd ever wear nail polish. I just didn't get the attraction of it. But I took her hand and looked anyway when Chance held it up. It was a pale, nearly invisible, pink gloss.

"Pretty, Becca. Your Mom do it for you?"

Right away a story came to me about a girl and her Mother. A rainy day with nothing to do but talk and paint each other's nails. The secrets they'd tell each other.

Becca put a nail in her mouth. "I should redo 'em, the edges are all chipped."

Chance asked her, "Next time you do can I watch?"

"He wants to dance on TV," I explained.

I WAS GETTING way more bored than Chance was, with the talk of hair and nails and all that stuff. So I asked, "Read any good books lately?" Then, it was her turn to be more bored.

"Oh, I dunno, I can't remember the last book I read."

"Duff's got tons of good ones if you wanna read one," Chance volunteered.

Becca was very gracious. "Yeah, maybe I will, later."

The talk wound down and I sent Chance back into the house, then I walked Becca out of the backyard to see her home.

"I been in this house before. Mrs. Enriquez? The lady before you? She was like eleventy-hundred."

We were walking down the driveway; headed back to the Market. The sun smelled wintry bright, but it was still mostly cold. I wrapped my hands in my sweatshirt, trying to pull it down over my thighs. Becca had to go home; she'd pulled a watch out of her pocket, just yanked it out and read it. Like it was nothing, knowing it was time for lunch. I thought that was so neat.

"I used to bring her groceries to her on Sundays. She always saved a dime for me, every time. Never forgot." Becca grinned at me sideways. She took off running and called back, "See you round the schoolyard!"

A girl's watch. Like real girls have, I guessed. She didn't look both ways when she ran either.

"WHO'S THE PADDY?" Barbie asked when I came inside. She stood peeking out the window and tapping her foot.

"You're a paddy, too, Barbie." I said, hopping and rubbing my legs to get the cold out. "Look at youse guys' hair. *Blanquita.*" She hated when I called her whitey.

"*Estúpida.* Not on the inside I'm not." She hissed, "Little *sin grona.*"

Chance ran at her and punched her, "She is *not* no brains! And she's not scared of *you*!" He wiped at his nose. "She pinched me when you were outside saying 'bye, Duff." He showed me the red mark near his skinny elbow. "And I'm telling Mama."

I tsked, "*Tssst*, Mama, gonna get you now, *chica*. And besides, everyone knows, *I'm* not the one with no brains . . ." Then I said, low and mean, "Paddy for a daddy."

"NO DADDY AT ALL!" she screamed. She came at me. That's when Justine walked in, finding us, on the floor scratching and kicking each other. Chance standing guard in front of the TV so we wouldn't hurt it.

WHAT REALLY HURT more than my arm's scratches was Justine yelling I wasn't any better than Barbie. She yanked us up off the floor. I thought that was more painful than everything Barbie'd hissed at me, even.

Justine held us apart by our clothes, though she really didn't need to on my part—since I stopped struggling, soon as she made that crack. But Barbie still wanted at me. Justine shook Barbie a few more times till she calmed down; then Barbie shouted, "She started it with her big mouth. And I'm telling Mama!" Justine still wouldn't let her go even though she'd tossed me away from Barbie like I was Chance's size.

"*Chica*," Justine whispered, "Mama *never cares* who started what. When you gonna learn, huh?"

Barbie ignored that and looked like she was searching for a way around Justine to get a few more kicks in. Eyes darting all around, but aimed at me every time: "I'm still telling!"

I counted things in my head . . . *three doors, two sisters, one*

Chance. Then I grinned, *no hope.* I let out a nervous laugh.

Justine and Barbie, even Chance looked at me like I'd gone crazy. So I started telling them, soft, calm, but fast, my fingers out in front, ticking things off.

"I did say an awful thing. I'm sorry, but didn't you too, Barbie? I hate fighting. I go crazy. I hurt you more than the angry in me needs to. But Mama'll kill us both if we come tattle to her. That's the truth." That was six; I added on one more, "I owe you for being mean—what'd you want?"

Barbie looked at me. Total disgust in her eyes. She walked into the kitchen, kicking at a wall as she went.

Chance started in, softly chanting, "Duffy won, Duffy won, Duff's the champ."

"Don't," I said. He'd grabbed my hand for a twirl. "Be good. Nobody wins."

"Are we done here?" Justine shouted.

"*Fine!*" Barbie yelled from the kitchen. And I let my breath out, hard. Because it wasn't done, not for a while yet. I knew Barbie.

ROY'S CAR CAME pulling up. By then most of the damage'd been straightened. Things looked pretty much like we all liked each other just fine. If you ignored the puffy welts on Barbie's arms and mine.

"It's a good thing there's no furniture," Chance whispered, he stood at the window watching Mama get out of the car. No one disagreed.

Mama and Roy came inside. Roy went right to the icebox with his six-pack. Mama leaned an arm against the wall and reached down to slip her high heels off. One, then the other, clunked to the floor. Roy walked back into the living room saying, "Hi, Sport."

To me, not Chance. I was the one he talked to the most.

I kind of felt sorry for Roy; he was still uneasy with us most of the time. Nervous, 'cause even though Mama chose him over Luis, her old boyfriend, he knew we didn't want him around. And to make it worse, Roy and Mama never talked much to each other. At least not when he came to our house. I tried liking him calling me that, *Sport*. But it made me feel like maybe I was being conceited for liking it. Mama hated it when she heard it.

ME AND CHANCE ran to the bathroom to watch as Mama got ready for Roy. Chance took the best spot—standing on the rim of the tub, so I stood off to her side, sometimes up on my toes to see.

Us kids found it hard to figure out Mama with Roy, together. She put a lot of effort into her face and her hair for him, doing things just right. But sometimes, the way she talked to him made me think she didn't want him at all.

I liked Luis better. He read to me and Chance a lot. He always asked Justine, "What's exciting in your life, *chica?*" And no matter how long Mama made him wait, he always let out a whistle of true appreciation when at last she'd come out to the living room; all made up, finally ready to go out for their dates.

Maybe all of us missed him. But I tried to be respectful with Roy all the same.

Barbie figured Roy just wanted to be friendly. Justine said he wanted more than that, but she wouldn't say what else. Artie didn't care about Roy at all. The two of them were like big boys in the schoolyard who'd come to throwing blows. And now they had to sit next to each other in class, acting like nothing hurt or nothing rough had happened. Artie was probably the most sad that Mama'd told Luis to go.

Chance kept asking for Mama to do his face, too. Till she just slapped down her hairbrush, picked him up off the tub rim, and huffed, "*Ay, como friegas!*" with a smile. She set him down out in the hall, closing the door in his face. That left me, so I kept extra quiet while she worked.

First there was a soft thump, Chance probably sat on the floor out there with his back to wall. Then, there came a little scratching noise, like a puzzled kitty wanting in. It got quiet. Mama acted like she hadn't heard a thing, but my heart grew sad at Chance missing out on this when I got to watch it all.

"Should we give him another try?" I whispered to her face in the mirror. Without looking at me she shook her head, *No*. And worked on her brows.

Chance knocked a very polite little knock on the door. Mama told me, "Go do something with him." So I opened the door and we went into the living room to talk to Roy.

From there we could hear Mama moving into Justine's room, where she kept her clothes. Chance leaned against the wall like Roy did; one leg crossed the other like a movie-star teenager waiting for his girl to come out of a malt shop. Chance drummed the wall with his little fingers, cleared his throat. He lifted his eyes, looking hopeful, thinking this time the answer might be different from all the other times. Chance asked, "You sure you don't like reading, Roy?"

"ROY THINKS IT'S a good idea for *Sport* to start school next week," Justine said to Mama, when she saw her come from the bedroom with her flowered overnight bag.

"Don't start with me young lady," warned Mama.

"What?" Justine smiled. "You'll be back by then, won't you? I won't need to call Mr. St. John for food stamps, right?"

"Justine, ¡*Tu eres un pedacito de mierda*!" I winced; people shouldn't call other people that.

Roy pushed off the wall and on to the fridge to get a beer. "Hey, Sport, Chance, what'cha get crossing an elephant an' a rhino?" He tossed a joke back at us, for distraction. It didn't work. They were at it again.

"Do I have to show you the pinch mark Barbie put on Chance, or tell you about the fight I broke up coming home today to get you to stay put for once?"

My heart stopped. Justine was ratting us out! Using us like ammunition. Chance and me froze. From the corner of my eye I saw Barbie trying to slip out of the kitchen through the laundry room.

"I'm warning you, *cuidado, chica.*"

"—or what? You'll wait till your kids all demolish each other while you're out with *him*?"

"Jesus!" Mama said. "You guys won't kill each other if I'm gone a day." She wasn't taking it; that was good. But Justine wouldn't let it go.

"What're we gonna do for food the rest of the weekend, Mama?" Justine raised her voice, making it echo in the empty room for Roy's benefit, just before Mama dropped her bag, took a swing, but connected only with air before Roy was there. Steering Mama into the kitchen. Justine following like a cat with a twitchy tail. Roy jumped back, shouting, "Ouch!" so Mama probably scratched him.

How Horses
Became Llamas

ROY SUCKED AT his hand. Then, he pulled his wallet from his back pocket. I thought about helping by holding his beer can, or telling him to set it up on the top of the icebox.

He said, "Well, here, let's just give Sport here a five, Rennie."

Mama glared at Justine. Roy ignored the look, concentrating on me, "Get some ground round, potatoes. Some cereal too, or eggs." I counted the things off, tapping my fingers against my leg; he talked nervous, higher and fast, "You got lard? Something to fry with?" I just kept nodding. "Well, you're the pro at this, right? You know what to do. Go get your shoes on first. And keep the change, Sport."

Mama walked out of the kitchen, Roy right behind her, like he hadn't even been talking to us.

"Stop calling her that." Mama said, sharp like a snake, she grabbed up her bag and purse. Bent to kiss Chance on the head. "Bye, Baby. Be good."

"I'm not staying!" Justine shouted.

"Rennie…" Roy tried reaching for her elbow. But Mama snatched her arm away. You could just tell she was going to be yelling at him in his car. Poor Roy.

When I slid out the door in front of them, no one closed it behind. Justine was probably still in the kitchen with Barbie, cracking up because through all the fighting she'd gotten Roy in trouble with Mama. I didn't know why, but Justine hated Roy.

"A HALF-POUND OF ground round, please, Mrs. Bettencourt." I'd already brought the milk, oil, and cereal up at the counter. Now, I was looking in the bins for a good onion to go with the two potatoes I'd picked. Becca must have been upstairs because I didn't see her anywhere.

At the register, before I got my change from Mrs. Bettencourt, she asked, "How are you liking your new school, Duffy?" My face went red; I couldn't tell if she was making fun of me or not. She stood there holding out the coins, smiling big, her eyes friendly. But still, I focused on her mouth, 'cause eyes can most times lie.

I told her. "I like it a lot," and that walking up the hill was fun. That there was somebody who played the same song every morning. "You could hear it from the sidewalk. Over, over and over, out their window every morning. Maybe they'd lost someone, 'cause it's such a sad song. I can tell they're listening to it for to cry."

I don't know what made me do it, keep lying like that, but then I looked right into her eyes and added, "Friday at school, for a treat, we saw a filmstrip about how horses got here to America. Some of them came from Asia, with the wandering migrators. The peoples who walked across the Bering Straits and moved all the way to Los Angeles from

Alaska, they brought the shaggy horses, the ones used to the cold. Big red arrows showed how they did it. The way they came. And the other kinds, the skinny shiny horses, the ones who wore the silver saddles, they came over in ships with the Conquistadors. Some horses got loose and spread all the way down to Peru and over time became shaggy llamas, cause it's cold up there in the Andes."

I didn't know for sure if that last part was right, but I figured, *she's stuck in this Market all day long, and from France anyway*. Maybe she didn't know either.

She nodded, handing me my coins, and saying, "I bet you're very good at oral reports." She closed her cash drawer. "Becca's upstairs right now, but she was very glad to meet you today. Any time you two want to walk to school together, just come round the back to the gate. We're right up those iron stairs."

"My mom sometimes keeps me pretty busy in the mornings with my baby brother. But, okay. And thank you, Mrs. Bettencourt." She was still smiling and I could see that maybe her eyes weren't so good at lies, like mine were. She looked real sad just then. I picked up my grocery bag, "Well… Bye."

I stepped out of the Market to see Roy's car was gone, so I guessed I didn't need to hurry back any more. I slipped the whole amount of change in my pocket 'cause he'd said to keep it all. I hoped Justine was still there, but figured she wouldn't be. I slowed down, taking my time, looking both ways before I started across the street. The bag was full, and I held it on my hip, baby style, instead of in front of me against my stomach. So I didn't see the little brown dog that ran up to me until he barked his high yappy bark.

You'd think I'd sat on him, surprising him out of a sleep or something. He growled, lowering his head to the sidewalk, like he was going to look under someone's dress.

"Yeah, yeah, little dog," I told him, shifting the bag to my other hip, "bark-bark to you, too." I stamped my foot at him, "Leave me alone or I'll get Mama so mad she'll get you, too."

Then he jumped up at me.

I dropped the bag. And screamed, "*¡Ay, yi-yi!*" when he lunged again, grabbing onto my calf. This little bitty brown dog. Dangling there. Not letting go. Making my leg burn with the pain.

I reached down, grabbed him by his little collar and pulled. Still he growled, not letting go. His back claws scratching at my ankle. Blood dripped from his mouth where he had me. I grabbed up the bag of groceries and staggered across the street. Yelling for Chance as I got closer to the front door. Barbie and Chance were at the picture window, eyes wide.

I cried as I pounded on the door, but they wouldn't open up. And still the little dog kept hanging from my leg.

"Justine!" I yelled, "Justiiiine!" Pounding and pounding, but they wouldn't open the door.

Then he let go. I kicked at him to make him run away. But he stood there on the porch with me. His barking echoed high and shrill while I kept pounding on the door to be let in.

"We can't let you in!" Barbie screamed through the door. "He might get us next!"

Chance was crying too, "Let her in, let her in. You can tell Mama if you want!" I took the first thing out of the bag I could reach—the bottle of oil—I threw it. It shattered on the walkway. He yelped, backed away, then turning, he ran off. I heard Mrs. Bettencourt then, calling my name. "Duffy? Honey, are you hurt?"

She was still across the street, but hurrying this way. Frowning. I couldn't let her see me crying or the mess of my leg. Not after I'd just lied to her.

I yelled, "I'm okay, ma'am. I'm gonna go in and show my mom. She'll take care of it. Thanks though!"

She kept coming onto the curb, but I waved her away as the lock clicked at last. The front door opened behind me and I slipped inside.

Chance locked the door after me and jumped back to the window to look again for the little dog. He waved at Mrs. Bettencourt. Then he ducked back out from the sheet curtain. "There's oil all over out there. Wow, you're bleeding bad, Duff."

"It's okay," I breathed. I dropped the bag, twisting to see my calf. "I'll be alright. I'll get it in a minute, Chance— just need to clean up, use some peroxide. Clean up. Ooww…"

There was a knock. I don't remember falling.

MRS. BETTENCOURT WAS driving me somewhere. I opened my eyes as we were pulling off the freeway. Palm trees swam by us as we made a sharp turn. My head bumped into Becca's shoulder. She was with me in the back seat, holding ice to my leg. She cleared her throat, I heard her say, "Mom, her eyes are open."

"Honey, your Mother must have just left," Mrs. Betten-court said, looking at me in her rearview mirror. She smiled big at us, but her eyes were nervous.

"Sit back, okay, dear? We're taking you to the hospital. Just relax, now. That's a nasty bite and I want to cover all the bases."

I struggled to sit up right and look like I didn't need the hospital, but doing that moved my leg from Becca's lap onto the car seat and it stuck there, the pain making me cry out when I shifted, trying to look okay. "I don't think I need the hospital, Mrs. Bettencourt. Really."

There was a trail of my blood from Becca's lap across the seat to my leg, and Becca's face was looking very pale. Her eyes kept blinking. She swallowed, glancing up at the back of her mom's head. I didn't want to get her in trouble.

"Nonsense. The dog may've been small but that bite certainly isn't. Becca saw the whole thing from her bedroom window. She ran down and called me. We're here, girls. Wait till I come around there. Becca, hold her still, Hon."

"Was Chance okay when we left?" I whispered to Becca, as her mom hurried around the back of the car, opening the door for us.

The thought of what Mama would do if she found out I'd left him alone with just Barbie, plus the trouble I'd caused getting blood all over Mrs. Bettencourt's car started me crying. Hard. So hard I felt the sobs catching in my chest's jagged parts. Making it tricky for me to breathe. They just didn't understand. She'd kill me for sure.

When Mrs. Bettencourt picked me up off the seat, holding me cradled up in her arms, crying and shaking, Becca scrambled after us, still pale and blinking at our side.

"Mrs. Bettencourt," I sobbed, as low as I could in her ear, "M-my mom can't pay for a h-hospital." She made a clucking sound low in her throat. Knocking the car door closed with her hip, she carried me like a baby through the electric doors of the Emergency.

"IS YOUR MOM working today?" she asked as she set me down in a plastic chair. Becca stood next to her with the bloodied ice bag held up to her chest in both hands, like a catechism prayer book. A little copy of her mother, the same worried look on both their faces. A nurse hurried over, kneeling in front of me. She reached for my ankle, turning me with such a gentle touch I didn't even feel her fingers on my leg.

"What's your name, honey?" she asked. Her hair was that same shade that Mrs. Bettencourt's and Becca's was. She wore a badge: E. Sartori, R.N. She had owly eyes and a pointy chin.

I laughed, and thought: All these blonde ladies paying attention on me. I must be in heaven. Then I laughed again and again. Hearing it getting higher and higher. My breath more shorter. Then it went hiccup-y, until I just gulped, holding it—to stop the foolishness.

THE NURSE LOOKED up to Mrs. Bettencourt, who said, "It was a strange dog. I've never seen it before. I iced it. Got her here as quick as we could." She paused then added, bold as anything, "This is my niece. She's visiting—for the month."

I felt so embarrassed to see she'd picked up lying so quickly from me. That was no way to get me to be a real girl.

THEY TOOK ME to a room. While the nurse cleaned up the bite I sat with a blanket over my shoulders, I was that cold. A plum-purple bruise had started: a thick figure eight, going right around the two big teeth holes in my puffy calf.

Had I had a tetanus shot recently? Nurse Sartori asked us. Everyone looked to me. "No," I said. "I haven't had any shots for a long time."

Mrs. Bettencourt added, "I'd have to ask her mother for sure, can we get her one now, anyway—to be on the safe side. Is that allowed?"

Nurse Sartori nodded, "Oh, yes, the Doctor will ask for one I'm sure." She lowered her voice, "If the animal isn't found, you'll need to get her a series of shots. It's imperative that the first be given as soon as possible after the bite's occurred."

Mrs. Bettencourt told the nurse she would get in touch with the dog pound as soon as we got home. That it must be a neighborhood dog. There were so many kids on the block someone would surely know of it. "Such a bitsy little dog," she said, shaking her head at the size of the growing bruise. I think it looked bigger because my leg was so skinny.

The gauze and tape over the bite pulled as I stood up, leaning on Becca. I hissed, pulling my heel up off the floor. My rear hurt from the shot the doctor'd given me. There was blood on my tennis shoe.

Later, in the car, both of us up front with Mrs. Bettencourt, Becca wouldn't look at my shoe to agree with me or not, but I thought the blood looked kind of neat there. With Chance I could always point to these shoes. I thought, that would be a great moral for the Dog Bite Story: Just because you're smallest doesn't mean you're always nice.

MAMA HAD THREE things to say about me going to the hospital once they got her back from Roy's.

Becca and Barbie found Justine over at her friend Lydia's house. Mrs. Bettencourt drove her to Roy's to bring Mama back the same day I got bit. She must have been killer mad about disappointing the rest of Roy's weekend.

One of the things she said directly to my face when I sat in the bathroom, my leg in the tub—I'd been there, feeling lightheaded, waiting for Justine to get back from the drug store with gauze and some more peroxide. But Mama walked in instead; she tossed the roll of gauze at my face, spitting mad, and hissing. Low, so no one heard: "Stop bleeding."

Mrs. Bettencourt and Justine were right behind her, so I didn't get slapped like I expected.

I overheard the second thing, through the bathroom door when she turned, walking out. She asked Justine, "Did they give her that tetanus shot in the arm? It hurts more there."

The third thing she had to say was just to Mrs. Bettencourt. Well, a lot of the neighbors may have heard it too; Mama and her were standing in our backyard. There was yelling for parts of it, like: *Bullshit, Alice! I did come back. I'm here now, not like either of them.* And: *You don't have the slightest inkling what I've lost keeping this circus going!*

I could hear them all the way from the front bedroom, where Justine had tucked me into her pallet under the picture window in her room; extra blankets, donated from Chance's space, up to my shivering chin. And the winter sunlight in through the curtains we'd made from sheets, glowing bright over my head. It was such a thing of beauty to see.

WHAT HAPPENED BECAUSE I got bit in the leg, and Mama got spoken to in the yard, was that Justine walked me to the school the following Monday. With a note from Mama. And they let me in. Mr. St. John, our social worker, started making more visits than usual. And we finally got some furniture.

I'D BEEN AT the new school in class with Becca for a full week. I expected they'd make me wait, then put me in the same classroom with Barbie. But I got lucky and in right away. Barbie waited, for Mama and till Thursday, so she got Mr. Hoffman; room 32-A. While me and Becca were in room 30-A, Miss Oliver's class.

They even retested me, putting me in the blue group: for the smartest ones. Miss Oliver called it Mentally Gifted Minors, but the kids, they called it MGM, like with the lion. I liked that. *Grwaar!*

ONE SATURDAY MRS. Bettencourt invited me over to make Valentine's Day cards with Becca for our class. How she said it was, *Classmates.* You could nearly hear the capital in it. It'd just stopped raining. At her kitchen table she layered newspaper to cover everything; then she set out red and pink construction papers for us, silver glitter, pink and white yarn, and little bottles of white glue, one for each girl.

For lunch she made sandwiches. We got cups of hot chocolate and she set a red apple on my plate, too. Her sandwiches weren't anywheres as good as Mama's; she didn't use tomato slices, or sprinkle on salt or pepper. Or mix mustard with mayonnaise, or stack them in a pyramid on a bigger plate or even cut them on the angle, for presentation.

Like even I knew to do from watching Barbie and Mama. But I didn't say anything, except, *Ummm*, when I bit into it. It tasted like a white lady made it, that's for sure.

"You know what Becca used to call this?" she asked, picking up our finished plates, apple cores and cups.

Becca's face said, *Mommm*.

Mrs. Bettencourt smiled. "Becca was maybe seven, she'd just made her first holy communion. She'd turn red whenever I'd remind her: 'Eat your crusts before you can get up from the table.' And I could never figure out what the problem was, till one day she tripped and whacked her shin, and I found her in the storeroom, hopping on one foot, yelling, "Dammit! Jeezus Crust! That hurts!""

I turned red along with Becca, and rolled my eyes. Even though I really liked Mrs. Bettencourt, being up here with Becca, making cards with glitter and drinking the hot chocolate.

I thought maybe Mama would've been like her—all the nice talking to us but none of the cussing—if Mama'd been lucky enough to have a market of her own to run. Except, I knew that with Mama, there'd be way better sandwiches.

I'd been telling Chance about Becca's house a lot since I got bit. But I kept the part about thinking that they probably fought a lot less than us all to myself. Some parts of Self-Knowledge were safer just inside my head.

Becca and I spent our time writing lists of who we wanted to hand cards out to. Since they were handmade and all, there weren't as many as there were kids in our class. She added Barbie to her list, just before she got to the end of it. I thought that was really nice. Both of us had each other's name first on each of our lists. That was best of all.

ON MONDAY, VALENTINES Day, I was so lucky; I came home with twenty valentines from school even though new kids usually don't do so well. Most were from girls. The few ones from boys were from the kids who kept asking to see my dog bite. So, maybe the bite, that was it.

At school, all the boys and some of the girls liked to peek at my calf. At the slowly fading figure eight, all clumping yellow and pea-green and spreading purple. And at the two maroon scab holes, there at the centers. Five of all the Valentines came from boys—two I hadn't made cards for, even. So, yeah, it was probably the bite.

I WAS PRETTY popular for that, since the doggie turned out to belong to an old lady down at the end of the block. And she swore he'd had the shot for rabies. Kids from up and down the block, and their Mamas with arms crossed over their bellies, stood out on their curbs watching when the Men from the Pound came.

No one liked the old lady and most of the neighbor kids laughed, following down the hill after the men in their uniforms who'd came to round up her dog for the holding and watching. They told her they had to do it. It was the Law.

The old lady, she cried: "*Mi pequeño peroito, mi bebé, Ay, Dios, NO.*" And held her apron to her face when they made her hand her doggie over.

It didn't look so big from where I stood now. The Mamas, they got nervous at her crying and prayers. They all turned to look back up the block in the direction of the Market, clucking with their tongues, like there was some big noise they had just heard over there all of a sudden. And they just didn't have time to watch a crying *bruja* just now.

ANY OLD LADY crying is never as witchy or mean-looking as they say she might be. The sun was setting; I snuck out of the house. Limping on the downhill, down the block, I knocked on her door. To tell her I was real, real sorry her doggie had to go for the Hold and Watch. That I was sorry for her pain. That I was sorry for the ladies on the block staring.

That I was praying for him.

Then I just stopped talking and tried real hard not to cry. Being a real girl was so much harder than I expected.

She called me *Precioca*. She wanted to give me a dime from her apron pocket. I didn't feel precious at all, not after seeing them take her doggie away.

I told her, "No, Ma'am. It's okay, I've got two at home for emergencies."

AFTER SCHOOL THAT day after Valentine's, we turned the corner onto Becca's street, heading to the Market. A clock sign was hanging from its front door, pointing to the *Back in Thirty* section of the clock's face. That's when I saw the big truck, with S&D First Street Furniture on the side of it, backed up into our driveway.

"*¡Ahora le!*" I shoved my books into Becca's arms and went running.

Chance was dancing around on our lawn. "Duffy! Bunk beds again!" he yelled, when he saw me. "And that guy," he jumped up and down, pointing to one of the movers, "that guy was cussing, cause the sofa's too dammed heavy, cause *¡Chingala!*, it's got a God-dammed full-size bedspring in it.

Duff—What's a full-size bedspring?"

Right then Mr. St. John drove up in his little blue and white car. Chance just loved that car. He stopped off cussing like a mover and went running to the curb to jump and get a new peek into the little round window, in the side of the car's white roof part, yelling louder with each jump then about the bunk beds: "Hey, that's neat! No back seat! Whoa, that's neat! No back seat! H'ray, that's neat! No back seat! Mr. St. John! We got bunk beds!" Until I came to scoop him up, carrying his wiggly little body into the house with my hand over his mouth.

Five, Plus Mama

MAMA WAS HOME, wearing her jeans and a white shirt that was tied at her middle. She'd tied her hair up in a scarf, like she wore for house cleaning. And the movers were bumping into each other trying to watch her shape and where she pointed at the same time. They nearly stepped on Barbie as she came scooting through the front door after me.

Mrs. Bettencourt came out of the kitchen, saying, "Rennie, that dinette is a perfect fit in there. Just excellent. What else can I help with? Hi, girls, go have a look at your new bedrooms."

"David, you old reprobate," Mama was saying to Mr. St. John, "I told you just give us time, and I'd get it done... 'Lise, this is David, my warden and conscience."

Mama loved new names. Even though I was really Defoe, she let everyone call me Duffy. Barbie was really *Alicia*. And now Mama was calling Becca's Mom *'Lise*, instead of Alice. She must have been in such a great mood.

IN THE WAY-BACK bedroom, our bed pallets were shoved into a pile over in the corner. Like Chance had been yelling:

we had bunk beds again. But this time, instead of a rollaway cot for me there stood a third real bed, with a headboard, too. Artie picked me up as easily as I'd grabbed up Chance and tossed me onto the top bunk, "There's yours, Muskrat."

Then he fell back onto the other bed, feeling the mattress on both sides of him, saying, "Thank you, O Lord, for these, Thy gifts…"

THE MOVERS WERE finally finished wasting time trying to sneak another peek at Mama. Mrs. Bettencourt and Becca'd gone back to the Market. Mama invited Mr. St. John to stay for dinner, but he had to go, too. Chance walked him out to his car for one final look through that round window. So in the end, it was just us five, plus Mama, at the new dining room table that night.

"I've got the seven-to-three shift during the week. They'll also let me work mid-shift till eight on Tuesdays," Mama said, after dinner, all of us still sitting, not wanting to move off. "Justine, that means you do dinner that night. And they switched me, no more mornings; I can walk Chance to school now. I'm on from six to eleven nights on Fridays and the swing-shift weekends from now on."

"Can I do what we learn in Home Ec?" Justine asked, about the dinners she had responsibility for.

"As long as no vomiting is involved, you can feed 'em your algebra for all I care." We laughed. "It's gonna be a tight fit," she said, "A real tight one for a while, till the furniture's paid."

"I'll start looking, too, if you want," said Artie, "Or see the guy at the truck place; he might have something."

I added, "I can ask old ladies around this block if anyone wants me to bring them their groceries from the Market." I figured that might be a dime each time. Not as good as what I kept from Mama each time, but it would help.

I looked around at us sitting, talking, at the new dining room furniture, and thought: *We fit just excellent.*

"Okay," Mama pushed her chair back. "We have a plan." She stretched, arching her back. "Now you monkeys get these dishes done."

Mama made the point of keeping her threat about her pound of flesh from the girls: Justine had to be home to make sure we all ate the dinners Mama'd made each Tuesday afternoon then froze for us to thaw out and heat after school.

JUSTINE REMINDED ME it was my turn to fold out Mama's sofa bed, when she handed me the last plate to dry. Mama had set up right up on the wall next to the front door, *for falling into* she'd said. I knew it wasn't my turn to do it, but I kept quiet, letting Justine think she'd fooled me. I dried the plate then reached up on tip-toes to put it on the stack in the cupboard.

"Okie-dokie." I acted like it was nothing, while I took the garbage can from under the sink. Because she wasn't trying to threaten me to make me do it, she was just being sneaky. I felt proud anytime one of us used our wits instead of being a bully about things. Artie taught me that.

She scrubbed out the sink as I knocked the garbage can against my knees, then she added, "I still have algebra tonight." So that made me glad I hadn't whined about it.

"You want help?"

She must've been feeling guilt, 'cause she told me, "Nah, you're doing enough, Muskrat."

WHEN I CAME back in to the kitchen the light was out. So I slipped the can back under the sink and headed to the living room.

"Mama's gonna be home in another half hour, Chance. You should be in the bath."

He answered, "I'm waiting to help you with the full-size bedspring." And I thought to myself, *Wow! Two displays of wits in one evening, that's so neat.*

Of course, sometimes it was nothing but bullying. Those times made me so sad.

It didn't matter who started it or who was to blame, or even who got hurt the most. If they were both nuns from the same silent order, Justine and Barbie would've said something out loud and they'd've gotten into it.

So us littler kids just stood back and made sure nothing serious ended broke too bad to fix. It was Artie's job to wedge himself in between and try to pry them apart. What was sad was how often he ended up doing it.

"I gotta study!" he'd yell, coming from the back bedroom to push Barbie against the hallway wall to get her off of Justine. He'd hold one back with his leg, as he'd snatch a hairbrush from the other before she got to throw it.

"Artie! It was—"

"Me?! Oh, no! Artie it was—"

"*¡Ustedes son dos tontas!*" Holding the weapon up over his head, "Just stop it! *I gotta study!*" Then he'd toss the hairbrush to Chance, who ducked it like it was on fire, letting it skitter all the way to the front bedroom.

I'd pick it up from the other end of the hallway, taking it back to the bathroom, setting it on the sink. Leaving the door open, but thinking, *Jeez! Girls.*

Artie got the job driving the truck. I think he chose it just to get away from our house. And Mama signed some paper saying he could work after school. For a while it seemed like Artie and Mama were the grownups. Justine seemed nearly one, too. Only Chance acted like a kid. But the furniture was getting paid. The family's first job, we all knew it.

I was still in charge of Chance, coffee making and the Market. Most times Justine and I traded keeping watch on Mama's work schedule. So that her sofa bed would always be opened up when she got in at all hours. And Barbie spent Tuesdays and Wednesdays after school with Mama, planning dinners, making lists for what to get for those meals. The two of them poring over recipe books. Talking about spices, about something important called a freezer wrap. That meant folding foil around stuff in a simple way so the food inside the icebox wouldn't go bad so quickly.

Saturdays, Barbie took over making the big breakfasts for us all, and she did a real good job. Which was funny, 'cause she tried so hard to get out of everything else. She still left the pots for us every time it was her turn for the dishes.

This house was probably very good for Barbie. The yellow bedroom all her own with its door to the bathroom made her unusually real human-like to me at school. And at home, too, when it was just her and Mama in the kitchen or at the dining room table, reading out loud to each other about scalloped potatoes or that freezer wrap. The two of them seemed like high school girls talking about boys, their eyes shining. And it hit me that everyone's more human if you give them something they'd love doing.

Roy stopped coming around as often. All of us bothered him. He never said so to us, but he had quiet remarks all the time. And he used them in really sad ways, a grown man having to be sneaky against kids; how come adults didn't know better? Seeing that made Justine laugh. But me, I felt guilty to be part of his downfall.

With all us kids around he let it be known we weren't doing enough to make Mama happy. It was kind of strange; Mama usually liked us more when he wasn't there. Justine and Artie said, "Roy's the one not making Mama happy." Sneaky against us or no.

"You're a big boy, read it to yourself," Roy told Chance when he came up to him with the "S" encyclopedia. That volume has a full-color page for shoes and snakes. Chance was real interested in both.

Justine for a first time wasn't really yelling at Mama as much as trying real hard to convince her. Of course, Roy was right in there using Barbie to make a point against Justine.

Roy took another long drink to empty another beer. "*Otros*," he always said, when he burped. Like he couldn't finish one can without telling us he had.

"Rennie. She has enough clothes now."

"Roy this is between my mother and me," Justine said back, "okay?" not even in a sassy way.

But that didn't stop him, "Your Mother works hard enough for what she brings home to you guys; you wanna new blouse go out and earn one. At least Barbie is here always cooking. What do you do for this family?"

"I'm *part* of this family, Roy—not like you."

Artie laughed, walking out of the kitchen. Even Mama hid a grin. It was good her back was to Roy. She let out a big sigh, telling Justine, "*Chica*, not this month. I haven't got it."

But Roy kept right on, since he'd pulled a newer beer from the icebox, "Damn, Rennie, Sport's tennies here are practically falling off her feet—When are you gonna spend money on her? Huh?"

And I froze. *OH, No! Don't drag me into this.*

Mama turned then, with the wooden spoon in her hand and told him, "Don't call her that, Roy."

CHANCE WANTED TO know a better way to get Roy to read him a story. Artie said, "Roy's just a punk. You got Duff or me—you don't need Roy for any stories."

"But, but sometimes I *like* Roy," Chance said, while he hung onto the bunk-bed post, swinging his leg front and back.

"Well, get over that 'cause he won't be around long," Artie said, flopping onto his new bed like an acrobat falling into a net. His hands behind his head on the new pillow.

"Why come, Artie?" Chance asked, his leg froze in the back pose.

I lifted my head up from the book I was reading up on the top bunk to see if Artie'd say that Luis might be coming back.

"Just 'cause, okay?" he said. "He's just a punk."

I thought about that, because sometimes Artie's right and sometimes he's not. So I said, softly, back into my book, "Maybe Mama likes 'em like that."

And Artie yanked the pillow from under his head and

threw it at me so hard my book flew from my hands. Chance had to scurry for it across the linoleum.

"What do you know? Squirt."

But I wasn't mad when Chance handed me my book and I traded him the pillow to carry back to Artie. Artie really missed Luis, that's all. That's what made him throw it. "I'm not calling Luis a punk, Artie."

"You better not," he grumped, punching at the pillow and stuffing it back under his head.

Later I read some of my myths to Chance. Artie'd fallen asleep. Since it was a Saturday I decided to practice being normal. Me and Chance lowered our voices to whispers, we talked about ways to like Roy. Chance liked the myths.

I TOLD BARBIE I'd be over at Becca's. Then I ran across the street to the back of the Market and up the iron stairs to their door. Me and Becca had a card game going. A big boy from one of the Foster Homes used to play it all the time, and even though I was small I'd watch and I was pretty sure this was how he'd played it. Kind of.

I called it Danny's Game for Threes. And it had to do with putting down cards in rows of three, face down, North to South, then also East to West. Then the goal was trying to get the very top ones you put down faced up to make patterns, like with gin, three in a row or three of a kind.

I spent a long time getting Becca to understand it but now she liked it. We played a lot. She told me sometimes even her Mom would play when I wasn't here.

"Don't you go messing this up for me," Becca warned, as she laid a red five down. But I was working on the eight, nine, ten so I only pretended to hover over her five. She smiled, like she'd been saved by luck. Then, I switched to the row I really wanted. I knew the whole game was memory. Most card games were.

"Hey girls, why were the numbers Five and Six scared of Seven?"

We both looked up and waited; Mrs. Bettencourt smiled real big before telling us, "Because Seven ate Nine."

Becca shook her head. "Mom, that is so corny!" She closed her eyes, like she wanted her mom to disappear now. "Becca is an orphan, Becca is an orphan," she muttered. But I slapped at her leg under the table.

"That's not funny."

"My mom sometimes loses her mind, Duff. So, thank you for being kind, for not noticing." But she was still smiling. You could see that she liked the corny joke.

"Good one," I said to her Mom. Then it was Becca's turn to slap at me under the table.

"Don't get her going," she warned and set down her third five. "Hah!"

"COLD AND WET. And cold," the guy on the radio said while we ate breakfast. "It's 35 degrees, and rainy at 7:15 in the City of Angeles, Burrrr." Mama was still asleep. We turned the gas on, had the oven door open to warm things up. It was so cold even eating hot oatmeal and warmed-up milk wasn't helping.

Barbie scraped the last of the oatmeal from her bowl. "This March is gonna rain from the first to the thirtieth." She took the crust from Chance's plate and ate that, too. "I bet you it might even rain till next Easter." She closed her eyes, in a spooky voice she said, "I see rain until the year

1976."

And Chance said, "I'm gonna ask Mama if I can stay home today."

"You can," Artie told him, "Just don't go waking her up, okay? Let her sleep till she's done."

"Sure Artie. Can you put the TV in the front bedroom for me before you go?" Chance asked. "So I won't make too much noise?"

"Who said I'm going out? I'm off. We're all in for the day. You heard the radio, cold and wet. And cold."

BARBIE MAY HAVE ended up right; it was like the rain would last the rest of our lives. And walking up that hill to the school in the downpour was real hard going. At least on Hockert Street the long nine blocks to school were all on one level. Here the blocks were less but too much of it ran up and down hills. None of us had raincoats. Not even Justine or Artie.

"I'm going anyway," I said "I can wrap my books in foil. That'll keep 'em dry."

"You're an idiot," Barbie said, pointing with her spoon like Mama did.

Justine put her bowl in the sink, running water and said, "Yep, Muskrat—you are."

But Artie said, "We'll fix you up, Muskrat. You won't get too wet."

So Artie dug around in all the closets and came up with some of Mama's dry cleaner bags and with tape and scissors we made me a raincoat. Like a hooded poncho. And I could hold my books up against my chest so we didn't need the foil wrap idea after all.

Kids at school were probably gonna laugh at me as much as Barbie and Chance were doing, but Artie shushed them because of Mama still sleeping. Then he walked me through the living room. My arms were in the poncho so I needed help with the door to get headed out into the weather. There was a soft knock.

When Artie opened it was Becca. In a real pink raincoat, with red rain boots and a flowered umbrella, standing there. She knew that Mama slept right behind the door so she glanced at Artie as the door guy and then at me with my books to my chest. Then, she lowered her eyebrows about my poncho, whispering, "You guys wanna ride to school?"

IN THE CAR, Mrs. Bettencourt asked Becca about Barbie and Chance. I'd had a tough time getting into the back seat with my arms under the plastic. But I explained, "Mama says they're running low-grade fevers—so she's keeping them home in case it's stomach flu. She gave me notes for their teachers."

Mrs. Bettencourt looked at me through the rear view mirror, not saying anything. Just driving through the pouring rain down the hill to school. Maybe I should have added about picking up Barbie's homework to make it sound more real.

Becca asked, "What's all this?" about my poncho. And I just looked at her, then nodded to out the window. I said softly, "It's raining, Becca."

But she was still waiting so I told them that Artie did it for me. Becca wasn't as impressed with his ingenuity as I thought she'd be. But I guessed having your own umbrella and rain boots, or even a car to drive your loved ones to school, well, a little miracle like Artie's rain poncho out of near nothing probably wasn't much of a deal to you.

I felt kind of sorry for Becca, but I didn't let it stop me from saying thanks to Mrs. Bettencourt as I squiggled out from her back seat once we got to school.

It rained all day and only let up just before school got out.

IT WAS GETTING dark. Me and Chance were sitting out on the front porch, waiting for someone to come home. Chance was real hungry, so I was trying to keep his mind off of that by telling stories, or anything else I could think up. I knew about there being nothing in the kitchen to fix for anyone.

We talked about lightning and Tony Randall from the movies. How burrs stuck to the fur of animals who took them from neighborhood to neighborhood. How that's the way the same type of trees ended up all up and down the blocks. I kept away from talking about food though. That always made things worse.

The empty kitchen happened about every few months when Mama's paychecks got tangled up in too many bills, so we ended up behind in the food. And the icebox stood empty till things balanced out again. They always did balance, but we had to be patient waiting for it.

But still, Chance was hungry now. The sun moved further down and no one came home with any bright ideas. At least it wasn't raining, I told him. And he said, "Uh-huh." And picked up a pebble, rolling it in his palm.

"You know, Duff—You got sad eyes." We'd run out of things to discuss and he reached up and ran his finger light across my brow.

"No I don't."

"Yep. You do, Muskrat," he said, like Artie.

"Maybe it's the shadows." I waved to them coming closer up the walkway. His stomach growled so loud I could hear it.

"Maybe it's old age," he said, serious, his chin down on his knees. Squinting back up at my face.

"Okay," I said. "Maybe it's that."

From our porch you could smell the cooking from the houses to the left and right of us. It was murder. Garlic, onion, and meat smells came up into our noses. I thought Chance would start crying. I looked down the street for Mama or Artie, then up to the other side, to the market's sign – JOHNNIES' MARKET—FRUTAS Y VEDURAS FRESCAS.

"…just come round the back to the gate. We're right up those iron stairs," she'd said.

"Wanna wait for Mama at Mrs. Bettencourt's?" I asked.

"Hey, yeah!" he said, hopping up. "We could do that, huh?" He got busy, dusting off his seat.

"Yeah. Lemme lock the door first."

So we walked up their stairs and she let us in. It ended up a nice visit. We were polite. We said, "Yes, Ma'am, that would be nice," when she waved towards her kitchen, asking if we'd like to join her and Becca, they were just about to sit down. So together, we made four.

Mi Alma, Mi Corazón

OR EASTER SUNDAY, Mr. St. John came in a bigger car he'd borrowed. He took us little kids to Lincoln Park for an Easter Egg hunt. The car was Jeff's, his roommate's, an Impala, so Jeff came too. But he let Chance and me sit in the front seat with Mr. St. John on the way to the park.

On his radio a boy sang about April coming. And Mr. St. John sang along. He knew all the words. It surprised him when I joined in with the line about July. I liked that part of the song 'cause July was my birthday month. I knew I'd fly someday; it was on the radio, in secret form, for just me to understand, so that no one could pipe up and say I wouldn't.

Jeff the roommate wasn't a social worker like Mr. St. John. He taught school, in a place called Rosemead. That sounded very, very white to me. Maybe that's why he owned the bigger car. And Jeff sounded very white, too. The way, From the back seat with Barbie, he kept calling Mr. St. John, *Dave.*

When Chance pulled his head back into the car from holding it out in the wind, he asked, "Hey, say, Dave, how fast'er we going here?" We all laughed and laughed.

We passed along the shops and markets on Boyle Avenue. I said, "Mr. St. John, you can get *boy*, *by*, and *be*, *bye*—like 'so long'—*lob* and *lobe* all from Boyle. That's six, beat that!"

Mr. St. John thought on it but couldn't come up with any others. "Yep, you can. One point for you, Duff."

"Unless you use Avenue too." from the backseat Jeff said, "Oh, wait—there's *bole*, as in tree trunk, too."

But that wasn't how Mr. St. John and I played this game; it was for one word only. There wasn't any *w* in Boyle to make *bowl*, so the roommate just didn't get it.

I got flip for the interruption, "Yeah, well, why not use the Los Angeles, California, too? Make up whole sentences?"

Mr. St. John explained the rules, saying how I was real good at this. And Jeff, he got flip right back when he turned to look out the window, muttering, "Too bad we're not cruising up on Huntington."

I kind of liked Jeff after that crack.

JEFF AND MR. St. John walked us all through the park looking for the Easter Bunny part of things. There were Lady Folklorico Dancers up on a bandstand with their handsome dancing partners in those tight black suits and frilly shirt fronts. And a mariachi band, with their huge hats, too. Chance nearly forgot about the Easter Bunny. He dropped his empty gathering basket to go running when he saw those dancers. And if not for Mr. St. John saying, "What about the candy, Chance?" over and over, we'd never've pulled him away.

But we both kept looking over our shoulders, walking through the park. Each of the ladies danced in those fluffy dresses. Like *pan dulces* come to life from a bakery, walking around in sugar colors: turquoise, hot pinks, yellows, and that blood red that made me want to trill out a row of rrrr's from just looking at them.

But we'd moved on. Because Jeff there seemed so white. It was his car that brought us. Well, for Mr. St. John's sake I acted cool. We found the Bunny stuff. Barbie and Chance got very competitive, running to be the first to get to the field for searching. I took my time. So I looked harder and in less places than all frantic, but not very thorough.

And then I saw it, up in the crook of a tree: a golden egg. The sun shining right on it. At first I looked all around to see why no one else noticed. I thought about calling Chance over to point it out to him, but then I just got greedy and plucked it for my own basket. *I'll share the candy with them both*, I told myself. *Just keep the gold egg for a box to save things in.*

You could hear the mariachi music floating over to us from the bandstand. I figured after the splendid Gold egg, why keep looking and be any more *codiciosa*, all greedy. I stopped searching, going to find Mr. St. John and Jeff.

Both Jeff and Mr. St. John were pretty excited about the golden egg when I pulled it from my basket, giving them a peek. "Don't tell them I found it," I warned, shielding the egg in case anyone was coming up behind. Putting his hand on my shoulder to see it, Jeff whistled, "Why not, that's a pretty shiny prize you've got there?"

"I don't want 'em being upset—'cause I'm lucky." And I looked to Mr. St. John, since he'd understand this. "Okay, Dave?" I shoved the golden one under my other eggs, down below the crinkled cellophane grass.

"Duffy is practicing the serious art of 'hiding her light under a bushel,'" he said to Jeff, and I nodded, *Yeah, that.*

Jeff took his hand and put it back on my shoulder, saying, "*Oorpay idkay, ethay eekmay allshay inheirateway ethay earthway,*" in some other language. I could see he might be a good teacher, he was good at it.

I looked up from my basket, "Huh?"

"Latin," said Mr. St. John. He took my basket to hold while he walked me to the Carousel for a little talk. Jeff stayed at the edge of the Egg hunt, waiting for Chance and Barbie to finish searching.

Mostly he stood me in front of him at the bench he'd found and started by saying, "When we have gifts, whether we worked at them or they came naturally, like being lucky from time to time, well Duff—" he sighed, squinting up into my eyes from his seat. "You shouldn't just go around ignoring those gifts in case someone else wants to be jealous."

It hurt hearing him. It started down below my feet's arches, and ran up the sides of my arms. He went on from there, saying more, but by then I was safe. It was all mariachi music.

I just looked past his ear and thought: *Easy to say when your gifts don't get you pounded on.* But I nodded like it was more of that Latin of Jeff's, like I got it and understood. Saving it to use later. "Sure, Mr. St. John. Okay." But he wouldn't stop.

"You know, dear, there's a lot more to Duffy herself than just making the coffee and running to the store for your mother." That made me look the other way even more. I nearly pulled my hands out of his and ran. I hated hearing that kind of nice stuff about myself. It felt like such a trick to get me set up to be punished for agreeing with it. 'Cause then I'd be trapped into being conceited. Like *"Hah! We knew you liked yourself way too much."* Then whap! *"Well, knock it off, damn you!"*

So I decided to be honest with him, even though it hurt my chest bone to even think the words, "But she asks me all the time," I said; it was a small voice that came out. Soft for just him to hear, "'cause she can trust I'll do it right."

"Sure, you do nearly everything right," he said, "You're too bright not to; I'm just saying here that there are many more things to do right; if you look around, choose some of them. That'll be just because you want to do them. Not because it's a job to do right for someone else. But because it's fun to do—just for you." He pointed at my heart. "Like writing in your Journal. You know?" He sat back as the others came hurrying toward us. "How's that going anyway?" He smiled.

Journal questions, wow, I'd nearly forgotten about that: "I'm thinking on things. Okay?"

He shielded his pretty blue eyes in the sunshine. At least this wasn't a sad look like the others, "Sure Duff—Okay."

And because he didn't get on my case, I took a breath. Tried thinking about what he'd said. And about my Quest. So I told him, real low, first looking back in case the others had come close to hear, "I'll try all you said, Mr. St. John. Real soon, too."

"That's my girl." He smiled, standing up.

When I opened the egg at home, I found three dollar bills rolled up inside it.

MAMA STILL LAY asleep on the sofa bed. We weren't sure about waking her up for *menudo* money since she didn't need to be at work till three.

"Better not," I voted.

But Justine, she said, "I'm gonna."

"Wait," I said and ran to my room for the three dollars Easter egg money. Justine was the only one I'd shown that to.

"Big provider," Justine taunted, but with her it made me feel proud. She added, "She'll give it back when she's awake."

We pulled the biggest pot from out of the cupboard, searching awhile for its matching lid. Trying to keep the clanging down in the kitchen as best we could. Then we went out the back way, quietly headed down the driveway.

Chance came running out after us, barefooted, delicately picking his way on tiptoe through the wet grass that ran down its middle strip.

"Where 'ya going?"

"Go back inside," I shushed him. I held up the big pot. "We're gonna go get *menudo*."

"I wanna go."

"No, you don't," Justine told him.

"Yes, I do."

"You don't even got your shoes on," I pointed out.

"Please?" he begged, hopping foot to foot. You could see he needed to go pee.

Justine told him, "Go back now and I'll bring you something neat the next time me and Mama go to the Lorena Drug Store. Deal?"

"Deal." he nodded.

"And don't go waking Mama," I reminded. So he turned, just as carefully, making his way back indoors.

To Chance's dancer's steps, Justine shook her head. *"Qué triste, niño este."*

The big pot was easy 'cause it was empty. As we walked down Elliott Street, then up the next hill from there, I dangled it at my side. Justine held the lid at its center, spinning it between her fingers like a wheel going fast. We sang as we went, just because we agreed that the sky overhead, an especially nice shade of April blue, seemed to call for songs as we walked.

THEY SOLD *PAN* there, too. The warm, yeasty smell of bread covered us when we stepped inside the shop. I thought I'd never stop inhaling; it was that wonderful of a smell. From the counter at the back, full to the shop's front door, people were waiting with their pots: for the kitchen to fill them and the lady to take the money.

Inside the bakery cases pastel-colored sweet breads were lined up in rows, making me wish I had more than just the three dollars to use.

Like I'd explained to Mr. St. John on the way to the park, weekends you could come in here with your pot, to get some *menudo* for your breakfast. Guys in line with the littler pots I figured either didn't have much money, or didn't have Mamas to teach them which pot to bring.

The closer we got to the counter, the more you could smell the warm corn tortillas. I put the pot up for the lady, and asked Justine, "Can I carry it back?"

"If you spill it, you burn yourself."

"No, I won't. I can jump back if it splashes."

"And what'll we eat for breakfast if that happens?"

I begged. Hands touching like the ceramic ones on the wall.

"Maybe," she said, putting the lid on the steaming pot that the counter lady came back and shoved at us.

"Next."

But Justine didn't let me carry it out of the shop. She took the pot by both its handles and used her elbow to push the paper bag full of cilantro, onion, lemons, and tortillas at me. "*Hace esta.*"

But I didn't want to do that and I whined, "Justine."

"Duffy! You do *that.*" And we walked slow and careful out onto the street, Justine holding the full pot just out far enough not to feel the steam escaping from around the lid. I was pretty mad, but still, I sent up a prayer that she wouldn't trip.

But she'd betrayed me, so I followed down the hill feeling it in my soul. Feeling it in the back of my neck, in my heart. Until that bored me. So I jumped ahead, landing facing backwards at her side. Two quick steps to my left and the rest of the way downhill I walked that way.

In front of her and the pot. Making gorilla sounds. Swing the bag of tortillas and grunting.

"See?" she said "You couldn't walk that way if you were carrying this."

I turned my head away and lifted my chin, "You won't even let me try."

"I know your arms—You're not strong enough."

"But, you should know my heart, too!" I pleaded; I wanted it so badly.

"Okay, yeah," she paused, "in that way you're very

strong."

"So? Can I? *¿Por favor, mi pequeña col?*"

She must have liked the little cabbage part because she said, "When we get to Elliott Street, a house from our house. You can carry it then."

"*¡Mi corazón! Garcias. Mi alma.*"

"We're a team, no? *De nada, mi hermanita.* You're gonna learn how heavy it is. One way or the other."

BECCA STARTED TAKING me when she went to Friday afternoon catechism. Not the ones for the little kids making their first holy communions, not the ones for the kids who had their confirmations coming up. This was for the in-between ones—our age.

If you were a boy who took too long getting into your seat, Father Rudolph, he'd pick you up by your shirt to help get you there faster. We were on the Stations of the Cross, the Third Station: Jesus Falls the First Time. All us kids knew the whole route, so sometimes there'd be questions out of order of where we were.

Patti, a girl from our block, who had crossed-eyes and a mother who was rarely home at nights, raised her hand. Around us most of the boys groaned. I think even Father Rudolph would've too, but he had a job to do here.

Patti scrunched up her face and wiggled a finger in her ear. Then she started in all in one breath. "Father, if maybe, when Jesus was up on the cross, and the huge nails were hammered through his hands and feet to fix him there, well, since his Father was God and Jesus knew that this heavenly torment here on earth was what God, his parent needed," She paused to check at what her finger'd picked out, then kept on her path, "well, maybe, I mean, could some of Jesus' pain been, well, yeah, pain. But—maybe, too, do you think, maybe, God could have let it be a more—delicate pain?"

Some of the boys snickered at her saying *delicate*.

Father Rudolph quoted: "*We adore you, O Christ, and we bless you. Because by your holy cross you have redeemed the world.*" As if any of the boys could understand that.

Then Father Rudolph told us all, "We're on Station Three right now: Jesus Falls the First Time. We'll get to the torment soon enough."

WRESTLING WAS ON channel eleven. Roy and Mama were lying on the sofa watching. The rest of us hated wrestling, but it was Roy's TV. So that's what was on. Justine and me were on our stomachs on the floor, and Artie sat in the big chair. The others were in bed.

Roy had lined up all the beer cans on the floor in front of the sofa, "*Otra*," he kept bragging. Another. She'd set her bottle of soda next to his empties, with her ashtray, too, a cigarette burning away.

During the commercials you could hear Roy kissing Mama, behind us. Like we weren't in the room. Like we weren't even kids. Once, I forgot, turning to say something and saw he had his hand down inside the back of her capris. I could feel my fingers and feet go cold. I didn't turn around at all after that.

The pounding on the front door made us all jump.

"Rennie! C'munnn ou' here! I gotta talk t'you! *¡Ay, Chinga!* Rennie!"

It was Luis. Roy sprang up. But Mama pushed him at Justine and me. "Get him out of here," she spat, when we froze. She snapped her fingers, "The back door! GO!"

Roy wasn't steady on his feet, so with just us two girls, we bumped him into a lot of walls trying to get him into the hallway.

"Rennie!" Luis was bellowing, behind us.

JUSTINE GAVE ROY a big push down the hall, telling him, "You heard her, the back door, you stinking *viejo borracho*." And we turned to rush back to the living room for Mama.

"Luis, go away!" She yelled through the door. Artie came from the kitchen with our big meat knife in his fist. He pushed Mama aside, reaching to undo the high lock. But Mama moved in his way. She yelled at Justine, "You girls stay out of here!" And like cowards, we minded, running straight to Barbie's room.

Roy was there. In the dark. At the edge of Barbie's bed. Reaching to stroke her hair, the same way he'd been touching Mama on the sofa. Barbie was up on her knees backed into the corner, and we both saw Roy's pants were undone.

No words, we didn't even have to look at each other, me and Justine, we just grabbed Roy up and ran him hard into a bunch more walls, getting him out the back door for real.

Justine kicked at him and he fell the last step down into the backyard, "Fucking *maniaco*," she cursed, "I hope Luis breaks your nose." She locked the door. Then, we shoved the dresser up against it to be sure. Justine told me, "I'll go see to Barbie. You help Artie." And she ran off down the hall.

I scooped Chance out of his bunk, blanket and all. The

pounding on the front door wouldn't stop. The thumping, BAM-BAM-BAM, shook the house.

"Rennie! I see his car out here. Dammit!" Luis bellowed from the porch.

"Like settlers in an Indian raid," I whispered, heading for the hall closet. "We're surrounded, pard'ner. You gotta be quiet, and hidey-ho-hide in this here root cellar, 'kay? No noise, right? I'll be right back once we get those pesky varmints. Practice ABCs in your head till I come get you."

I set him down on the toys, blankets and hangers, but left the closet door open just a crack. I ran to the living room.

Artie was out on the porch with that knife and he was telling Luis, "She doesn't want you here so get the fuck gone, man." Mama had hold of Artie's arm, pulling to get him back indoors.

The porch light made bad shadows on Artie's face. He stood shaking, practically crying, when Luis told him, "Aww, little bro', now don't be like this. You ain't all that big, y'know?" Luis raised both his hands, swaying, his head moving like a sad, wet dog.

"Big enough to throw down and jack you up, old man, *¿Verdad?*" Artie flicked his knife. "Truth," he'd said, and it glittered. "I mean it. *Vaya.*" He took a step forward. Behind Artie, Mama made a sound.

Luis straightened but kept his hands out low in front, his fingers spread wide; he looked past Artie to Mama in the doorway. "You see what that *hijo de puta* is teaching your son, Rennie?" His hands dropped and his shoulders went with them, like he'd start crying next. Then he twisted around; Roy'd made it to his car, screeching away from the curb.

Luis sighed, "Rennie… *Mi alma. Mi corazón.*" He threw his chest out, "I…I would've treated you all like gold," he cried. Then he backed up, staggering down the walk, back to his truck.

Mama pulled Artie in off the porch and pushed the door closed behind him. Turning the high lock with her shaking hand. She leaned, her hands behind her, flat against the door. You could hear the truck rolling away down the hill.

Before she could say anything, Artie tossed the knife down so hard it stuck in the floor's boards and wobbled there. Angry. Sharp.

Artie said, "*Tomelo*, 'cause you'll have to use it next time, Mama. Or your precious *novio* will." But she wouldn't touch the knife.

"*Ay, m'hijo*—"

He backed away, "*¡No! Me acabo con usted.* Finished! This ain't my job. Not no more." He walked out of the living room. We heard him cussing, dragging one of the suitcases out from under Justine's bed.

Mama sat down and lit a cigarette. Her hands still a little too shaky. But she wasn't crying, like Artie was starting, and me and Justine were doing. Like Barbie already was.

Her eyes found us girls there, all of a sudden, waiting; like she'd missed us before. "*¡Ay, como friegas!* Get to bed, damn youse!"

We went, because we couldn't tell her about Roy anyway; it would hurt her feelings way too much.

By the morning, Artie was gone. Without Artie, who else did she have now? There was just me and Justine to be the strong ones. Most nights I remembered to pray to Jesus that Artie still had his dimes with him.

Dead for Awhile

ON THE PLAYGROUND, we stood in line for the horizontal bars after lunch. Becca was behind me, because I may be small but I'm faster than most and I got there first. When you're in our grade you don't wanna be on the rings anymore; the boys can see your underwear. And they never let you forget it. But the horizontal bars area is at the end, near the fourth-grade rooms, and mostly you just have to give the littler kids a boost when it's their turn and they'll let you stay on as long as you like 'cause they know you.

It got to be my turn and I said, "Let's do Propellers."

Becca said, "Ooo, yeah! But lemme be on top."

Propellers is for two. Both of you on the bars at the same time, one under and one on top. The top person sits on the bar with her hands a little farther out than usual, 'cause the bottom person puts her hands next to them, on the inside, and hooks her feet on the top's ankles. Then you drop your head back and let yourself lean waaay back and the gravity of the top spins you both backward around and around and around, like propellers.

Mostly, gravity keeps your dress down.

Becca liked being on top. She's taller, and if you're tall

and take bottoms you can graze your head every time you go around. But I said, "No, I call tops, just duck your head this time," and she said, "Okay, Duff, but you owe me tops next time."

She weighs more than me, but I just liked tops more than bottoms, even though she pulls me down with her weight, and it's harder to get us started.

We must have spun for, like, fifteen minutes straight, the faces of the littler kids whipping past the back of my head like they were bats hanging upside down. We were bar hogs, staying on and spinning until the bell rang for Line Up.

"That was so much fun, my stomach hurts," I said, holding my side while we stood in Line Up to go back to class.

Becca leaned in over my left shoulder and whispered in my ear, "So much fun I went bald."

"So much fun I broke out in a rash," I whispered back, giggling. The stitch in my side grew sharper. "So much fun I wet myself."

"Quiet in Line Up!" The boy monitor for Sixths warned from up front.

"So much fun my leg fell off." She reached around to poke me in my side and I groaned, doubling over.

BECCA AND A girl monitor from the Sixths had walked me to the nurse, and Becca told a lie to Miss Oliver, who showed up out of nowhere; that us being cousins, her mom should be called, 'cause she had a car.

So, while I kept still on the cot and held the thermometer at the right angle, and felt how the nurse's cool hand relieved a bit of the pain, Becca apologised to her more than once for me throwing up so much. I listened to them whisper that my mom's work number wasn't any good any more; that stomach flu was going around. Well, calling Becca's mom; that's what they finally did.

Becca went back to class with Miss Oliver, and I got carried into the backseat of Mrs. Bettencourt's car.

Telephone poles and treetops and a cloudless sky rushed by the car's window, and though I tried my best not to moan, because of the rocking of the car, I failed. She glanced back at me then, but my eyes kept fading from seeing her face to where there was only white in my sight. Maybe she turned front and kept driving, I don't remember. I heard her say from far, far away, *Oh, my God.* Before I gave up. In my head, I added "...*I am heartily sorry. For having offended thee...*"

Someone shouted, "Okay, it's burst, let's get her in there," and the rolling cot I was on went rocking down a bright hall: the motion of it pure murder. Then we were in a very cold room. I heard, "So this is our barefoot countess, humm?" A face came up over behind me, he smiled, and put a rubber smelling thing over my face, asking, "Can you count backwards from one hundred, Bright-Eyes?"

I nodded, but thought that I might never see Mama again in this life, so instead of counting, I breathed in and began, "Ah, *Mi Dios*—"

I can't remember if I made it to the part that goes: *I firmly resolve, with the help of Thy grace, to sin no more and to avoid the near occasions of sin.*

I WOKE TO Mrs. Bettencourt and Justine right behind her; I

guess Mama hadn't made it. Justine didn't realize my eyes were open, and I heard, "She's just gonna ask, *'Who's gonna pay for this? Huh?'*" And I knew they meant Mama.

The second time I woke, I hear them like from a distance, Mrs. Bettencourt saying to Mama, "Later, Reina, in the hall," She'd tucked my covers tight or maybe that had been Mama.

WHEN I WOKE up I was on my back and my feet were freezing. It was the hospital still. The curtain thing around the bed was pulled nearly all the way closed; just a sliver of an opening at the foot of the bed. I wanted to curl up in a little ball, but I was too stiff. I wanted to pull the covers over my head, burrito-style, like I did at home, so I could go back to sleep. My stomach burned. When I pushed against the mattress with my feet, trying to turn on my side, I couldn't. Moving stung. Bad. I put my hand to where the stinging was and touched a bulky bandage, taped low, lower than my belly button, the size of a paperback book, but not so thick.

I let my eyes look sideways and around, trying my hardest to keep my hand pressed down and my body still. And that's when I felt Mama there, her head resting in her arms on the edge of my mattress. Like we do when we put our heads down on our desks at school for quiet time, or when we play Seven-Ups. No peeking.

She might be sleeping, I thought. So I stopped trying to move. But I felt so cold I started to shiver again and couldn't stop. The trembling made Mama twitch and she lifted her head with a jerk, pulling back until she was focused on where she'd woken up.

Our eyes met, "Hi, Mama," I said. "It's cold in here."

She touched my forehead.

"I can ask them for another blanket."

"Where's my pajamas?"

"You don't need them."

"Okay."

We stayed there like that for a moment, in whispers. Mama, her eyes still all sleepy, and me, cold and stinging. She yawned. "They took your appendix out."

Propellers. So much fun my stomach hurts. "Oh." I was feeling sleepy again, myself. "Can I roll over?"

Mama stood and turned me on my side, gently, like I was an old lady, frozen and creaking, "There you go." She sat back down, propped on her elbows this time, chin in her hands. Her dark mascara was smudged, up under her eyes.

"You can put your head back down," I told her, and "I'm sorry," I added. She acted like she hadn't heard that; she stayed propped up. She yawned again. I wondered what would get her to listen. Then I said, "Can I go back to sleep?"

"Sure, Sugar. *Duerme ahorita.*" I looked at her longer, waiting. Maybe the slaps would be coming later. Then I pulled the sheet over my head. I kept my eyes open under there. My hands, in a prayer between my knees and my shoulders, cold and tight. Waiting. Finally I felt her lower her head down to the bed.

From under there, I whispered, "Mama? I'm really sorry."

Outside of the curtain there were shifting noises and little coughs. I heard footsteps moving past us. But they stopped short and stepped back to my bed. I held my breath. They were probably looking in at Mama sleeping;

maybe she shouldn't be here in the night.

"*Ay, no,*" a lady's voice whispered from the foot of the bed, "*Raul, mira, la niña. Esta muerta.*"

With a squeak of the curtain, Raul's whispered, "*Pobrecita… qué lastima,*" before they tiptoed away. I waited a second more before I peeked out from under my sheet – Mama's eyes were open, inches from mine. She was smiling. She lifted an eyebrow, and mouthed, "*qué lastima,*" such a shame. I smiled too at the story they saw; me, dead still, under the sheet and Mama's head bowed on the bed. Then I closed my eyes and fell back asleep.

The next time I woke up there was another blanket on me, but Mama was gone. I lay there wondering if I'd dreamt my being dead for a while and her tired smile.

"HER DRAIN'S NOT as productive as I'd expect it be," the Doctor was telling the other doctors who were standing around my bed looking in at my uncovered stitches. There was a little amber tube sticking out of the side of my stitches, near my bellybutton, like a miniature butterscotch lawn hose. And greenish-yellowish stuff was leaking out of it, no matter how often the doctor peeked at it. She flipped through the pages she held, saying, "Looking at the serum iron level, and iron binding. I'd add anemia, considering her actual age and this low weight. These people." She sighed, "We'll keep her a bit longer, till she's in better shape for discharge."

I looked down at my bare middle and exposed hip bones and tried to be funny, "Maybe if you stood me on my head and leaned me up against a wall I'd drain better." But no one except the nurse bothered to smile.

EVERY DAY I got helped out of bed and I'd walk, careful and bent a little, out to the nurse's counter. I'd look down the hall to the left and the right, but no Mama. One day a lady with a cart of books gave me one about origami; there wasn't any folding paper but it was nice looking at the steps anyway. It wasn't Mama, but the book lady was being nice. My smiling nurse noticed my origami book when she brought me lunch one day. I showed her the peacocks and giraffes, and the lion you could fold to show his fangs in his open mouth. The next time she saw me she handed me a thin telephone book, saying, "Knock yourself out, kiddo," before she checked my nonproductive drain again.

I folded every animal in the big book, careful not to pull the needle from the back of my hand. And gave the animals around to the other kids. Some of the parents who came visiting looked in my book and asked me for alligators and dragons 'cause they'd seen me doing the harder ones. So I was very popular when they came to take their kids home; the parents all hugged me good-bye, wiggling their animals "so long" at me, and some kissed my forehead.

With the bunnies, I folded them in big, medium, small, and smallest size. And my nurse took them to her counter and they stayed there, day after day, looking cozy sitting, all together, like a regular bunny family. I touched the smallest one every time I stood there, waiting in the hall.

THEN ONE DAY Mr. St. John, walked into my ward holding a yellow balloon that bobbed on a fancy curling ribbon. He looked smart and tall and clean, and, well, white. He searched all around then he saw me in my bed. "There she is," he said, as he handed me the balloon. "Are you ready to get out of here?"

I hadn't seen anyone I knew since that night with Mama, maybe eleven days ago. Someone did know I was still alive. I looked up at the yellow balloon and, like a little crybaby, I broke into tears.

IN THE CAR he found out about Mama, her not visiting after the first night. But he promised not to say anything to her when I asked him not to. I hate lying, but sometimes you have to ask folks to do it anyway.

So to make the time pass I started up an old game we used to play on Hockert Street—when he was just getting to know our family. We talked about the Best Life. The life I'd lead once we grew up and got out on our own. The life he was probably living right now.

Mr. St. John, he got it wrong again, and was saying stuff about ponies; how many he was gonna have and where he'd shop for them, where he'd be keeping them and all. So to help his story, since he'd promised about Mama, I acted like the pony-order guy, and asked, "And how will you have your pony served, Mr. St. John?"

"Why, with blue chaps and a blue vest of course", he said. "Trimmed with silver tassels, please, and umm ... A black and silver hat on the side, I think." We laughed.

"And you, Miss Chavez," he asked. "How would you like your pony?"

And I thought a moment, because ponies weren't really on my Best Life list, but I didn't want him to stop and not play anymore.

"Please bring my usual pony with blue and yellow and pink ribbons braided in her mane and tail," I answered.

"Yes, a little light brown one I think, and make sure my pony only allows barefoot girls to ride. No shoes, spurs, or boys, please."

Then he pulled to a stop at my house and we saw her coming down the block from the bus and Mr. St. John said, "Shit, your Mom," and I couldn't stop myself; I looked all around for a way to run before I remembered who I was with.

"She took a short day. I told her I'd be bringing you home."

And I realized, Oh, Man. A short day from work and just because of me. She was gonna kill me for sure. We both stepped out of the car and waited for what would be coming.

The pain arrows in my side from my new scar made it hard to worry and be strong at the same time. But standing there I felt lighter, like I could fly now, after the operation. "You don't have to lie after all, Mr. St. John," I said. "I'm not gonna."

ONCE MR. ST. John left it was just Barbie and me in the kitchen, talking to Mama. I slipped into a kitchen chair and just tried to catch my breath, my side was killing me.

"A half day off for this." Mama turned to me.

"You didn't have to, I would've told him not to call," I said, not looking at Barbie.

"The truth, Duff. What have I told you about that?"

"Don't do it without permission first," I recited.

"Don't you get smart with me, Duffy." She slapped at the tabletop and made me jump. "You think you can make me look bad? Get on his good side and make me look like shit? Well you can just go to your room and figure out how you're gonna get dinner tonight cause you're not getting any from my table, Miss-I'm-so-smart."

"But Mama—I—"

"No Buts—get out of my face. Now." So I went. And didn't eat dinner, which added to the feeling of being so much lighter now. But at least I didn't lie. And learning not to lie was something that *was* on my Best Life list. Even it if meant giving up a chance at good times with Mama, all sleepy and nice in the dark, her forgetting for some reason and not slapping me. The Best Life meant never being dead for a while, that was the other thing I added to the list.

"DUFFY, WAIT UP—"

Barbie and me were hanging at the playground instead of heading home after school. It was a dentist day for Becca, so I slowed down for Barbie to catch up and we sat on the swings and talked together, though usually she wasn't interested in being with me on the street. The two of us don't have all that much in common; we didn't even look like sisters.

So to make the time pass I started up an old word game we used to play on Hockert Street—before they put me in her grade and when I was less of an annoyance to her.

It was Thursday, I said to myself, so we didn't have to get home quick. On Thursdays Mama would come in from one job, change, and go right back out again for the next— we had time.

We both pushed off with our feet and the swings took us up and front, they seemed almost the right size for us again, not like we were sixth at all.

Then all at once she stopped and said, "Shit, Mama. It's a short day. She's waiting for me at home," Barbie yelled, as she jumped and scooped up her books and started out the yard.

"It's Thursday," I yelled, following right behind her.

"Wednesday—*sin grona*. The twenty-seventh?"

And I realized. Oh, man! Yeah, it was.

And we both went running as fast was we could.

"I'm gonna say a teacher kept me after to help work on the bulletin boards," she huffed and puffed.

"I'm not gonna lie." The pain arrows in my side from my new scar made it hard to yell and run at the same time. "We just forgot."

"Nu-nuh, you don't. You keep outta my lie. I'll lie if I wanna. You tell her anything different and I'll kill you." And she ran even faster up the hill for the last block to the house.

Barbie was in the kitchen, breathing hard, but already she was talking to Mama. I flopped down on a kitchen chair and just tried to catch my breath; my side was killing me.

"So where were you?" Mama turned to me.

"Playing in the playground," I said, on my way back to my room for no dinner.

FOR CINCO DE Mayo, Mrs. Bettencourt invited me to spend the night at their house. And Mama said, sure, even though it was a Thursday. "One less crazy Mexican hell-raising in the streets tonight." But I knew she was joking, 'cause she smiled at Mrs. Bettencourt when she said it.

We were gonna make cookies, and Barbie took some time and found her famous Sugar Cookie recipe from the checkered cookbook and opened the binder rings to let me take that one page with me to Becca's. Maybe she was sorry about the lie.

As I was headed out the door, Mama stopped me and made me hold my hands out; she gave me three red apples, dropping them one by one in my hands, like each was its own instruction: "Never-Arrive-Empty-Handed." She said, then whacked my rear, as she scooted me out the door.

Up at Becca's they'd set out the measuring cups and spoons and the bowls. And Mrs. Bettencourt was reading from a scrap of cut-out newspaper.

"Okay, lessee." She fixed the tiny pair of black half-glasses closer to her eyes, "Flour? yep." She patted a big sack twice. Becca nodded: Check. "Eggs. Hon, maybe you should go down and get some fresher ones." And Becca was off running, like it was a blood transfusion we needed. I looked over my page of recipe and then decided to be brave and I held it up, "Can we use this one I brought?"

Mrs. Bettencourt lowered those half-glasses to take my page, then slipped them on again, saying, "Sure, Dear—Oh, this looks yummy." She actually said that: Yummy.

"Where's your allspice?" I asked, holding the sifter over their biggest bowl.

Becca looked at my page and said, "That's not in there."

"That's okay, with spices sometimes it's fine to wing it," I quoted Barbie. "Or if you don't got any allspice then nutmeg and cinnamon will do the same thing." I pushed my curls from my forehead with the part of my arm near my elbow. "Really—it works." I added. Seeing them looking at each other, checking: Nah? Yeah?

Then, "Allspice." Becca's mom said, "Huh."

So Becca went running downstairs again.

We sat and talked about all kinds of things while we waited for the already baked cookies to cool. The conversation ranged all over the place, Mrs. Bettencourt answered everything we came up with. I felt so comfortable I even asked what the difference was between the "TM" and the "R" in the little circle, and found out about Registered and Trademarks. Becca wanted to know about the definition for "Void Where Prohibited." It was a great talk.

And the cookies were yummy. Even I said it.

Then the talk turned to names, when Mrs. Bettencourt held out the plate of cookies for us to have another and said, "After you, Alphonse." And me and Becca started cracking up. She tried explaining, but we just kept giggling higher and higher till Becca was spewing crumbs and milk drops; we thought it was so funny.

When Mrs. Bettencourt said "Rebecca Jennifer" in that mom way, I thought Becca had to calm down. But she wagged her head at her mom, and said back, "Alice, Dear…"

Rebecca and Alice, names for blondes from stories about gentle girls. An excellent fit, I thought.

"I love names and their origins," Mrs. Bettencourt was saying.

"Can I do your hair, Mom?" Becca asked; she'd gotten a hairbrush from her room.

"Sure, Sugar," Mrs. Bettencourt said, sitting back in her kitchen chair, "Go on, Duffy, we're listening."

Becca took up the hair brush and her mom closed her eyes and listened while Becca brushed, from Mrs. Bettencourt's forehead down to her pale ends. "Umm, these are sooo good," she said about the red apple. I wanted to mention they'd come from her Market, but I didn't want to break the nice of the room. I kept going.

"Justine, well, that one came from a book by a guy named—Durbel, I think."

"Durrell. Lawrence Durrell," Mrs. Bettencourt said to the ceiling, soft and lazy.

"Yeah. You know that book?"

"It was one of my favorites." Becca was still brushing down, long, long strokes, and her mom's eyes stayed closed now. "Go on."

"Artie was named after his gran'pa. His Daddy's Papi. And Barbie's real name's Alicia, but Justine says even though Alicia's a Mexican name, Mama calls her Barbie 'cause she's blonde and nearly all white." I stopped and blushed, hearing what I'd just told them.

"—I mean—not as Mexican as me and her are—my Mom—"

I kept going, thinking maybe they wouldn't notice the bad manners, "Chance wasn't born when I was around; Justine says Mama never had a story of how we two got named, except that our Daddies named us; before they went away. I heard the name stories of the big kids when Justine and me were both in the same Foster Home for awhile— just before we came back to Ma—my mother."

"My grandfather's name was Arthur, too," Becca said.

And her mom sighed, and said, "Yes, it's a very strong name."

With the Noise of It

I WANTED TO take her hair in my hands and brush for a while, and Becca, she gestured, c'mon, with her head, and I took over on the upstroke, Mrs. Bettencourt didn't even notice. At least that's what I thought until she exhaled real satisfied and sleepy and murmured, "That's nice Duffy. You've got very soft hands. Becca, turn that song up higher and hand me a napkin, please, hon."

Becca sat on the chair and watched me brush more, her feet swinging under the table to the music. She put her chin down on her arms and yawned, then she asked, "Mom, tell Duffy what my Daddy was like."

"Daniel was tall, skinny, and good-looking, and he had a wicked smile for a man so gentle."

Becca added, "He was my uncle's best-est friend. Like twin flames, huh, Mom?"

Like me and you, I thought. "Yep," was all her mom added, till I was done and I put the brush down.

"Duffy," she told me, "Let your Mom know she's welcome to come visit any time, too. Okay?"

I said, "Okay." And she reminded us: *Brush your teeth before you get into bed, girls.*

ON ANOTHER EVENING, Mama and Mrs. Bettencourt were together drinking coffee, talking and smoking cigarettes in her living room over the Market, and Becca and I were playing gin rummy in her kitchen.

I was working on losing to Becca so we could keep the game going. But that was harder than trying to win. Becca was so very bad at it. Barbie had asked to come too, but for once Mama said, "Not this time, precious." Barbie glared at me. I could just feel the bruise from the pinch I'd get later.

Mama was laughing in the other room, and I heard her saying, "'Lise, you know if my choice in meat was anything like my choice in men, my kids would be long dead from ptomaine by now."

And Mrs. Bettencourt said, "Ah, Rennie, c'mon now."

I liked that, how Mama used *Lise* for Alice. I thought one day I'd be brave and try it out on Mrs. Bettencourt myself.

I gave up and laid down my four kings in front of me and the extra two of diamonds on the stack and told Becca, "Rummy Dummy."

Becca yelled out to her mother, "Mom, come quick, we got a card shark in our kitchen!"

They walked in with their coffee cups, and Mrs. Bettencourt whispered, "Just like Daniel," as they moved to the stove for refills. Becca's Papi must have been a sore loser, too.

Mama said I could stay the night, and after Becca came out of the shower, her mom braided up her hair while she sat on the floor up against their couch. It startled me when Mama reached around my waist, holding me like she usually did only for Barbie. I stiffened for a second, then tried to let myself relax. My mind off, standing there studying how Becca leaned against her mom's legs, her eyes closed. I almost felt Mama, there with her arm around me, not pinching or hitting. But just like she loved me.

Becca was already in her room when I came out of the shower. I could hear Mama and Mrs. Bettencourt still laughing like girls out in the living room. I stopped in the hall to go on tiptoe to look at an old picture on the wall when I heard Mama saying, "Oh, yeah, 'Lise – you know these *chingada chismosas* around here would have me for a meal if I up and went the other way. You and me both? Good God, you thought college was hard."

Mrs. Bettencourt answered, "I'm talking about going to a *place*, to *dance*, not a full conversion here, Dear. And frankly, Rennie, "*Ne le frappez pas jusqu'à ce qué vous l'ayez essayé.*"

I knew about those mamas on the block, how they stared at that weeping old lady with their arms tight on their chest. How Mrs. Bettencourt felt about them, and I figured all that French meant: *Chinga las chismosas, let's go dancing, Rennie.*

Becca's bed had room for two, no problem. We just pushed all the stuffed animals down off the edge. I was on the inside, against the wall. Her feet went farther down the mattress than mine, and it reminded me of sleeping with Justine, cold nights in her and Barbie's old room, back on Hockert Street. My nightgown was twisted up high from scooting over and rubbing my feet together, so I wiggled trying to smooth things down under her covers. Becca was on her stomach, her face turned away from me. Her hair nice and thick in that braid over her shoulder.

"Hey, jiggle-butt, keep that up and you can sleep on the floor," she complained.

"Sorry, just—gimme a sec—" I hopped up on my knees, and that pulled the covers from off her, "Oopps." I yanked my nightgown down. Her braid was so creamy colored. I pulled the covers back up over most of her and still kneeling, I asked, "Can I unbraid your hair?"

"Sure," she said, into her pillow. I moved one leg over her rear to sit up behind on her and reached for the rubber band, "You must weigh, like, half of me" she said, "I can barely feel you. Don't pull."

"I'll be careful," I promised. With the rubber band on my wrist, the three wavy strands fell away from each other and the silky ends tried to wrap themselves around my fingers. This is what *amber waves of grain* is all about, I thought. "Hey, did I tell you the time I had hair down to my waist, like now, and I was gonna cut off one of my curls to give to this other girl, Marilyn? She had red hair and wanted black like me, and we figured we could wrap the top part of it around a bobby pin, and she could wear it that way. I had her convinced to take a curl or two. 'There's enough, really, take one, I got plenty, one won't matter.'"

Becca, chuckled under me, "Man, I can just see you trying to explain that to your mom," and I bounced with her rising laugh, falling forward, my chin at her shoulder.

I wanted to fall into sleep there. Her hair loose and soft under me. I looked to the door, then whispered, "Hey, wanna do propellers? I owe you a top."

She made a big shrugging move to roll onto her back and slid me right off of her, pulling the covers back up to her chin. On her back, she thought about it, her eyes glittered in the light from the streetlamp, "Not tonight, Dear."

And we thought that was so hilarious, her mom had to come in and tell us, "I mean it girls, pipe down now or else."

MAMA WAS MAKING up her face in the bathroom, and she let me watch while I stood on the tub edge. She had her hair curled and the smell of the Aqua Net hair spray was like perfume to my nose. It made it itch.

She opened her eyes wide and drew mascara along their undersides. Then she stepped back, looking into the mirror from one eye to the other. She made a face, like, "Oh, what the hell," at herself and reached for her lipstick. I made the "OOO" face she did, as I watched the lipstick tube glide around her mouth, spreading like red frosting on a warm cupcake.

She plucked a bit of toilet paper from the roll. "No use gilding the lily," she said to me through the mirror, pressed it between her lips, and started blotting what she'd just applied.

I couldn't take my eyes off the rose-colored kisses she tossed in the trash basket,

"Mama, what's girls' night out?"

"It's girls going out together and no boys are allowed."

"What'll you *do* out?"

"Well," she thought to the mirror, "I'll tie one on, and maybe do some dancing."

"Ahhh." I stepped down from the tub. And she stepped back and looked again into the mirror, straightened down her tight black skirt.

"And maybe if I'm lucky, I'll get a kiss—or two."

CHANCE AND I had all the playing cards faced down on the floor in the living room, and we were playing Memory. He was getting better at it, but still I cheated a lot and said the names out loud of the cards I turned over and back again, to help him remember where they were so he could make matches.

Justine looked up at the clock and said, "Bedtime."

Chance threw down another two cards that didn't match and said, "Good, this is junk." And I kissed him goodnight before he went off with Justine for his bath.

I laid down on the floor with all the cards, my back up against the sofa and drew in the nearest cards spread on the floor. Then I just gave up on moving to gather the others in and closed my eyes. Justine came back into the living room and said, "I'm gonna open Mama's bed. Shove a bun, Duff—I'm too tired to goof around."

I said, "Open it up over me, I'm tired, too." And she did just that, snapping the overhead light off and checking the front lock before she went off to bed.

IT WAS PITCH black when I heard Mama's key in the lock. I sat up and bumped my head into the sofa mattress over me. Mama and Mrs. Bettencourt came in, and Mama was saying, "Where'd you get Bettencourt, anyway, 'Lise?"

And Mrs. Bettencourt answering, "Same place I got the Market." And they both laughed, like I hadn't heard Mama laugh, in—well ever.

Then Mrs. Bettencourt was sitting on the mattress, saying, "All laid out—Boy, you've got them trained well, Hon."

Mama's black skirt and her silky print blouse dropped to

the floor near my hand, and I shrunk back, making myself small and trying hard not to breathe too loud.

"Yep." Mama's weight at the other side of the bed sagged the mattress from there, "Between our Daniel and your brother we've got six pretty great kids."

"Our Daniel—" Mrs. Bettencourt echoed. "Who'd've thought …" Then I saw her red dress fall across the coffee table and slide down to the floor. "Duffy has so many of his moves, it's frightening to watch. And all that jet black—"

"—curly hair. I know. Try living with that reminder, night and day. On his birthday I can't stand looking at her—it hurts so much."

Mama said, "Here, let me get that." And their mattress sags came together in the middle, Mama's feet off the floor on her side. One of them giggled, and I felt my chest go warm with the sound.

"Oh, Miss Michealson, how you act." Mama's voice was a soft whisper over me.

The mattress shifted, "It's okay, Hon. Hell, Rennie, it's not like this is the first time—the boys together, the girls together, consider it a family tradition."

"You've gotta be out of here before any of 'em gets up. Auntie Alic-*hummph*."

They were kissing up there. Together. I could tell.

Mama and Mrs. Bettencourt. Soft noises and quick breaths, then the mattress got heavy saggy all in one space, more soft noises for a bit, then faster ones, and still it wasn't sounds like Roy and Mama, like that one time with the wrestling, when I'd looked back in accident. This sounded nicer; it sounded fitting somehow to me. I laid my head on my arms, and thought: This sounds right. Girls' night out.

I closed my eyes and relaxed, over me Mama murmuring, "Ahhhh—*Lise…*"

WHEN MAMA GOT up to go take her shower it woke me, and I sat right up, nearly hitting my head on the sofa mattress before I remembered where I was. But no one was up there now, I could tell by the no sags over me. And Mrs. Bettencourt's red dress wasn't on the floor anymore.

I wiggled out from under there and stood up. The sun was barely making light in through the side window. I could hear the shower running. I remembered Mrs. Bettencourt telling Mama: *You've got them trained well, Hon.* So I went into the kitchen and put some water on for coffee.

I took her cup and saucer out to the coffee table, and folded up her blouse and skirt from off the floor; then I padded down the hall to crawl into my own bed and slept until late.

"DUFF—" CHANCE WHISPERED, warm boy-breath in my ear. "C'mon, it's afternoon, get up."

Even though my eyes were closed tight under the sheet the noises from the bird conference outside on the wires had me wide-awake.

The sun must have been up and on the windows for a while because the bedroom was really hot and stuffy. My sheet was twisted and sticky where it bunched around my neck. I stretched under there. It would be nice to get outdoors where the wind was.

"Hey, crabby," he said, tickling my feet, but doing all the giggling himself. "Get up."

I pulled the sheet from over me and dangled my legs

over the top bunk.

"Shush, let's not wake Mama up."

"Mama's already up—you're the sleepy head." He slipped off the rung of the bunk-bed ladder, making a soft thump on the linoleum. "Do this," he demanded, holding out his tennis shoe. Another job for the knot-un-tie-er.

I handed Chance back his un-tied shoe and went along the cool floor of the hallway to the bathroom.

The door to Barbie's room was open; I could see most of her clothes all over the floor, even blocking open the door that went from her room into the bathroom. I wanted to be like her, have all my stuff right out where I could see it and get to it all easy. But back in the room with Chance and all his boy stuff—well.

I don't know why I do it but I slipped my arm through the crack in her door and ran my hand on the smoothness of the paper on the wall; even with my eyes closed I could feel the bright yellow pattern. And I thought: even wallpaper had such a different sound than stucco.

MAMA CAME BACK from Mrs. Bettencourt's in a mood one day, so I stayed in the back bedroom, and didn't show her my homework where I'd made up my own crossword puzzle using most all of the Southern American countries, and several of their indigenous animals, too.

I could hear her from the kitchen when I went down the hall to use the bathroom. "It's stupid that's why, when do I have time for a thing like that?" Mama was saying to Justine. "Like Miss-I've-been-to-France, Miss close-the-market anytime-I-feel-like-it, over there."

"I just think a Tupperware party would be fun. You did

the Avon real good in the old house."

"I knew them there; this street is full of nothing but *viejas amargas* and *chismosas*, who am I gonna invite from that crowd?"

But Mrs. Bettencourt, and Justine and Barbie both, worked on Mama day after day till I thought she would up and yell at them.

Barbie was secretly planning and re-planning what hors d'oeuvres she wanted to make with Mama. And when Mrs. Bettencourt sent a note back home with me for her, Mama opened it and a ten and two twenties fell out of it.

Mama read the note and blushed, but she finally said out loud, "Okay, I'll do it."

So, first she sent me to the store over on Lorena for party napkins and colored toothpicks. Then back to the same store for new ice trays and two packs of invitations. Then, when the Tupperware party was a week off, on a Sunday she called, "Duffy—"

I ran into the kitchen with one of my shoes in my hand.

"Cool those jets, Duff, I'm taking you with me."

"You are? Where?" Barbie asked. *Yeah, where?* I thought.

"What? I can't do that?" She spread her hands wide, "Look again, Head of Household." She tapped her chest, "It's my prerogative."

So I sat right down, there on the floor, the way Chance always did, and whistled as I put on my other shoe.

We walked all the way to the First Street Department store. Man, was it far. And all the way Mama talked to me about the Tupperware party and what she thought she'd do to spruce up the house, like the way I'd heard her talk to Barbie with the recipes: like she really liked me.

I was the one who found the doilies for the armchair. She liked the idea when I held them up saying, "*Mira*, Mama. How would these go?" And she let in a breath and rubbed them between her thumb and finger and said, "Ahh, yeah. *Qué linda.*"

So in the end we had a new glass vase, avocado green, and the pretty doilies, and a new set of green glassware that she said were *Highball* glasses. She had ordered new gold panel drapes, for the picture window. But we didn't have to carry them, they could be picked up the following Wednesday.

Then I helped carry the bags, and walked with her down the sidewalk, on the curb side, 'cause it seemed the thing to do when out walking with a Lady. Then Mama stopped in front of a Leeds shoe store and pointed to a pair of navy blue high heels in their window; they looked like the real leather kind.

"Pumps," she said.

She stepped in to try them on while I sat and waited with the bags on my knees. On the way out she reminded me that she'd have to drop off her dark dress to the dry cleaners as I promised to make sure she remembered which day to have me pick it up.

It was going to be a very classy Tupperware party. I knew it by the way she said "Pumps." And still we talked, as we walked on home from First Street, me and Mama, all the way back home to Elliott Street.

Walking down Marisol Avenue from the corner, she said, "When we get home I'll need help picking the stuff for the punch."

And I said, "I'll go."

"No, I mean, choosing which kind of punch to serve."

That was the help she always got from Barbie, "I'll help, but—"

"Yeah?"

"But, maybe, can Chance and Barbie help, too?"

"Share the wealth, huh?"

"No. The fun," I said, seriously. But she laughed at me anyway.

THE DAY OF the party Mama made sure that Chance stayed out of the backyard and kept neat. Barbie had ironed her best white blouse, and she had it on under what she called a hostess apron. I'd gotten Mama's pretty blue dress from the dry cleaners, and I folded the plastic bag in with all the others in the hall closet. To keep things neat.

Then we all sat in the living room and waited. All the neat colored bowls and canisters and the plastic rolling pin and bright green lettuce keeper were set out on the dining room table, next to the party food Barbie had made and the games Mama had found to play, for breaking the ice, she said.

But it got to be one and then two hours past the invitation time and still no one had knocked. Becca's mom kept getting up and going to stand every once in awhile, at the gold drapes that were pulled open, letting the sun shine in, but no one walked up to our red door.

Finally Mama said, "Kids, if you want, take the food into the back room and have yourselves a little picnic. Okay?" We looked at each other, and Chance, Becca, and Barbie got a party plate each and filled it with the colorful foods, using the colored party picks I'd walked so far to get.

Then they trooped back to the hall. Barbie's shoes the only noise on the floor. I stayed at the dining room table, not moving, and hardly bringing in breaths even, 'cause I was sure there was something more I could do, I just wasn't sure what it could be.

Mrs. Bettencourt pulled a cigarette from Mama's Chesterfield pack, lit it, and handed it to her. Mama drew in a drag and said, "Well—" Becca's mom didn't answer, just went back to the window and stared out at the street, one arm across her middle, like ladies who are waiting do, while Mama finished her smoke.

As quiet as it was, Mama leaned forward, reaching for another cigarette and lit it silently, like she was on guard of waking herself up with the noise of it. She crossed her legs at the ankles, and uncrossed them when she sat back into the chair and then crossed them once again at the knee, inhaled, and let her navy blue high heel dangle from her toe. She held her cup up, shoulder high, even though she kept her head down.

"Duff—coffee. You want a cup 'Lise?"

Mrs. Bettencourt looked back into the room from the new gold of the draped window and the empty street. At Mama so still and elegant there in the chair, with the doilies on the arms, a sad, sad look as I took her cup. I looked to Mrs. Bettencourt, and lifted Mama's cup. "Coffee?"

She shook her head.

All she said was, "Nuh-uh."

BECCA NEVER SAID anything about it out loud, but we both knew that Mama and her mom weren't talking to each other any more.

Mama had taken her pretty dress off and put the navy pumps away in their box after Mrs. Bettencourt packed the Tupperware things up and called for Becca. Then they left our house that afternoon.

Mama sat in the living room with her feet tucked up under her on the sofa bed. Still as ice. I took more party food in to Chance and Barbie, and their faces were like mine so I knew neither of them would be coming into the front of the house. She'd have time alone. That was good.

Love and Sorrow at the Same Time

I CLEARED ALL the rest of the party off the dining room table and freezer wrapped what I thought to save. Until the icebox was too full and I had to get creative about where to shove things. While I did the dishes, I heard Mama from the living room, shifting from the sofa, and turned to see her kneeling on the floor, in front of her records.

She sat back on her heels. I saw the blue album she'd pulled. A blonde lady on the cover, with her head tilted, her fingers to her neck, like she was remembering something soft that might have been there.

Mama leaned forward and set the record going with a click: And a sad, sad man's voice sang to her, about how he couldn't stop. It was one of the really sad ones from that album. I'd heard it a time or two since she'd first brought it home. His growly voice was full of love and sorrow at the same time. The house filled with his grief and regret.

I sang along in my head while I dried my hands on a towel: and when that one song ended she just picked up the needle and played it again from the top.

Then, I went to the living room, asking, "Mama... you

want anything?"

She looked up from the album in her lap, and brushed her hair from her forehead. "A whole new life would be nice." She reached, turning the volume up higher.

—*Please,* he sang to her, *please*—

WHEN I WALKED to school the next Monday that record was still going. And I realized that the little part of the lie I'd told Mrs. Bettencourt a long time ago, about someone playing a song and maybe they'd lost someone wasn't really a lie after all: I was just way early in telling it.

Mostly it was Chance and me who noticed how much Mama hurt.

"Let's do something to make her happy," he whispered as we stood in the doorway, watching her stare out the big picture window.

I wasn't so sure. But he pulled me into the living room, saying, "Mama we got a show for you—to make you smile." But as he started to dance I missed grabbing his hand for the twirl and he went tumbling into the coffee table with a big bump.

She turned toward us, saying in the scariest, soft voice, "If you can't make it better then just leave me be." She moved her eyes to the window again.

"Mama—" Chance started, but I pulled him away.

We went outside to play Monsters in the backyard. She was sad now, but any minute that could turn to mad. And Chance was the first job I had responsibility for, not Mama.

I LOOKED INTO the living room where Mama was still sleeping. She lay face down on the sofa bed. The light through the picture window made her hair alive with a dark, red-like jewelry, like glowing gems. She still looked like the most beautiful woman in the world. Even when she frowned. Or came at me like I was gonna be so sorry, *chica*. She was still beautiful.

Her record player was still playing that same song.

It made me wonder if only really sad or mean people were beautiful. Like Mama and Barbie, I wondered if that was why no one thought I was a prize; because, mostly, I was okay if I could make the sadness into a story and push it away that way.

There was a half bottle of soda and an empty coffee cup on the floor near where her hand hung. And the room smelled like too much smoke. The little TV played on low. I turned it off, picked up the cup and ashtray from the floor, tiptoed into the kitchen.

JUSTINE FIGURED MAMA needed to get out of the house and go walking with her up to the Lorena Drug store for a little window shopping. So that's what they did. Us kids were pretty happy about that because when they went up there they usually came back with a toy or something else neat for each of us. Mama was usually in a good mood when she had things to give us. They usually took their time and made a journey of it, so I went to see Becca.

IN BECCA'S ROOM I told her that maybe if I found the right time I could ask my mom if we could have a sleep over at my house, and spend the night some weekend. "There's the whole extra bed now, so there's room." I said.

"You miss him?" she asked. "Artie?"

I hadn't thought about it in a real long time. "Sure," I lied. But the truth was I hadn't thought about him in a sad way since nearly forever. Certainly not in a day-to-day missing him way. I hadn't learned how to do that in the Foster Homes.

Becca watched my face. It was hard to put into words, I guess, but I'd never missed any of us, 'cause we were always going away from each other; we had been all my life. Even Mama wasn't there when she was sad, like now.

So I'd decided to be as real as I could—even if it made Becca look at me funny. "I only miss him in my poems."

MAMA SAT ON the sofa with the bag at her feet and said, "Duffy, coffee."

But Justine touched my shoulder. "I'll get it." Then she headed for the kitchen as the rest of us gathered around Mama.

Mama was grinning because she knew we knew there were presents for us in the bag. She raised her voice to Justine in the kitchen, "Remember that store with the pretty green dress we saw?"

But Barbie stamped her foot. "Mama!"

Then Mama finally gave in, saying, "Well, I guess there's a few goodies here for you little monkeys."

First she pulled out a red pad of paper for Chance, the kind for school with the faded dotted-blue lines for helping you to print your letters all the same size.

Chance grabbed it from her and fell to the floor to get a look at it. "What do you say?" she asked the back of his head, but he was flipping though the pages and wasn't listening anymore.

Then she stretched, saying, "We walked all the way to First Street; these heels are killing me." She was teasing Barbie. And she winked at me. Then she reached into the bag again and brought out a 45 record for Barbie. It was Motown, I could tell by the white map and the blue of the label.

"The Supremes!" Barbie cried. "Thank you Mama!" She gave her a kiss.

"You hear that?" Mama said down to Chance, but he was still going from page to page in his pad.

Then it was my turn to be teased, Mama took her hands from the bag and crossed them in her lap and started to tell us about some girl who had waited on them behind the counter at the Drug Store, "Oh, wait, I was doing something here, wasn't I? Gotta be quick, work in another hour."

I nodded, real slowly. She finally pulled out a box of chalk, for me. They were the colored kind. The box read 8 COLORS. This was neat, Chance and I could play school with this and his pad of paper.

"Thanks, Mama. Thanks a lot."

But then Chance stood up and he threw his pad of paper at Mama, "There's no pictures in this! I want something pretty!"

Mama flinched. No one made any noise.

Chance yelled again, "Mama! I want something pretty!"

I knew what I had to do. I was mad that I had to do it but I knew it had to be.

"I want the colors!" He pointed. Mama's face looked like she could cry.

I looked at Justine there with the coffee, and I handed my box over to Chance, "Here, you big crybaby, take the fucking things!"

And Mama just went nuts.

She grabbed me *DON'T YOU!* by the neck first, *EV-ER!* then pulled *LET ME!* her high heel off, *HEAR YOU USE!* I bent at the knees, *WORDS!* leaning my head back, *LIKE THAT!* making the letter 'C' with my body, *AGAIN!*

But I forgot *GET YOUR HANDS!* about my hands, *DOWN!* her nails, digging *ONE CRAPPY!* into my shoulder, *LITTLE GIFT!* and her shoe swinging away and down, *AND YOU!* away and down, gouging *CANT!* a hole *BE!* in my palm, *THE!* causing *LEAST! BIT!* a delicate pain; *GRATEFUL!* just like Jesus'.

Then things got better for me, 'cause I simply wasn't in her grip any more. The whole of the room moved far away, down below me. Now I was safe. I could hear cries and screams but it was all okay because it was only sounds; I was somewhere else now.

Higher, over Mama's shoulder, as she worked so hard with her beautiful new blue pump. It was okay. Except that Justine was screaming something. But none of that was making any sense.

Then they pulled her off me. She dropped me and the room came back in a rush. I looked at the floor. Moved my knees. Slow, in case. And crawled to pick up the pieces of coffee cup that Justine had somehow broken.

BECCA AND HER mom were both at her door when Justine walked me out the back way and over across the street. "She's gone to work. I'm not staying. Can she spend the night with you?" Justine asked, pushing me inside, but watching behind her on their stairs just in case. Mrs.

Bettencourt looked puzzled, as she drew me in, but I winced when her hand landed on my shoulder. She pulled her hand back, "What happened?" Justine turned me around and Becca cried out seeing my legs.

It hurt too much; I couldn't twist to look myself. Mrs. Bettencourt whispered, "*Mon Dieu!*"

But by then Justine was heading down her stairs. I hurt too much to turn and see if she even looked back to see Mrs. Bettencourt closing her door behind me.

Mrs. Bettencourt put me in a really warm bath, and Becca sat with me while I soaked on my stomach. "What do you want to do?" she finally asked.

I said, "I dunno. Sleep?" I kept my hand under the water, 'cause I didn't want to see Becca cry again.

"No, I mean after that?"

"Be better?"

I dried off. Me and Becca asked to walk over to the church. Her Mom didn't think it was a good idea but I told her I really needed to. She offered to drive us but that didn't feel like that was the right way to get there.

When I looked her right in the eyes and said so, so she nodded and let us go.

"You—you be careful okay, Hon?" We both said we would be.

Becca was worried because my hair wasn't dry yet, and I had to smile. Because it was the first time I'd ever let it be braided and wrapped up on my head—to keep it off of my back. I was doing lady things for all strange reasons. And it dawned on me maybe all ladies did things for all strange reasons.

We walked back down those iron stairs. To the street.

On the way to church.

I started with the station we'd just finished learning the month before with Father Rudolph, The Fourth Station: Jesus Meets His Mother.

I knelt slow and easy. In a whispered voice I put my hands together, where they hurt the most. And I prayed the opening prayer: *Lord Jesus Christ, take me along that…holy way…Take my mind, my memory, above all my reluctant heart,…let me see what once you did…for love of me and…the world—*

Because these stations were for meditating on, it had dawned on me in the confessional, that Mama couldn't cry, no matter how much she listened to her song over and over again.

While Father Rudolph said things around me, I saw Mama's pain, till it was spilling out into the street and into everyone's soul. She'd kept things so to herself—Artie, Luis and Roy, and the party no one came to, her ungrateful daughter—that these pains were something that now were a prison of hers.

So just maybe, Mama was bound into hurting me; she was forced into making me do her crying for her. And she'd be doing that with my whole life.

I figured that must be a whole lot of pain to be holding back. So while I was there, on my knees, I said some more Hail Marys for her at each station than the usual. And finished each of them with *Amen* two times, for extra. Then, at the end of it all, as I started to rise slowly, another *Amen*. Whispered once more: for me.

Before I stood up to get on with it.

BECCA AND ME walked back to her house that night after

Church, and neither of us said anything the whole way. I thought that was the most kindest thing of all.

THE NEXT DAY, Justine came back home after dark and pulled me into her room from the hallway, where Mama couldn't see me. We sat on her bed, and she said, "Duffy, this is gonna sound real bad for me to say, but you should fight with Mama more."

I turned my eyes away from her face. What she was saying was wrong—I knew it. All the wrong things to do. But it didn't stop her from saying more.

"Yell once and a while. Don't let her do stuff like this to you. Get mad."

I didn't even bother to shake my head. I just waited for her to stop it. All those instructions that could get Mama to kill me next time instead of just hurt me real bad. Why didn't she tell me she'd protect me next time? Why didn't she say she'd be the one to save me from her?

"Be mad. Get mad all the time."

Justine didn't understand what I already knew. What I didn't have the heart to tell her, 'cause she loved me so much.

Mama would let the others fight with her because deep down she loved them, and she showed it when they all fought. But if I fought with her, me, Duffy, even once, she'd kill me. Dead. Because without me, how could she get all that crying out?

"I mean, if you have to, next time take a dime and go to a phone booth—"

I'd never meant the same to Mama as the others did. 'Cause no one in the family thought I meant anything at all.

Anyways, fighting was what Justine did. That was something else I didn't have the heart to break to her—that I didn't want to love that way, like her, by hating first to get it going. *Ever.*

I was just too different from them all. And not just my hair and my last name.

IT WAS TUESDAY afternoon, after Mama's morning shift, that Mr. St. John's car came pulling up in front of the Market, instead of our house. Mama was in the kitchen with Barbie, working on dinners for the week so she never knew he'd been in the neighborhood.

Becca told me later that she'd listened at the kitchen door and she remembered Mr. St. John saying something to her mom like, "This summer the kid needs a few days where she gets to be eleven instead of thirty-one."

And because Becca didn't think first from her listening spot, she said right out loud, "You're dammed right."

Her mom leaned into their hallway and told her, "Thanks for your contribution—but we've got it from here. Scat, Missy."

So that was all she could tell me about their talk.

MAMA'S MUSIC KEPT going and though Becca and me tried, we couldn't get her Mom to come to my house. Or Mama to go there.

Partly, it was their falling out over the Tupperware party. And the sadness built up from that. But right under that was something the two of us just didn't get, I figured; they've got a pride problem. But Becca, she thought, no, it's more deeper than that. We tried to figure it out because of what Father Rudolph had said—that it was our job to honor our father and mother, and since we only had a mother each, we figured all the honoring should go double there.

It was pretty obvious to us that the both of them were upset and not talking.

"She never says bad things about her," Becca assured me.

And I said, "Mama's just sad about it—not mad at all. That's why the music is always going. For the pain."

Becca tried recalling all the times Mama had visited, but we couldn't see where it went wrong. She asked, "Did anything bad with them ever happen at your house?" I thought back to being under the sofa bed and the kissing over me.

"No, nothing bad."

"Then I just don't know," she said.

SUMMER WAS COMING so I left off about honoring everyone and focused on how lucky Becca was to be going to camp all summer long. It was something she said she did each year. Though this was the first year, because of being friends with me, she said she'd rather not go. At least that's what she told me, but she might've just been saying that. Because of the beating.

'Cause her eyes really shined when she showed me the new two bathing suits and the shorts and tops her mom had taken her to get for camp.

"There's horses there. We hike and sleep out and put on plays for the staff twice while we're there. There's lots of singing and no boys at all." She said that while folding her five training bras into the little flowered suitcase. I figured her saying that part was just for me, on purpose. Since here we were going to be in seventh by September and me still in undershirts, and she knew it.

Part of her felt guilty for the fact that I was having to stay at my house. But I quoted Mr. St. John, about "When we have gifts," that this gift her mom could give her was not one to be sad about. Becca looked down into my hand's scar, then away, and she blushed.

IT MEANT POOR kids, but the words Mr. St. John used on Mama were *Disadvantaged Children.* But she knew. Even though it was there in a nicer way on the forms he handed us. I read it over her shoulder. Poor kids could take creative arts classes over summer vacation: writing, violin, guitar, things like that.

Mama shook her head. "Baloney-sauce, David. I need her here, not running over to the library all summer. And when was the last time you heard of a concert violinist from Boyle Heights?"

Mr. St. John told her, "Now, Ren—Mrs. Michealson, I'd think you'd be proud that she's got these talents—"

"—sure, during the school year," Mama butted in.

But he got tough, I'd never seen him do it before, and it was really uncomfortable to be there while he was being on my side.

"Look." He slapped his hand down on the table, "Her IQ is scoring near the 130s, and she may be holding back on that to please you. She's testing out two grades above her age group, *which* you are ignoring.

"This is the summer she turns eleven. The last year for being a kid, for having fun, for all we know, for being interested in anything at all. C'mon, Rennie, give her this break."

He sat back and then he added, "You've been to college; you know there's more out there than this. You'd jump at the chance if it were Barbie." I thought of Roy. I thought that was a low blow, the Barbie part, even if it was true.

All I knew was Mama was going to be extra mad at me for not being around to get her coffee or run to the Market. Also I'd be losing a lot of change from running for her. But inside I felt guilty and happy and special all at once. I made a promise to myself that if I got to go I'd be so good Mama would think I was an angel, and not just an *idiota*, always getting her mad.

Justine walked Mr. St. John out to his car, but then they walked past his car and over to the Market. Later, Becca reported what he said to her mom, before he got back into his car and went for reals.

Mrs. Bettencourt apologized to him that Mama wasn't talking to her any more, so she couldn't just come over to broach the subject. Becca told me that Justine just kept quiet.

SCHOOL LET OUT for summer on June the seventeenth. A Friday. Becca had skipped the last day of school 'cause the camp was gonna last for six weeks.

Mrs. Bettencourt had to put her on a train to Colorado, down at the Union Station near Olvera Street.

The night before, Mama had let me spend the night even though it was a school day. Becca sat on her bed and pulled her second pair of tennis shoes out from under her bed. "Can you do something for me?" I figured she was gonna say, the new packages of socks with the little yellow pom-poms at the heel still in the living room on her sofa, but she asked, "Will you still come over as much as usual, to see my mom in the afternoons? I think she's most lonely then."

"Sure, Becca. I would've done that even if you didn't need me to."

"Cool." She smiled, tossing her blonde braid back over her shoulder, "Thanks." And I knew for sure she meant that.

In the Green and
Purple Shade

O N THE FIRST Saturday of summer vacation I sent up a very strong prayer. If I was lucky, I was supposed to start the Creative Writing at the public library the next week on Tuesdays. Violin would be at the Evergreen High School auditorium Wednesdays and Thursdays.

I'd pulled my Journal out from its hiding place and wrapped it in a sweater to take over to Mrs. Bettencourt. I had some questions to ask her. Questions I thought not even Justine could answer. But maybe someone who knew French might understand.

The questions were about being a person good to myself, like Mr. St. John wanted. I needed to ask how to do that and still be Duffy, who was good to the family, all in the same life. I figured she'd have some good *chingada chismosas*, let's-go-dancing type of advice I could get from her.

"WELL HI, HON, Becca's not—" She stopped herself and whacked her forehead. "Oh my! How silly." She laughed,

"What am I saying?"

I stepped inside. "Not used to it yet?"

"Umm-hum. It's not easy, dear."

As we walked into her kitchen I told her, "Yeah, I know what you mean. Justine said Mama kept forgetting and yelled for me to go to the Market a week into me being in the hospital for my appendix."

"Yes, well," Mrs. Bettencourt nodded, "That sounds like Rennie, God love her. You want a soda pop?"

"No, thank you. They make me too thirsty." I sat at their table, "I guess all moms are like that, huh?"

"In ways," she agreed.

"Has Becca written yet?"

She looked back over her shoulder at me from her icebox, "No, not yet. A Popsicle?" But I shook my head, no, again.

I thought about what I'd come over to talk about but got too shy to begin. I changed the topic in my mind. Instead, from nowhere, I asked, "You think you'll ever talk to my mom again, Mrs. Bettencourt?"

She straightened up and put her hand to her throat, like the blonde lady on the cover of the blue album Mama kept playing. I got goose bumps. She paused. And her eyes got kind of shiny. "Oh, I suppose, in time we will. You know Rennie though."

"Yeah," I said.

"Well put," she said, one hand on her hip. "She'll want to talk soon. I think."

But it sounded like she was asking, not telling. Like she was confused. So to cheer her up I pulled my Journal from the sweater to show her. "Wanna see something really neat?"

"DUFFY! GO TO the store and get—"

Tuesday was finally here. I was nearly ready to go to Creative Writing at the library. Chance leaned his head into our room where I knelt, searching under the bunk bed for one of my lost tennis shoes.

"She's-call-ling-you," he sang.

"Go ask what she wants," I stalled, my face still under the bed, trying to see my shoe in the mess of toys and dusty socks.

"She *vants* you to go to the *marrrket*," he said in his vampire voice.

I punched my leg: *I should've asked first thing when I got up!* Maybe I could do what she needed and still not miss anything. But just in case under my breath, I prayed, "Please God, don't make me be late."

I tried not to be mad, like Justine says I should be more. No matter what nice things Mr. St. John said in some sunny park, I knew how I was Mama's helper. Who else was there? Barbie? Well, yeah, but no. Even if Justine said different I knew it was just easier to go on and do it, rather than fight about not wanting to and be punished anyway. Then there I'd be; having to go after the fight was over. My way would be faster. That was the best I could do for myself right now to make me happy, like Mr. St. John said when he'd spent that talk pointing to my heart.

Chance stood in the hall bowing low. He giggled when he waved his arm like a gallant knight to show me the way. He was still in his striped T-shirt and underpants, even though all the morning cartoons were over.

I could've been mad, but then Mama would see it on my face. What if she thought up more than just the Market to send me to do?

I figured my luck was changing, because I saw my shoe under the hamper in the bathroom.

"DUFFY!" she yelled from the kitchen.

I ran into the kitchen and leaned against the sink.

"How many things?" I asked, jiggling my foot to get into my shoe. Mama stood in front of the open icebox. She had on her green-checked blouse, tucked in tight to her jeans, and she hummed to the radio. She seemed happy.

Barbie sat at the table, taking pin curls out of her hair. She frowned, like my smell bothered her, and didn't look at me.

Mama turned and said, low and mad, "You come when I call you." The she started ticking things off on her fingers: *Leche, pan, manteca,* Kool-aid, coffee, and a half pound of baloney. Six. She told me, "Go get my purse from the sofa."

Mama turned back to Barbie and her stack of bobby pins. They both started humming again. I ran past the dining room. Jumped the coffee table for her purse. *Whack,* the top of my foot scraped the table as I spun back around with her purse. Then, *oooff,* I ran smack into Justine headed for the kitchen.

She was still in her blue robe. She grabbed me to keep from falling and chuckled, "Who set you on fire, Muskrat?"

"Mama needs some stuff from the Market. I gotta do it before I'm late for the library," I breathed, tearing back quick to the kitchen.

I held onto Mama's purse and lifted my knee up to see my foot. Balancing against a kitchen chair I could see a bruise starting already. I peered at it, and touched it light with my fingertip when Barbie kicked the chair from under the table. My leg slipped from my grip. My foot thudded down hard. It sounded like the heavy plop of Mama's open hand on a table when I got too involved with reading encyclopedias.

My shin vibrated a sharp pain all the way up to my appendix scar. My noise made us all jump.

At first I felt embarrassed, when Mama reached for the purse, giving me a look over Barbie's head, telling me, "When are you going to use your head?"

At the table, Barbie smiled and stuck her tongue out. But Justine saw that as she came in. She patted Barbie's head, in passing, and said, "*Fea.*" I felt just a little bit better. Mama frowned at Justine and handed me the Market money.

Outside in the hot air I ran for the corner, then cut across the street. Trying to keep the six things, but a Spanish song from the radio was in my head. Held there as tight as the money in my fist. I couldn't get rid of it. The words were ones I'd heard every morning but it dawned on me that I didn't know what they meant. It was weird; my ears knew the words, yet my mind didn't.

I said Spanish words I knew out loud, to see if any of them were in that song. *Flaca*, that meant skinny. *Sensitiva*, too sensitive. *Fea*, ugly. *Metiche*, nosy. *Sonsa. San grona*, big idiot. And it made me stop running. Weird to see the only words I knew for sure were the ones that would get me beat up or make someone cry.

But I couldn't think of the full way how to say, *Watch out for that truck*, or *Half a pound of baloney, please*. Or even, *We'll be together soon*.

Maybe Mrs. Bettencourt could show me those in French over the summer. Maybe I was too late in this world for my own language.

In her Market it was dark, cool, and the same Spanish song was on her radio, too. I wanted to tell her about Mama listening to this same song at home, but didn't know how to put that, in any language. I couldn't see for a second, but I knew where everything was by heart. So far this summer I had counted, and the most was four times to the Market in one day.

I nearly asked, "How's Becca doing?" but thought maybe she'd be really missing her about now; it would make her sad. That was the last thing I wanted to do to such a nice person.

So I just dumped all but twenty cents of Mama's change into the brown bag, said thanks, and ran for home.

"I'm go-ing to the Li-bra-rrry!" I sang to the tune still in my head, dropping a dime, then another, in separate pockets, "*Cu-cu-rroo-cu-cu.*"

I didn't even look both ways for dogs.

NOTHING'S GONNA GO bad today, I thought. *I'm going to the library for an adventure that's lasting three hours.* I was gonna be in a quiet room with ALL THE BOOKS in the world. The sun's shining. Justine had called Barbie ugly for me—right to her face. My foot hurt with every step I ran, but even so. Life would be best if every day was like today. Even better if there was no fighting in the kitchen when I got back.

Chance was watching more TV in the living room, with his hands over his ears. He frowned at me and his eyes said: *It's all your fault.*

Mama and Justine were going at it in front of the stove. I put the bag down on the coffee table. "Tell Mama the change is in the bag," I whispered to Chance.

"Chicken," he hissed, as I tiptoed into Justine's room. I crossed my fingers that he wouldn't tell them I'd been back. I hoped to get to the way-back room for my permission slip. Then sneak out the back without getting dragged into it.

I thought that maybe the first story I'd do would be about a family that liked fighting with each other so much, a guy would come by and give them checks for doing it so well. They wanted lots of money. And they'd always use the littlest's name to hurt each other. But the littlest would hate all the fighting, and would vow to live in poverty. So she'd fall asleep on the couch while everyone else was busy around her, yelling and raking in the cash. I was fuzzy on the middle and end, but the moral would be: *If you're so mad you're gonna fight someone, use your fists—not shouting.*

I liked that idea. On the way down the driveway I added in the family motto: *Pound their heads into the ground till their nose bleeds.*

Yeah.

FROM ARTIE'S CLOCK in our room I saw it was nearly ten o'clock already. I'd looked at a map the week before and counted; the library was ten long blocks away. I had to go up the giant Sixth Street hill, and across the freeway overpass, to a whole new neighborhood.

Most of the houses on the way down Elliott Street had their front doors open wide because it was hot. Music, all kinds, came from one yard after the other as I passed. Like my feet were changing a radio dial up and down as I walked.

It made me feel like magic. I thought: *that's a good part for the Mad-Getter Story—she makes music instead of fights.*

Little old people stood in their yards with water hoses; they smiled at me. They nodded to themselves when I waved and clicked their tongues at their lazy yard dogs, lying right where the trembling sprays of water were aimed. And one *vieja* threw a kiss to a little yard kid who danced with his baby sister on their lawn, begging in a high voice, "Gra'ma squirt me, me Gra'ma." "*Mira,* Gra'ma—A ladybug!"

Everything was hot and clean, like this street was feeling as good as me about not being trapped indoors.

The library was gonna be a long hard walk from our house. The Sixth Street hill I had to go up was known as Bike-Killer Hill. The steepest hill on earth. Artie and me, before he went for good, we were here on this hill one day when some poor kid lost control of his bike's brakes.

The kid was shouting for help, loud and scared, as he whizzed past. We turned, watched his trajectory, a word Artie used later for me. Kids all up and down the hill around us frozen at his passing. Stunned as the kid's feet tried to catch up with his spinning rubber pedals.

A few boys, from the top of the hill, shouted, "Davey! Jump off! JUMP OFF!" And even Artie called out, "Swerve! Swerve into the grass!" Then a little girl, way smaller than me, who'd stood shocked, still, next to me, she piped up, yelling, "Davey, Look out!"

My teeth hurt as we watched the kid and his bike, colored handlebar streamers, finally come to a stop. All tangled at the bottom of the hill, munched-up on the hood of a parked car.

No one could help. The smaller girl next to me had the

last word, after that Davey kid hit, she whispered softly, "*Jesus*—"

My knees shook as the kids at the top dropped their bikes, and we all went running. Artie was the strong one who carried him to the nearest house.

And now, every time I walk the hill, up or down, I feel pain on my teeth and hear the echoes shouting. I remember it all in my spine. Quiet like a ghost, her whispered *Jesus*— Too bad that memory of Artie wouldn't make a nice story.

After I reached the top of the hill, I started across the freeway. It's a long way across, very windy with the cars rushing below. Like it must be at the Grand Canyon, I thought. Although I'd only read about that from the encyclopedia. I almost closed my eyes as I walked. The sound of the cars below me felt like my dreams of a fast flowing river at the bottom of a wide, winding canyon.

It was so windy that the permission slip in my hand nearly got sucked away. Out and over the cars by the updraft. Mama had given me such a dirty look when Mr. St. John made her sign it in front of him that the thought of losing it to the freeway had my stomach grabbing at my heart, like the wind was doing to the little slip of proof.

At the green light I ran fast across Lorena Street, the big wide street that the freeway runs under, to a little pathway that cuts through to a quiet street that the library's on. Three more blocks, I thought, holding my side, trying to walk faster. These last three blocks here in this new shady neighborhood didn't look anything like my Elliott Street on the other side of the freeway, down at the bottom of Bike-Killer Hill.

There were huge trees all the way down the block in

front of me, covered with light lavender flowers, on both sides of the road. These trees must've had some special name. Like Artie's word, I needed to find the right one here, they were too magnificent to just be called *tree*.

The trees, they went up higher than some of the houses. A few of them tried to meet from both sides to over the middle of the road. The lawns all seemed greener than I'd ever seen in my yard. Artie could make the rent, I bet myself, on mowing this row of lawns alone. But I got the feeling that maybe not many people spoke Spanish on this street, or let music out of their front doors to meet someone's feet if they might be passing by.

Most of the houses I passed had different colored roses growing, just like on my block—but all of these were behind fences, and in tidy rows along the bricks of the house sides. I remembered the word *trained* I read; about roses that grew like that.

I slowed my walking and smiled at a lady who was getting into her car, "Excuse me, Ma'am. Do you have the time, please?" Mama would be glad all those conversations in the kitchen made me sound so good.

The lady frowned and squinted at her wrist then said, "Fifteen after ten." She smiled back when I thanked her then moved on. I had time; that was good. I kept walking but slower now, humming, running my hand along the fences here and there, like I knew the place, like these trees were everyday to me. Then, at the corner, there was the library.

It was a very old brick building, and, under a window, ivy grew towards wide steps that led to heavy double doors. More of the umbrella trees stood on its lawn. The path to the front door was shaded by them. It made me think of pictures of buildings in England I'd seen. That must be like this, I thought. Over the doors big words were carved in the gray stone of the archway:

ROBERT LOUIS STEVENSON

<> PUBLIC LIBRARY <>

1932

I figured, Mr. Stevenson, he must've mowed tons of lawns for money for a place like this.

AFTER THE LONG hot walk I was so happy to be in the shade of the purple trees. The sign in the window of the door said the library hours started at 10:30 a.m. *I'm okay; I'm early.* I smiled to myself, *I'm okay.* My breathing came out roughly, from the hill and hurrying across Lorena. The stitch in my side didn't get better now that I'd stopped. So I dropped to the grass by the path and sat soaking up the green and purple shade.

A breeze hit me and dried some of the dampness off my hairline. It felt wonderful.

But sitting there in the coolness and beauty I started thinking. I scrunched up my eyes, peered overhead through the purple light, *What if they don't like me?*

What if they say I'm stupid? Or too Mexican? Or that this neighborhood isn't the one I should've come to? I thought, *What if Mr. St. John had made a really bad mistake?* In the form he'd given Mama to sign. What if they hate me for no reason? Like Barbie does sometimes? I wished Justine was there on the lawn, waiting with me.

I wished I wasn't so dark, that I was lighter, like Becca and them. I got up to make my way back to the front door, to see the hours again, in case I read it wrong that first time. There was a small brass plaque next to the door. Standing on my toes I read it out loud:

I will make you brooches and toys for your delight
Of bird-song at morning and star-shine at night,
I will make a palace fit for you and me,
Of green days in forests, and blue days at sea.

"Hello," came a voice from behind me. "Are you here for the Creative Writing class?"

I raised my eyes to the window's reflection. It was a lady, with bright red hair down to her elbows. Tall, like Mr. St. John, she wore a scoop-necked black dress. It was real short. I turned to answer, and she smiled at me. Sunlight reflected in her hair just like Mama's. She held two big, heavy book bags and a ring of maybe fifty keys. I walked right up to her and took one of the bags. She let me, and invited, "Come on in."

The big ring of keys made a nice sound when she worked to open the door. She motioned me to follow. We walked into the coolness of the high-ceilinged rooms and made our way to the Children's Reading Room.

"HERE YOU GO. Have you read this one?"

She handed me another book for the stack she was building. Already there were ten in the stack. "Call me Patricia," she'd said. I had felt kind of funny at first hearing that. "Well, when I'm at work I'm called Miss Givens. But I think this will be fun all summer, so why don't you call me Patricia? And I'll call you——?"

"Pilar. Chavez." I'd been thinking of other names since I was seven. And decided that was a good enough pen name for the summer.

"Not just Pilar?"

I was trying to get her away from *just* anything, because of how it felt to think of her as *just Patricia.*

Big people were supposed to be called Mrs. This and Mr. That. I'd feel like I was at a party no one invited me to, wearing the wrong clothes that fell over my fingertips and no shoes, if she said to call her by her first name. Still, she was a real nice lady so I settled on *Miss Patricia.* She wore a gold symbol with three letters around her neck.

"I'm glad someone came early," she told me, pulling another book, handing it to me; we had a real rhythm going. "I can always use a helping hand."

I was comfortable with her right away. Except for the name part. Maybe this class wouldn't be so bad I thought. I wondered if she knew any French.

"Actually, I'll let you in on a little bit of information," she said, while she continued looking for books from the low shelves, "I may be the new Librarian at the Jr. High School when September comes; this Creative Writing class is basically a summer indulgence, like a sweet tooth of mine."

I patted the stack of books when she stopped searching and straightened up, "It's a good thing these aren't fattening," I said, "we'd both be overweight by the time summer's over."

I guess she wasn't used to children because first she looked at me like I surprised her then she laughed way too long for how good my kidding was. She reached out to touch my head, "Well, well. A sturdy mind inside such a slight frame."

I moved quick like cat when I saw her hand coming at me, then I tried to stop myself from flinching, but she saw it anyway, the way I froze. She took her hand back. "And you've got the blackest curls I've ever seen."

And Toys for
Your Delight

TO COVER UP being so goofy about her hand I let her know that I knew the Dewey Decimal System. That I understood how to put books in alphabetical order by author, or by numbers if they needed it. Both my hands were on the rolling book cart. I kept swinging my foot as I tried to brag in a gentle way but still not be too proud.

Then five or six other kids came into the Children's Reading Room. Some of them happy to be there, like me, and some boys looking like they were bored already. I recognized Georgie, from my class in sixth. He plopped into one of the chairs set up in a circle. At least there was someone I knew, even if he was a boy.

Miss Patricia first looked at the big clock; it was 10:30 now. "We'll be starting in fifteen minutes." She looked back to me, and saw how shy I felt to be noticed as the first one there. Her lips came together, she glanced from the kids looking me over with suspicious stares; my head was lower on my neck. I got red in the face; my feet weren't swinging now.

"So what have you been reading lately?" she asked me.

Like we were still the only ones in the room. I didn't even stop to think it might be a trick to get me in trouble, like when Mama asked to make sure I wasn't getting into her books from the book clubs.

I said, "The Prophet, we got that at home for Christmas. A Tree Grows in Brooklyn. Maggie Now. You know The Listener? By Taylor Caldwell? It was cool, there was a moral for every vignette. That's the right word, right? Vignette? I looked it up—it's a real funny word. First it means, like, a running ornament, now what the heck does that mean? But farther down in the definition it means, the act of a play, but in books or stories it's just a scene. Man, that was a good one—that book. Even better than the Stations of the Cross. We're on those right now with Father Rudolph." I took the last book she'd pulled but held on to it while I was talking, letting it give me some bravery. "What ones have you read?"

She nodded, handing me another book as more kids came though the door, and she asked real low, "MGM?"

I blushed, "Yeah, I'm one of the lions." I whispered, "You won't tell any of these kids, will you?"

"How old are you, nine, nine and a half?"

"I'll be eleven end of July."

She paused, looking at the kids who waited; then she winked, "I can give you a real good list to go from when you run out of things at home."

It wasn't till I was walking home, repeating her words in my head, that I noticed she'd said: *When* I ran out, not *if*.

"HERE, DUFFY, YOU'LL need these—"

Justine stood smiling and from behind her back came a

blue-flowered book bag. She held it out, "Go on. For reals." I grinned so big my cheeks squinted my eyes into small and happy slits.

"Wow, thanks, Justine." But when I took the bag it wasn't empty. It felt heavy, a lot heavy. And I stared at her, eyes big now.

"Well, open it, silly, See what's inside."

"Oh, Justine." Then my hand dug into the bag as I sank down onto her big bed. Looking back up to her I made an *Ay, Mi Dio*, face, eyebrows high: out of the bag came a pink zippered pencil case, then a tiny blue box, full of paper clips and silver thumb-tacks. I had to hug her again, this time with my eyes tight and hands full with the presents.

"Thank you," I whispered.

With my chin up on her shoulder I squeezed her tight, then opened my eyes: the small treasures were still there.

"C'mon. Dump it all out on the bed," she invited, pushing things away to make a clear space. I turned the bag upside down and shook it; out poured a rainbow of still more little things: a package of yellow school pencils, a set of different colored writing pens tied up in a thin maroon ribbon. I couldn't believe it, there were index cards, and a palm-sized spiral notebook with a red rose on the cover. And then still more, a thick package of 3-hole school paper. A pencil sharpener in the shape of a little spotted dog in a red dog house.

"You like 'em? Huh?"

"Yeah," I nodded, "I really like 'em, wow—"

"They're for your writing. Writer's tools. Mrs. Bettencourt and Mama helped me think what to get."

Mama? Mama and Mrs. Bettencourt? They were talking again?

"They're beautiful." I felt like crying. And nearly did as one by one I picked up each thing, turning each over and over.

I wiggled, kneeling there on the floor. I stuck a fresh pencil into the little doghouse and twisted.

"You deserve them, Duff—Maybe this'll be a starter to get you to try the Journal. Now that you've got your tools and time for all your words. I can tell you'll be excellent in no time." But I couldn't think of any words right then.

The Journal was something I hadn't thought of since Easter and the talk with Jeff and Mr. St. John. She added, "I thought with your birthday coming up, I'd combine the two and surprise you now."

"Oh, Justine," was all I could get out. I touched everything spread out around me there, just for me.

She sat at her white and gold dressing table, leaned forward, to look closely at her face. I came to kneel and looked into her reflection in the mirror, like Mama let me do in the bathroom when she was getting ready to go out. She smiled the same way Mama did when she was putting on her face. Her cheekbones going up in the same tilted way.

"Tell me more about your library lady," she said.

"It was great!" I said, "She has keys to the front door on this big jangl'y ring. She let me in early with her. I helped pull books for her. I got to put them back later when everyone was gone. This library's nothing like the little one we got over on June Street. There's posters of all kinds of stuff on the walls and on the ends of the bookshelves. And," I breathed in, "the chairs are set up in a circle."

"Really? What for?"

"To-encourage-the-freer-exchange-of-ideas," I quoted,

almost sure I'd gotten it right, "That's what she says."

"Does she?"

"'Member how we used to sit an' go page to page in the encyclopedia? Talking about everything we saw? She's like that, like you are, full of facts and ideas, knowing neat stuff," I said. "'Member how heavy the book on our laps was? 'Member on the back porch the wind would try and turn the pages for us? An' you'd help me sound out all the big words and then one day I got good enough to help you?"

"That was so neat," she said, and I could tell from her eyes that she was remembering, too: how we'd discuss anything our eyes came across, as the sun went down behind our house and night came on. She ran her fingers through her light hair and asked, "Did you write anything today?"

I shrugged and picked up the pale blue hairbrush off her table. "First we listened while she read us a story. It was a real baby book, with pictures on each page, but a neat story anyway, with a moral. It had bits of poem in it, too. About a boy who could dance; it was a gift, but he didn't know he had it. That's where the moral came in. Hey, guess what? Georgie and Richard's in the class. They tried to act like they didn't want to be there, but I kinda think Georgie does—I remember one of them, wanna hear it? A poem? From the book she read us?" I didn't think so much of my writing as Justine did.

"Sure, Muskrat; go ahead."

So I kneeled a bit straighter and started in my best voice.

OUR EYES LOCKED in her mirror as I recited. Justine was looking at me like I was the smartest girl in the world. And when I looked back to her I felt I was.

Alone, just the two of us here in her room, it was easier to feel smart and proud. I blurted out, "If this room was my whole house, or if I lived alone at the library, I think I'd be the happiest girl in the earth."

"What if Chance and Mama and Barbie started to miss you?" she asked, "Then what?"

"Well—maybe I'd visit, bring presents from the library—so's they wouldn't feel bad. Colored paper for Chance, and for Mama, lists of good books to read."

"You could write them stories. Or poems—"

I frowned and shook my head, "Nah, Mama would want a real gift, like stuff Barbie would think of—something bought, or like Chance could make from wood or rocks."

She leaned towards me till our foreheads touched, and whispered, "What was the moral of that story?"

I grinned, and put the hairbrush back on her dressing table, "Yeah—Well…"

Justine set her elbows on the table and looked in the mirror; she took a big breath, "Tell you what I think, Miss Chavez," she murmured.

"And what's that, Miss Michealson?"

"Just keep being wonderful Duffy, 'cause you are. One day Mama'll love you as much as I do." Our eyes locked in the mirror, "You gotta remember that all the times in the Foster Homes she didn't get to see us much, that's a lotta time missed, a lotta understanding that never got practiced."

"I always try—real hard." I said, "I just wish—"

"Give it time, Muskrat, 'kay?"

"I will." I promised.

"Okay—Now tell me—" She crossed her eyes, showing her bottom teeth, "Did you *write* anything today?"

I laughed, shifting into holding one shoulder up like a hunchback, my arms out like a hypnotized zombie slave. "Yessss, Master. I did." I pretended drooling. "I dragged it all the way from the Library here to the castle for you to experiment on, just as you commanded!"

Out of my back pocket I pulled a folded sheet of paper and handed it to her. "It's a poem," I mumbled, turning my face away, it hurt so much to show her. But she was studying her face.

"You read Duff—I like your voice when you read."

A scary feeling went up my back; Miss Patricia had said nearly the same thing in the class today. I unfolded the paper. In the same zombie voice I started reading.

"Ah, Duff—Do it for reals, *mi corazón.*"

So I started again, "Leaving the Pretty Hills, by Pilar Chavez."

"Pilar?"

"Lemme alone about that, okay?"

"Okay."

"—AND HERE, TODAY, as I relate to you."

Justine sat quietly and stared at her hands, then picked up her blue brush and held it in her lap. Not even pulling blonde hairs from it like usual. "That was great," she finally sighed, "I wish I could write that good." Her quiet tone embarrassed me.

"Did I use that word relate right?" I asked. "That means to tell somebody—right?"

"Oh, yeah." She nodded, leaning up to the mirror to study her face again. "Yep, telling somebody. You got that right." I put my elbows on the dressing table, watched her search her pale features. She paused, then caught my eye through the mirror, like Mama does, "I'm breaking out," she sighed.

I looked first left then right, then over my shoulders, "*When?*" I whispered, secret agent style. She pushed me over. "Can I come too?" I giggled from the floor.

"Silly." She chuckled, shaking her head. "Pilar—wow."

Still giggling, I crawled back to her bed and inspected my presents. Justine said, "I got a what-if for you, Muskrat."

"Hummm?" I was concentrating on opening the little blue box.

"Listen Duff—I mean it." I turned, getting comfortable, my back against her bed, my knees up. Foot tapping, leaning my head on the bedspread.

"Yeah?"

"What if I moved outta here and in with Lydia's family next year when I can get my work papers?" She asked it real fast, all in one breath.

I wanted to say. *I'd go with you, right?* because she'd surely take me too, wouldn't she? I couldn't look at her. I'd cry for sure. Afraid of knowing that this what-if was one like Artie.

That it meant I'd have to be the one who stayed. She was more my Mama than Mama even wanted to be. I thought of Artie being forgotten and of all the times Justine'd stuck up for me against everybody.

I tried to be brave, 'cause I don't forget things. Like Justine's kindness spread out in colors on the bed behind me. Like Mama's yelling in the backyard about losing. I knew I couldn't let Justine end up yelling to someone later, in some other yard. Not because of me.

"I guess—I'd write you letters all the time, and ask

Mama if I can help her move her things into this bedroom.”

ON THE FIRST day of violin class, I walked all the way to the Evergreen High School Auditorium on my own again. But this time to the west instead of back up the Sixth Street hill. I'd been there once before with Artie. To the high school; the school he went to when we'd first moved in on Elliott Street. That one Sunday we rode the long blocks all the way down Fourth Street then up to Savannah Street, with me on his handlebars. We biked even way past Mama's new second-shift work at the Coffee Shop, to see his new school, see how long it would take him to get there each day.

We just rode and rode for blocks way back on that day in February. It was remembering stuff like that when I really missed Artie. Missed doing things—just us two, like true explorers. He'd be happy to see me walking his same route now on my own.

In the Auditorium there were some of the same kids from the writing class. Some others I didn't know at all. Mostly, of this group, everyone seemed a bit older than me. I walked my second permission slip to a man in a white shirt who sat smoking a cigarette at the piano near the stage. He said, squeezing his eyes narrow to read my slip and mark me down in his roll, “Another one.”

“Miss Chavez? A pleasure, I'm very sure. Let's see, violin or cello?” He reared back to take a good look through all his smoke. I followed his gaze down all of me to my feet—“Definitely not cello.”

“Afraid not, sir,” I answered to that, and smiled. 'Cause he seemed like an easy-going type of teacher, especially the way he made his cigarette do that bipping and bopping when he talked.

He smiled, handing me a music book from one of the stacks there on his piano, then pointing to where I should sit on the arc of folding chairs in front of him.

I sat in the row where he'd pointed as another kid walked up. You could hear the grin in his voice as he said, "… and still another one."

When the rows of chairs were nearly all full with us, he stubbed out his cigarette and stood at his lectern, eyeing each of us for a second, while we all watched him look from face to face.

Then he pounded once on the book in front of him and held it up in the air. All of us jumped at the noise echoing up to the ceiling. He raised his voice up loud, "The cellos and violins you'll have in your possessions soon may well be the most difficult instruments for each of you to master. Why? Two major reasons: One, because in today's world, the radio is the only way most of you know how to make music. And B, especially in your early efforts of *hee-ing* and *haw-ing* donkey notes, no one at your house is going to want you to practice much. Ignore them! Tune all that negativity out! Anyone in this room can play music. And I'm here to see that all you end up doing just that."

He pointed. "Stand up." And the kid did, it was Richard, from sixth with me and Becca, seventh in September. "Do you want to know how to play cello—" he leaned, to read his names list, "Mr. Montez?"

And Richard, wiping his hands on his pant legs, said, "Sure Mr.—"

"Simon. Mr. Simon to each of you. I'll return the courtesy in kind."

"Yes, sir. I do, sir." And we laughed because Mr. Simon said that sounded like wedding vows to him. That we should all take our tasks as seriously over the course of the summer.

Mr. Simon went on, moving from really serious teaching to making us all laugh. He went though about five more cigarettes, too. At one point near the end, he held his full ashtray up off the piano; quick as anything I stood and emptied it and handed it back.

"Not at all necessary, Miss Chavez. But thank you all the same," as he kept right on with his music advice.

It was a great class. I liked Mr. Simon as much as I did Miss Patricia. It was going to be an excellent summer. I was especially glad at the end when he didn't ask us to read any music from the books.

JUSTINE WAS DEAD serious about moving out like Artie had. She'd told Mr. St. John and Mama and neither of them said, "Oh, no, young lady, this will not do." Or anything like that, like you'd expect from the TV show families.

Mama said pretty much the same thing she'd been saying from the day she got us from the foster homes, *'At fourteen I was working full time. You'll be too, and be out of here by seventeen tops.'*

Only Mr. St. John wanted things to slow down and step back, and *please let's take another look at this situation.* The rest of us had known all along that this is how we do it, here in Boyle Heights.

In the end, he walked with me out to the porch as he patted his pants pockets, then his chest once, he said, "…could've sworn I had more gum," then he raised his voice. "Rennie, We're heading over to the market for gum, be right back."

We walked a lot slower than we needed to. Mr. St. John said, "Duff—Remember that film last year? *A Patch of Blue?*" He had his hand on my shoulder. He looked both ways before he'd let us cross.

"Sure, I learned the word *tirade,* from it, 'member?"

Mr. St. John nodded, "Right. Tirade. An—"

"—un-safe time." I finished. "Roseanne was always in a tirade." I used it in a sentence.

"Well, when your Mama gets going like Roseanne…" I thought to myself, *Oh, no, way worse than that.* "Well, keep a very low profile, Okay? I worry about you sometimes."

"Sure, Mr. St. John. I can do that."

He bought his gum, offering me a stick, but I didn't want any. He went away from our house that evening very sad, for coming in as a white guy with such high hopes.

IT WAS REALLY late. Me and Mama were the only two awake in the living room. I felt a silence you'd get from stories. I thought you'd never feel this from real life, but here it was.

She called it a *rare night* and I knew what that meant.

The coffee; she needed me to make some every once in a while with the slug in it. The slug was Imported, it said so right on the red and yellow label, above the words *Kahlúa,* and *Licor Delicioso.* The slug smelled real pretty, but once Chance and me tried a taste on the tips of our tongues. It was as awful as tasting vanilla straight from the bottle when we baked cookies that one time. But Mama liked it, the *Licor Delicioso.* I'd melt a slug into her hot coffee: on rare occasions, as she put it.

So here was one of these occasions. Justine was on her

way gone, Mama's coffee was hot and slugged, and I wasn't sleepy, and for some reason, she didn't mind that.

I sat at one end of the sofa and wrote one of the assignments for Miss Patricia's class, and Mama, at the other end, just sat. Sipping. Her stare on nothing at all.

Then from somewhere, Mama just started talking. She pulled her knees up under her and drew her cup up to her face, inhaling, then offering me an inhale across the sofa, too. Boy that was such a pretty smell.

Then she said, "You know, Duff, when I was little like Chance, maybe six or seven years old, I used to write poems." That brought my pencil up off the pad. I looked over at her and didn't know what to say.

"Yeah," she laughed. "Me."

She took a long sip from her cup, she grinned. "I remember once, I sat on my front porch with a poem I wrote. Gee, from the time school let out till way after dark, waiting for him to come in from work so I could show him." Her voice was like one of her records, a song sad and far away, though she sat right there talking.

Sweetness from Her Cup

"'THE STREET LIGHTS came on, it got real dark, my stomach was growling, but I wouldn't go into the house. Nope, I just sat there with my poem waiting for my Papá. Finally, your gra'ma came to our screen door and said he'd probably stayed on for an extra shift. He wouldn't come home till later.

"'So,' she said, 'You'd better just come on in here and eat, Missy, before you go to bed.'"

I thought to myself, *at least she wanted to feed you, Mama.* But I didn't say it out loud.

Mama kept on with her story.

"And while I sat with her at our kitchen table and picked at my cold dinner, I swear to God it felt like my heart would break. Your gra'ma told me, 'Lemme see this poem of yours.' I wanted to save it for him only, but she was *enojada conmigo*; I let her take it from my hand."

"Did she read it?" I asked; I didn't want to think about her tearing it up, not even from Mama.

"Oh, yeah, she read it. Then she stretched back in her chair and reached for a pencil from the sideboard. I'll never forget it, a red pencil. She sat back down with me and started to correct the spelling and grammar. To tell me I'd used all the wrong words. That animals didn't do things like I'd written. Then she said, 'My, Goodness, Irene, why don't you use your head?'"

I looked over and I saw how sad Mama's eyes were. Staring off somewhere I couldn't see. She went on talking and sipping on her coffee, "I never wrote anything after that. I never did show him that poem."

In a voice that suddenly sounded real small to my ears I asked, "Mama, do you remember how the poem went?"

She smiled and thought for a while, then she looked far off and said, "Nah, some little silly thing, about a cat, I think; probably one of the worst poems ever, now that I think about it."

I smiled, "I think it was probably a great poem." Both of us sat in the quiet, then she began talking again.

"You know, Duff, I depend on you the most of all. More than I can the others, even from the time you were little. Always wanting to know if you could do something else for me, you've always been a help to me." She sighed.

"Chance is just a boy, and with Justine… well. So with only you and Barbie left … I'm really glad that I can depend on you. You know?" She patted my foot, "If I teach you something, I know you'll learn it. You've got a good head on your shoulders, Nugget, not like me at your age." I could smell the sweetness from her coffee cup. It made her hand on me feel a bit warmer, too.

"Maybe I ask a lot of you," she was saying, "but it's only because I know you can do it. That's the only reason—you always listen; you're smart, like Justine. If you want to know about something, you just go and learn it, like with the encyclopedias. I never worry about you."

I sat and thought of everything she'd told me. I never really felt she liked me. I knew she loved me; she wouldn't have gotten me from the foster home if she didn't. But I was surprised by all that she'd said; my heart felt like a piece of a puzzle had just been found on the floor of a closet. I cleared my throat and asked, "Mama, would you like me to show you how we write good poems?

"At the writing class we get handouts and tips. All kinds of good tools. The Librarian put them all into a book, typed and everything. I'm pretty sure I can borrow it to give you a lesson. If you want. We could walk over to the library next Wednesday. I mean, would you like to? Write some new poems?"

Mama turned to me, now she was the one looking surprised, "I'd love to Duff. Thanks for asking. We'll make an evening of it—just you and me." She leaned in close, whispering sweetness, "Barbie and Chance can stay at home."

I thought for a second then whispered back, "Maybe we can order them Chinese food, so they won't feel left out."

She smiled at me, "See, that's why I'm so proud of you."

THE FOLLOWING DAY, after Mr. Simon said class was dismissed, I snuck into their High School library, holding my new violin case up in front of me the way soldiers do their guns. This was the Evergreen High School library. Way more books than the kids' section at Robert Louis Stevenson public library. All around me the shelves went higher than I could ever reach, even if I'd stepped up on the black rolling library stool. Maybe Artie would even have to get on tiptoes to get the top shelf books here.

I stepped down a row and inhaled and ran my hand along the spines of each book, wondering if these were every book in the world. More steps. Still I was in the same row, books going on for days. I was in the 800s. There were slim, typed, white labels, every once and a while on the edges of the shelves, for the Dewey Decimal System sorting: 810 –American Literature in English; 811 – Poetry; 812 – Drama. I turned a corner and started up another row, then another corner to turn, and still more 800s.

I walked all the way to 817 – Satire & Humor, before I stopped moving forward and decided to walk backwards, my violin case bumping on my leg. I tilted my head to read all the titles that caught my eye, all the way back to 811– Poetry. That's when I saw it, my head tilted to read sideways: *Songs of Travel and Other Verses* by Robert Louis Stevenson.

I think for a second I forgot to breathe, remembering reading those words on Miss Patricia's library wall: *-and toys for your delight.* Making the connection from here to over there across the freeway blew a wind though my brain. I felt lighter, ready to fly.

I set the violin case between my knees and opened the book, skimming the pages of songs, finally finding that one at SONG XI:

> *And this shall be for music when no one else is near,*
> *The fine song for singing, the rare song to hear!*
> *That only I remember, that only you admire,*
> *Of the broad road that stretches and the roadside fire.*

I could feel the sway and motion in the words as they spoke in my mind. Words like two hands swinging between folks out for a stroll past a cool stream. I wanted to write words that like that some day. Words that moved that way.

I WAS LYING on my stomach on the living room floor with my music book open in front of me. Changing all the notes to letters and numbers so I could remember the music and play my part of Brahms' "Lullaby," *Arrangement for Ensemble Strings, Difficulty five of nine* ♪♪, for Mr. Simon the following Wednesday.

Chance came crawling on his knees over to me with our deck of playing cards, "Wanna play Memory, Duff?"

"Can't. Working." I told him, changing the last of all the ones in the three low lines.

He sat back on his feet. "What'cha doin'?"

"Fixing this music book," I said, writing the final B over all those kinds of notes.

He got down on his belly next to me, propping his chin on his hands. "What's that one?" he pointed.

I counted up from the bottom, E-G-B-D-F-, but got a little lost because there were plain Bs, I wrote those as Just B. Then there were Bs that were sharp, and Bs that were flat; I was making the sharp ones B-2s. The flat ones B-1s, cause the number one was flatter than the number two, but my mind was getting confused.

"Maybe a G-2?" I said, looking to my notes for how it was supposed to go, "Nah, it's a B. Thanks, Chance." And I marked that one, too.

"Is it a code?" he whispered.

"Yep, only white people know how to read music, so I'm getting around it by doing it like this."

He rolled over on his back and brought his knees up to his nose, while thinking about that. "What else is just for white people?" he asked. I stopped marking my book and thought too.

"Having a bike from the Sears, instead of like how Artie always got ours–by swiping 'em. Having dandruff and allergies and athlete's feet," I added, from what I saw on commercials. "Having a car, like Mrs. Bettencourt. Knowing how to read music," I tapped my book, "—lotta things, Chancy. Just watch TV."

"Oh, yeah." He nodded, probably thinking about his favorites: the June Taylor Dancers. "That's right."

WEDNESDAY CAME, BUT Mama had to go over to Roy's. So we never did get to the library for the poetry writing. I told myself that was one more thing to learn; the way another type of pain felt. That my Quest was teaching me so much. That I'd use it someday in my writing.

Then I called Chance out into the back yard, and we played Monsters on the lawn till it was time for bed.

Mr. St. John was at our house for a dinner Mama made him. A special birthday dinner. Barbie had helped Mama make her famous Nopal and Shrimp patties. And there was Sangria for the grownups too. Jeff brought the Impala again. Chance was real put out that they hadn't driven the tiny blue and white car with the little porthole instead. For about three drinks of his red Kool-Aid he didn't say anything to anyone at all. Just swung his feet propeller fast under the table, like a cat's tail, when it's thinking about pouncing.

Then near the end of the meal, when I brought out coffee on the tile tray for the grownups, Jeff asked, "Hey, Chance, you ever seen under the hood of a Chevy before?" That was it—Chance was out of his seat and pulling on Jeff towards the front door. Mama laughed, and Becca's mom said: "There you go, Jeff, a new friend for life."

Mr. St. John and Mama and Mrs. Bettencourt moved into the living room and started lighting up cigarettes and settling down to do some talking on the sofa. Mrs. Bettencourt picked up my music book to flip through the pages. She kept looking at my marking, "What's all this, Duff?" she asked, turning the book out for Mama and Mr. St. John to see, too. All the notes were changed to my system. Mr. St. John reached to take it and see the job I'd done. I was pretty proud I'd taken the trouble to be neat with my penmanship. There were no eraser marks. And most of it was written out in a real straight line above the top bar lines.

Mr. St. John frowned. He flipped, looked, then flipped some more, going from page to page, puzzled. So I took a chance and moved in next to him. Pointing, "See, these are the whole notes, and here are the flats and these are the sharps, with all the twos. Get it?"

"But aren't you supposed to learn the actual musical notes within the staff?" he asked.

"I have to do it this way."

"Yeah?" He looked again. "Why's that?"

I didn't know how to explain it to him. I looked to Mama then to Mrs. Bettencourt, all of them waiting, "Well, I'm not white." I said, shifting from foot to foot, *boy who couldn't see that?* This was hard. I told him, "Mexicans can't read music."

Mr. St. John gave Mama one of those *See what you've done here?* kind of looks, but she just shrugged and picked a bit of tobacco from her tongue. Then, blew her smoke up over the sofa, telling him, "There's no disappointing this one, hum?"

BECCA'S MOM AND Mama, after Mr. St. John's birthday dinner, were kind of good friends again after getting past the Tupperware party disappointment. From time to time that summer they'd go out dancing. Sometimes I'd be getting up to use the bathroom, and I'd hear Mama's key in the door, letting herself in from being over there above the Market for the night.

But other times, like this week, they'd been fighting and Mama said it was just as well I wasn't around to go to the Market. Why spend her good money there anyway?

She'd go out with Roy, or other guys who we didn't even know what to call. Some didn't even get to come to the door. She'd call from work to give any instructions; then we were on a free night. Dinner was what we made, and TV was as late as we wanted. It was a good thing it was summer.

Nights like that, and the mornings that followed, no one mentioned that her sofa bed just needed refolding, and wasn't made when she'd come in early and shower, then go right back out for work. Maybe Chance and Barbie just didn't notice. Justine may have figured out she'd been gone all night, but as she mentioned once in the kitchen to Mama—not trying to be mean or anything—"Roy's TV is the only thing left of Roy."

Mama, she'd just finished ironing her work blouse, she said real mild, "We can just call the TV a settlement."

Before one of the fights with Mrs. Bettencourt, I was glad that Mama spent time there over at the Market. Because even though Becca asked me to, being so busy with writing class and the twice a week violin, I'd had to go more than once into Confession. And say I'd let my good friend down on my promise.

I LOOKED ALL around the library's Children's Room for a story idea. But nothing was coming to me. There was only books here to look at. That made thinking up a good story a harder thing to do, since a lot of my ideas came in through my eyes. The light through the windows helped some, but I still felt stuck.

Miss Patricia surveyed us all from her desk and motioned me over. She was always a help. I really liked her ideas for how to get things going. Or knowing when to stop. I was learning so much on how it was all done. Way more than *just emptying your head on the page,* as she liked warning us.

She had a list in front of her. Even upside down I could see my pen name and the title of one of my stories at the top of it. She tapped a chair next to her desk and I sat. She whispered, "We've got some good news for the group." Like I was one of the teachers or something.

So I switched over into the helper point of view, "Uh-huh?"

MISS PATRICIA FIGURED the parents needed to get a look at our work so she'd arranged with her Library bosses for a little reading night here in the Children's Room. That's what we were setting up. Us kids were gonna read our best work so far. Because some of us only wrote poetry, and some of us concentrated on short stories, it would be a *"mixed-bag event,"* she said.

I looked down at her list, with my name at the top, and asked, "When we do this can I be last?" She was doodling on a pad. "You don't seem like the shy type, but sure, I can close with you, good idea, the strongest last." She tapped her pad with her pencil. "Very good idea, Pilar."

I was real glad she thought so 'cause that "strongest last" reason was exactly why I wanted to be last. But that was too conceited, and if I'd had to, if she'd made me say so, I was gonna go with shyness for a reason. It was my way of keeping my Easter promise to Jeff and Mr. St. John, of slowly working my light out from under my bushel.

"MAMA, AT WRITING I got chosen for a reading, the librarian set up a night for parents. I can invite two. There'll be refreshments. And—everything. If you want, it's next Tuesday, at 7:30. You're off then. I mean, would you like to go? Hear me say my writing?"

"*Ay, m'hija,* I'm so tired after that shift, and I have to cook, too." She grabbed up her cigarettes from the end table, then looked around for anything she'd missed; she was running late. She'd come in less than an hour before. Now she rushed to get going. "We'll see okay?"

"Sure," I said, holding the door open, "If you can't go can I ask two others? Maybe Artie and Justine?"

"If you need to," she said; then she pulled the door closed after her, off down the walk.

"DUFFY, WAIT A second, Hon—"

Mrs. Bettencourt stood digging something out of her purse and I was waiting. The two of us were at her gate at the bottom of the iron stair. "Its right here, I just know it. Oh good—"

She'd caught me on the way home from the Creative Writing class. "It came yesterday, but I just today remembered." She pulled out a photograph of Becca, with her arm around some girl. They stood in sunshine near a cabin, the pair squinting into the sun. A leg of some other camper was a blur at the left, and I thought, *Such a good touch to show how much fun was there.*

"Cool. Thanks Mrs. Bettencourt. What week's this?"

"Week four. She'll be home before I know it."

We started talking about the camp. I figured the Market must seem pretty quiet without Becca there. She said the sweetest thing to me; "Actually, that quietness is because you have so many nice new things *you're* doing."

It sure seemed the best life to me. I stopped heading home. We walked around to the front of the Market and stood there talking more. I said, "If you got any other photos, I could make a picture frame for them with origami, if you have any wrapping paper to use."

At that, she touched my arm and I didn't flinch away, she told me, "I'm sure I do."

"SO IT CAN'T be Justine 'cause she's got a shift, and I asked, but no one has Artie's number, so I was wondering—"

"I'd love to g—"

"—if I could use your phone to call Mr. St. John—"

We both stopped there, and I felt real, real bad. Here she'd given me one of Becca's photos and said sweet things and I didn't even think of her first for the reading.

"It's not 'cause Mama—"

"—I know with your Mother—"

"No—"

"But—"

How many times were we gonna stop and start?

At least she was smiling at me still. She put her hand on my head: "You can use my phone. I do have Jeff's number.

If there's room, I'd really like to go. I don't mind begging an invitation. There—your turn."

I didn't say anything, just pulled open the Market's screen door for her, and waited till she'd stepped in ahead.

"BECCA WRITES BUT never as often as I'd like her to," she said. "And I must have shoved at least three sets of writing papers into her case when she wasn't looking. Three at a minimum."

I laughed. "Maybe it should have been while she *was* looking."

She laughed. "With me pointing and saying use these?"

And I thought a moment, because although the summer was my Best Life come true, how much about it had I shared with Mama? I was busy sharing it with people and teachers who weren't even my family. Father Rudolph would probably scold that it should've been the other way around. Even if I did like these strangers way better.

In her storeroom I asked, "Do you think Mama may be too busy because she doesn't know for sure how much it means to me?" Mrs. Bettencourt came back towards me with her apron tied on, and with her hands on her hips she looked real stern.

"Please Duffy, listen to what I'm saying here. It is not your job to worry about your mother. It's her job to do that about you. Like I do with Becca," she said. "That's a mother's job—to know what matters to you." She'd found the pretty wrapping paper and handed it to me. "I think, maybe there's just so many of you to know about for Rennie. It weighs her down that there's no room to reach all of you like she'd want to."

I though Mrs. Bettencourt would be a great teacher for Mama and told her so. She blushed, "Yeah, well…" She moved back behind the counter. Then, she watched as I folded the origami picture frame right around Becca's photo, fancy-wrap, for a queen.

"Okay, lessee." She had her tiny black half-glasses on now. "Oh, lovely," she said when I was done, "I have just the place for this, too," as she walked to the register.

MY BIG DAY. It dawned on me it was just going to be me at the reading.

Mama wasn't home yet. So after waiting as long as I could, I gave Barbie two of my dollars from my Market money and asked her to watch Chance. And not tell Mama. She said, "Sure."

I walked across the street and asked Mrs. Bettencourt if she still wanted to go and she grinned real big, saying, "Sure, but let me make a call, hon."

I'd remembered some of the things we'd talked about when I was making her the origami picture frame, and thought—*I should've asked her first and Mama second.*

And when she led me around to her car, I knew it wasn't a thought I'd give to Confession either.

Things My Heart Heard

I THOUGHT A lot about things while Becca's mom drove; how real girls go out and not always with their own families. How maybe real girls shared good times with loved ones, whoever those ones were. Because my Quest was showing me, whether I wanted to know or not: being real was really about being happy.

By the time she parked I figured that I must have gotten past another of the steps of my Quest. It had to be—it hurt way too much.

The parents clapped every time a kid walked up to the lectern, every time one finished a piece, every time they moved off to let the next kid come up. You'd have thought it was a sixth grade graduation and junior high was next from all the wide smiles and pride shinning in everyone's eyes.

Mr. St. John arrived in his own car, I thought he'd have forgotten too. But no. They sat together and that was almost nice to see.

At intermission, when the cookies were being held on tiny napkins and the punch being drunk from kid-sized Dixie cups, we sat talking about all kinds of library things while we waited for the second half of the presentation to start.

I felt sort of awful not having Mama or Justine there, but then I just took that feeling and shoved it away. Then it was okay. I even asked *Lise*, sitting in the little circle of chairs, to say hello to Miss Patricia.

I called Mr. St. John over too. Suffering though the three of them beaming down at me. Watching me turn red while they kept up with their *Author Someday Soon* conversation. I shielded my eyes. Nearly walked away, except I kind of liked it—in a bad way—what were they thinking?

Great talk to be doing in front of someone who hadn't read yet.

Miss Patricia got it into her head that this was Mama and a husband. I got real glad when their turns came to be going red in the face once I explained who it was that'd come to hear me. *C'mon*, I thought, *these are two white people you're standing in front of.*

My reading went well. The parents laughed, and I had to stop and wait for it to go quiet so they could hear the ending of the last line I had to read.

It caught me off guard. I wished Miss Patricia had told me it was funny. I thought if I'd known I would have read it different.

"Great presentation. Lots of talent in this group." Mr. St. John said on the way out, his hand on my back. 'Lise agreed as she dug in her purse for her car keys. I kept thinking I could do that every night of the week. Never getting tired of hearing the laugh at that unexpected place. Or the clapping after.

'Lise hummed while she stood on the Library steps. She said, "That went very well. Want to celebrate with a malt at the hamburger place?"

Yeah, it had went real well, especially the moment Miss Patricia had said, "Pilar Chavez."

I said, "Okay, I'll treat." Because I had some money with me, definitely enough for three malts. But she laughed and said no. "You're the special one tonight—my treat."

Mr. St. John, he tried to tempt us with french-fries, too. But my plan for being a real girl was also not to be a mooch. If I couldn't buy it myself, I didn't need it as a treat from anyone else.

So then he started bringing up me being in seventh come September, saying, "'Lise, you can see she should be in eighth, after hearing her tonight, maybe even ninth."

I opened my eyes wide at him, I bit down on my straw so he'd see the pain he was causing. But he missed it entirely. They went on talking as I pulled in, smaller and smaller into myself. My eyes began to burn. The cold malt dropped, heavy, it sank to the bottom of my stomach. And the pain in my shoulders felt such a powerfully heavy feeling.

With the two of them I couldn't drift away though. I had to sit and hear it all. Mrs. Bettencourt tried to touch me, but I had to shiver from the ache of their words. Finally their talk died down, and I squeaked out, "You guys gotta stop this now." I pleaded, "Like Mama says, seventh is good enough. And we better get used to that. Excuse me, please."

I picked up my malt, taking it to the trash can. I couldn't go back to the table. I went to stand by her car. Just to stand and look up at the stars. Not to cry. I used the time to pray a prayer of disappearing.

But God answered: No.

STILL, IN THE car I thought, it went real well; the reading, the audience laughing, even I saw that. But after our malts, in the backseat of her car, I tore up my pages on the drive home.

REMEMBERING MAMA'S NEVER-ARRIVE-EMPTY-HANDED rule as we pulled up to my house, I asked. "Wanna come in?"

She thought a second, then low, to the steering wheel, she whispered, "*¿Que la?*"

I thought: Is Mama home yet? Will she talk to 'Lise? But I was tired of them acting like sulky babies. Like Justine and Barbie over some silly thing like a hairbrush. They had to get over it. They were supposed to be grownups.

We walked up the path to the front door. I saw that 'Lise walked gripping her purse like someone going to see their Social Worker about keeping her kids. It came to me: she was like me, she didn't want to fight with Mama. She wanted to be liked. And if I took her in the house and Mama was still in a mood—well, it would be like sending her in for a beating. "Do you maybe wanna just say goodbye at the door instead?" I asked.

"No, no." She said, shaking while she still gripped her purse. She smiled a sad smile and promised me, "I can do this."

"'Lise?"

"Yes, Dear?"

"I don't think I can. Do this, that is."

And that stopped her for a second. But she must've been missing Mama something fierce, 'cause then she said, "Well, why don't you go in the back way? I'll just knock like

I came for a visit. She'll never know."

That seemed so crazy yet so brave, too, that I didn't even try to talk her out of it.

Indoors I thought about staying in the back room and acting like I didn't know she was even at the door. But then I thought, *No, I can't do that.* 'Lise was the one who'd gone to the reading for me. She'd wanted to go even before I'd asked.

So I crept down the hallway, listened, waiting to hear anger. But it was just her voice. With Chance's and Barbie's, no Mama at all.

WE FOUR STOPPED being awkward after a few seconds and she stayed and we all talked like normal. Like me and Becca did over at her house. Then, we played some Monopoly, with Chance and 'Lise against Barbie and me. Until we heard Mama's key in the door and I realized I hadn't pulled her bed out for her.

I jumped up and just said, "Mama." Barbie had the pieces on the board swept up into the box lid, Chance was right behind her with the board and the rack of play money. They slipped into Justine's room, not making a sound.

So it was just me and 'Lise standing there when Mama stepped through the door and stopped short. There was a guy in a car who honked as he was pulling away from the curb. She didn't turn, just gave a half wave behind her as she pulled the door closed.

"Alice," Mama said. Putting her purse down on the sofa, then looking at me when she realized it still *was* the sofa.

"Sorry Mama," I began as I reached to move her purse to get the bed pulled out.

"Leave it, Duff. Go on to bed," she said. She gave me the gentlest whack on the butt, "I've got it. Go on."

So I took one last look at Mrs. Bettencourt and, like a chicken, I went.

WEDNESDAY, WHEN I woke up the next day from sleeping 'till I didn't want to anymore, I was surprised to find I still thought the reading had been fun. I even slept so late I skipped violin.

FROM THE MARKET, you could hear Mama's song stealing across the street. Those lyrics strong as ever. Since there had been no yelling or slamming doors after I left the two of them, I figured maybe they were back to friends again. Except there was Mama's song still.

'Lise was sitting back by her register in the dimness, her hands in front of her, not holding anything, just being there to stare down at.

She must've been missing Becca real bad, 'cause I could see, even in the shadows, that there was a bit of a tear starting there, as she raised her head and listened to Mama's song come drifting in through the screen door.

She had been so nice to me, letting me use her phone. Talking to me like I was as real as any girl around. Coming to the presentation. And the malt afterwards. Then, even nice to Barbie and Chance, with the Monopoly and all. Before I turned to go, I reached and touched her lonely hand there, empty on the counter.

I looked her right in the eye, so she'd know I wasn't lying, "I'm so sorry, 'Lise."

Back at home I wondered if Mama would ever hear her song enough that she'd get to the crying part.

THAT SUMMER I found there was one better part of having to walk all the way to Evergreen High School for violin. Sure, I was happy about getting to go farther from home than anybody in my house ever had, even Mama. I laughed inside every time I passed the Coffee Shop on the way there. Way farther, even than Mama's job. And twice a week, too.

But, second, the really best part was that there were tons of signs to read along the way there and back. Some were in Spanish, some English. And plenty of time to read them all. The four-story brick wall was the best, its sign was painted high up, wide, right across the windows of the building, you could see it from about two or five blocks before you walked up past it: UPHOLSTERY. You know how many words I could make out of that? A lot.

MR. SIMON WASN'T smoking. Which was a sign he was getting frustrated with us and that was a bad, bad sign. He clapped his hands and stopped us from going farther, "*HolditHolditHoldit.* Just—Stop!" he said. And everyone put their bows up, like he'd taught us to during a *blessed pause for silence.*

"You, Miss, and you also. Up here, please," he said pointing to me and Richard's older sister, Sylvia. To the class he said, "You will all watch, listen and repeat, please." Some one behind me whispered, *parar, escuchar y repetir* to themselves.

Mr. Simon reached his hand around Sylvia to where she held her violin up in the start position. "Learning to hold the violin correctly is relatively easy for some of you, but like Miss Montez, here, the grip on the bow seems quite a source of, shall we say—*woe?*" He moved her hand into more a graceful bending and made her try again.

"To begin with, I expect that each of you is continuing to practice in front of a full-length mirror. We use *open* strings and *long* slow bows to start. *Place* the bow on the string at the heel of the bow. *Check* that the bow hair is flat against the string. Completely flat, Miss Montez. *Draw* the bow down, make sure that the bow stays in a straight line between the bridge and fingerboard. Better, not good, but better."

He nodded, smiled at her, then turned to me, "Next caterwauler, please."

Sylvia moved back to her seat but he tapped her with my bow as she went, "Practice those long bow strokes on all open strings, no fingering necessary. Maximum control. *Softly* and *slowly*."

And we all nodded. "Now for the Lefties, all two of you," he said. "Miss Chavez, your participation, please." He motioned to have me put my hand out and grip the bow from him, then stopped dead when he looked down into my palm.

"Fifteen minutes. Everyone out. Cig break," was all he said.

But he held his hand on mine. Kept me standing there while everyone else shuffled out into the daylight.

"That's quite a scar," he said, still not letting go. I looked down and thought I was seeing it for the first time. It had been there it seemed like for so long now. My little scarred hand. For some reason I thought my Quest had made it invisible to adults. I looked more. Looked at it like it wasn't mine.

"I'll work harder with the bowing, Sir." Looked at it like

it was nothing. "I can't feel anything," I reassured him.

But he didn't get it. He made us wait to come back in while he smoked three in a row.

THE FOLLOWING DAY was the first time I noticed Joanna in my violin class. When I saw her, I tripped over someone's case and hit my nose so hard tears came to my eyes.

We were all in our seats in the Auditorium and I'd gone to the front, up to Mr. Simon to ask if he had an extra sponge for my chin, cause mine wasn't in my case. When from behind me I heard low notes being played on a cello, someone's bow pulling some really sweet notes from their instrument: *Bum-bah-Bumbah, Bah-Bumbah-bumbah, Bah-Bum-Bah-Bumbah-bumbah.*

It was the *Wimba Way* song.

Except for the only ones here being us kids, you'd swear it was coming from an album. What was echoing from the sound holes, it was that good. And for the chanting parts she'd switched and began with pizzicato fingering, her left hand moving so graceful up on the neck and fingerboard that even Mr. Simon stood to see who it was coming from.

It sounded so cool. And she wasn't even looking at music, either.

I felt that my mouth was open so I closed it, taking the sponge from Mr. Simon without even saying thank you. And he'd been so nice about my scar and all. I couldn't take my eyes off her.

Walking back to my chair I went *SPLAT*—onto my face on the dusty floor.

I tried not to look at her for the rest of the class because each time I moved my eyes towards her my bow slipped.

Mr. Simon was getting fed up again. He'd said so, using the word *sloppy*, too.

But for the last peek I snuck at her; from out of nowheres, I said to my heart, *That's the girl I'm gonna marry.* Which was silly, I knew it. But—well, that's what my heart heard anyways.

Later, when we were all leaning over our cases, putting our instruments away, laying down our bows in the case lids, I went back up to hand Mr. Simon his sponge back. He called out, "Miss Delgado, a moment please."

As she came loping our way, Mr. Simon watched her move between the folding chairs a second. Then he switched, looking me up and down. Lowering his voice, he said, "Since you're a lefty, Miss Chavez, I suggest you find a seat somewhere to her right next time."

And I nodded: *Yeah.*

DURING THAT SUMMER it got to be my sneaky job to let Mama know what 'Lise was thinking, and then relay what 'Lise wanted to say to Mama but couldn't.

I'd ask, "How are you doing today?"

And Becca's mom, as she counted out my change, she said, "*Je suis bon.*" Which was code for *Tell her I'm doing fine but miss her.*

So after I'd put a few coins in my different pockets, I'd run home, and as I handed the bag to Mama I said, "Mrs. Bettencourt sure is getting skinny with Becca still gone. How come mamas don't ever eat if there are no kids to cook for?" And Mama, she got that code, but was stubborn about hearing it. She'd say, "Some folks just don't know how to deal with sorrow." Which was her own code for *I'm not gonna be the first to say I'm sorry but I miss her too.*

But I kept up with it even when they thought I'd forget to notice. Because it was all in the air, and everyone was noticing it except the two of them.

I WAS TELLING Joanna, "I'll be eleven, end of July." She paused our looking up books in the card catalog about architecture, then she winked at me, "You wanna do something special that day?"

I wanted to say yes, but just maybe Mama would have something for me, so I picked up one of the finger-sized pencils and stuck it under my nose like a mustache. I raised my eyebrows to keep it there, "Nah, I'm just making conversation."

I raised my eyes to the windows, way up at the end of the book stacks, past her pretty eyelashes and asked, "You ever seen a real architecture building? Like from another state or country?"

"—saw the Empire State building when I was real little, but I don't remember it."

She took her list and we headed to the 700s section for Joanna to go through her choices, which was The Arts section, though we both disagreed with the Deweys about putting Buildings there.

She walked with her elbow up on my shoulder. She was tall, like Becca and her Mom were; she probably didn't even need to stand on her toes for most of what she was looking for there on her list of books to pull. It was me and Mama and Justine who were real, real short. Even Barbie.

I faked a limp to throw her step off. To get her to smile at me; the sunlight from the windows hit the scattering of freckles on her nose. It was with all that sun in her face that I realized she had hazel eyes. When she held her book list you could see the green in her eyes flick from under her lashes, list to shelf, then back to the list. It was poetry right there in front of the 723 section.

Joanna handed me another book for her stack. Then she stopped and asked, "You want a few?"

"Nah, I'm gonna go over to poetry." Miss Patricia wanted us to bring in a favorite and I thought I'd try Robert Louis Stevenson. He didn't do lawns after all, I'd found out.

"Can you sleep over tonight?" Joanna asked, and I didn't even think to say I'd have to find out first.

"Sure, I just have to go home to get something to sleep in."

AT FIVE-THIRTY I walked right up to her door. Her mom answered, inviting me, "Come on in. JoJo! Your friend—" she turned and gestured a help-me-out-here circle with her hand.

"—Duffy. Am I early?"

"We don't do much clock watching, did you wanna be?"

"Huh?"

But then Joanna was there. I set my pajama bag down and followed her into the next room.

Her house was like the library. There were books in every room. Even in her bedroom there stood a full-wall bookcase. Hardly any stuffed toys like at Becca's. And the floor didn't have linoleum like in mine and Chance's room, either.

We sat in her room, and Joanna plucked at her cello like it was normal to have it out of its case when we weren't even in the auditorium. She let me go from book to book, reading all her titles. In a completely different way, it felt nicer than being at Becca's over the Market. Then we heard calling from the front of the house. Joanna pulled at me as I stood bent over and head tilted, still reading book spines.

Her parents were all dressed up for going out for the night. "To the Dorothy Chandler Pavilion," Joanna said, to hear someone called Zubin Mehta conduct the L.A. Philharmonic with some special soloist that her Dad felt I should have recognized, but I didn't. He made a sad face at that. It made me wonder if I should go get my bag and leave.

And as they headed out the door, Joanna's Dad got stern, "Keep it cool. Stay out of the liquor cabinet. And I don't wanna see any cop cars here when I drive back up."

I froze, then he hugged me bye as hard as Joanna, and whispered, "—pulling the leg, sorry 'bout that, my dear." Then they were gone leaving only her mom's light perfume and the fading sounds of their revving motor.

Joanna shut the door after them and put her arm around me and we walked back to her room for more books and cello. I was thinking, just us two, Joanna and me; a girls' night out. Just like Mama.

"YOU SURE LIKE books," Joanna said.

We were talking about all kinds of stuff while I tried to read every title on her bookshelf. I thought never being without books should definitely be on my Best Life list. I thought she was so lucky to have started her list so young. I told her so.

Joanna tilted her head, but didn't laugh at me, "My what

list?"

So I went and sat on her bed, telling her about Barbie's Best Life List. How she had plans for when she got older. What she wanted.

When Joanna got the idea I asked her for her list. She shut her eyes, pondering for a while. "Tell me yours first," she said.

"To never be without books. To not lie. To not be—invisible. To never be a bad mother." I blushed, and thought next I'll be telling her about Artie and my scars, about being on a Quest and my journal. "Okay, now you," I said.

And she started in, ticking things off on her fingers: To go to college. To be musical her whole life. To make her father proud of her. To beat him one day at chess.

I thought of how different her list was from Barbie's with the ponies and the aprons for the kitchen, for the hair dryer and stuff. How Joanna's list, full of things to do and achieve was nearly an opposite of Barbie's for things to get, to have.

Then I wondered about my own list—to not this and never that, and I got kind of quiet, 'cause it was simple to see mine was no better than Barbie's. I only wanted to *not* do things. I was so dumb. It made me wonder why Joanna wanted to be my friend, or even why Becca would.

When the Devil Knows Your Address

THE SUN WAS streaming into her window when I rolled over and heard Joanna stretching and saying, "We usually go to an IHOP on Saturdays, you wanna come?"

"Oh, man!" I yelled, and jumped up, pulling my nightgown over my head.

"Duff, what's wrong?"

"What time is it?" Saturday was Mama's day off. From the looks of the sun it was probably too late in the morning to be sneaking in if she might already be up. I was looking all over for my undershirt, "I gotta go, now!" I said and grabbed my pajama bag. Pushing my hair into a long messy braid. *Forget the undershirt,* I thought.

"Well, wait. My dad can drive you. He's up already." And she was out of her room, heading toward their kitchen. Without me even explaining.

"JUST THAT CORNER, I can walk from there." I said, pointing to the Market. I held my pajama bag in my lap.

Joanna in the back seat said, "Ah, Dad—"

But Mr. Delgado wouldn't let up, "I drive her to her house and say howdy or that's it for any more sleep-overs."

I pointed at 'Lise, who was stepping out of her Market with her broom, "There she is." I said in the saddest voice I could, hoping he'd think I'd given in. Then before he was parked, I scooted out and ran to her saying, *Help*, real low.

She looked from me to him, getting out of the car. And put her hands around me, like I was Becca, arms across my chest, guardian angel style. 'Till she saw Joanna getting out, too. She leaned in to my ear, "From him?" But she straightened when Mr. Delgado walked up with his smile and his hand out.

"We didn't know she hadn't told you she was spending the night. I'm sorry for frightening you like this," he apologized.

'Lise reached for his hand and shook it, telling him, "Her sister said she'd gone over to their house last night." She pointed right to my house. Goosebumps ran up my arms and across the top of my head, seeing everyone turn to look at my lawn. My red front door. "Duff, first say thanks. Then into the market, young lady. Now." And she whacked my rear as I went. Not for play either.

Joanna called out, "Bye Duffy. It was fun."

And as the wooden screen door banged shut behind me I heard, "She wasn't any trouble, I hope?"

"YOUR MAMA THOUGHT you were here last night. She sent Justine to find you." I stood with my pajama bag in front of my knees, looking down; sad this time for real. 'cause no matter what, 'Lise always seemed to pick up my lies and run with them. "Since it's obvious she's too proud to come face me and ask for her daughter back, she probably thinks you still are."

I looked up. "Thank you."

"Lucky you—that Rennie's who she is." Then she walked me to her door. Whacked me again. "Well, I hope it was worth it." The weary tone of her voice made me wish she'd been angrier, like Mama gets. And less disappointed, like she certainly was in me.

MAMA WAS IN the kitchen when I came in. She just looked at me from there, then turned her back. Reached over to the radio dial to make the music go up higher. I tried to just walk into the hallway and on to my bedroom, but she called out from the kitchen, "When you get in there you'll stay until I say so."

I hurried along the hall and shut my door as quietly as I could.

WHEN I WOKE up I didn't know what time it was. It was dark, but a light blue type of dark; it felt like sunrise was just about to get here, but I looked at the clock on my headboard. It read: one-forty-eight. The moon was full silver. Hanging right over my window, making the outdoors nearly as bright as a day. I'd slept all the day and night away. Mama hadn't come in once.

I'd pulled a blanket over me but I was still dressed, even my shoes were still on. I hung my head over the bunk to see if Chance was asleep, but he wasn't in his bed.

For a moment my heart told me they'd all moved away and left me there. Such a marvelous feeling to have, even for a second. But it didn't last long enough. I thought about Miss Patricia and how she liked my writing. About Joanna's dad with his "not till I talk to her mom," and Becca's mom. The way she'd come to my rescue like that, no questions first.

How Mr. Delgado wouldn't take no for an answer; he had to meet my mother or else. And that brought me around to thinking about Mama. How the whole day and night had passed and I was here alone in this moon-filled add-on room. Like I was a stranger.

Songs were going through my head and my eyes were getting used to the dimness And I stopped smiling. I lay there wondering what it was I could give up, like for Lent, what could I take on, or face, even. That might, in her eyes, be enough of a sacrifice for Mama, to keep her from hating me. And to earn her—*What?* I heard my voice ask me, *What do you want from her?*

No words came back to me.

I stretched my arms up to the headboard, and felt a book there. Waiting there over my head. I clicked on Artie's little reading lamp. It wasn't a novel I pulled it down for a read. It was my 1966 Journal. I'd promised to show it to Joanna. And then the words came to me.

My heart said: *This is the sacrifice.*

I SAT RIGHT up in bed. The covers fell from my chest. This, here. I'd figured it out—something I could hand over. Like Father Rudolph had showed us in Station Six, Simon Helps Jesus Carry His Cross, my doing this might help Mama. And on the greedy side maybe help her to like me more.

I climbed down the bunk ladder and made my way into

the kitchen for what I needed. Then, I moved back through the hallway, into the way-back bedroom for the Journal. Next was the slipping out the back door to the yard. Back to the old barbecue that still leaned against the garage.

I set the red carton of lard and a box of matches down at my tennis shoes. Looked around in the dark for the hose. I ended up going and getting it from the front yard. I wrapped the hose around me so it wouldn' make any noise as I carried it back, and the blue of the whole house and yard made me wish for night work, like Mama got sometimes. Everything around me so fine and calm. It just seemed a better time to be alive and moving soft from spot to spot.

I dropped the hose and dragged the one end over to the spout. Then I squirmed my hand into the oven mitt with the daisies sprinkled on its one side. I thought of Chance and me the day we found this barbecue. His helmet had a daisy on it too. I thought; Miss Patricia would call that foreshadowing, if this wasn't real life.

I STARTED IN with a whispered Prayer of Solace, because this was to help Mama: "...*till the shadows lengthen, and the evening comes, and the busy world is hushed, and the fever of life is over, and our work is done.*" The hose was running and I kept the fire small, but I thought that was okay. I didn't want God to see a prideful fire. Just a very sincere one.

THE NEXT DAY I was running down the driveway chasing after Chance, he was being Bruce the ocelot and I was being Honey West, like from the TV show, when we came barreling around the corner of the house. From up on the porch, Mama grabbed me up and dragged me indoors. One moment I was moving forward, then, *BAM*, I was moving sideways in her grip. Like a cartoon of someone running on air.

I was hoping Chance wasn't following, 'cause it didn't feel like a safe time. And I didn't want him getting it on accident if she decided to tirade and swing too wide. Suddenly aiming for all idiots, like sometimes happened.

The change from daylight to the darkness in the house had me blind. I stumbled for a second. Then she shoved me into a chair in the dinning room and said, "Hold still."

I figured if I was sitting she wasn't in the mood for a beating. So I stayed as still as I could there in the cool dimness. Being a statue, waiting.

She walked away into the hall then into the bathroom. In a second she came back with scissors and a towel. Artie's hair trimmers in her hand. She bent to plug the trimmer in and I heard the *hummmmm* sound it made as she flipped it on and set it down on the towel near my shoulder.

She twirled a finger and I turned on the seat so my back wasn't up against the chair's back. She held out my hair, up off my waist, her fingers tangling in it. She just started cutting. Bit by bit, from the ends as it hung on my back and on up to my head.

She kept quiet as she worked, moving around my head and I could feel the lifting, cutting, moving, lifting cutting, moving. I thought about Barbie's pageboy cut, and how Mama always said the words "Four fingers, all the way around," whenever she was trimming Barbie's hair.

Four fingers, all around.

She was done with the scissors, and now she pushed my

chin down on my chest and said, "Be still," again. Though I hadn't said anything or moved in anyway so far, except as she'd tilted my head.

The *buzz* of the trimmers went right around my ears, and then to the nape of my neck. It tickled.

Then, she stepped back with her trimmers, she said, "You're gonna ask first, next time. Right?"

I was looking down at all the black curls on the floor, like a dog and a half, there at my feet. I thought; I'm free, there's nothing else she can take off me.

"Right?"

"Right, Mama."

"Now, go get the broom for all this."

THE NEXT MORNING I woke up and touched the back of my neck, where I usually had a long thick braid hanging from, it was empty.

"C'mere," I told Chance. "Here, you be quiet. As soon as I make Mama coffee we'll go." He sat at the table with the mini-box of cereal and tried to empty the whole load into his mouth. "Use milk or don't bother," I scolded.

"You're not the boss of me. You an' your boy hair," he said. Turning away but munching the Frosted Flakes with his mouth open in the direction of the living room.

Then next time untie your own damn shoes, I thought to myself. But I made a note to remember I'd thought that. For Confession. Why was I mad at him?

The water was boiling for the coffee and I had a piece of toast ready with jam. Putting it all on a triangle of napkin, I took it in to Mama on my favorite tray. The one made from real mosaic tiles. The picture the tiles made was the

Holy Mother and Child. It was my favorite of all time. Not so much for the religion, but because I loved the way Mary let Jesus sit on her lap and touch her face.

"Mama? Here's some toast and coffee, okay? Me and Chance are gonna go out and walk for a while. Is that okay? You said to ask first next time."

For a second she didn't move. But I knew better than to ask twice. I waited.

"Duffy," she groaned, as she rolled over and struggled to sit up, "Do you value the fact that you can walk upright, without crutches?"

"Huh?" Chance asked, his puzzled face dusted with cereal crumbs. I stood still in case she was going to grab me again. My neck hurt waiting to see.

But she reached for Chance and gave him a hug and a swat on his rear. Then she smiled up at me and said, "Thanks for the breakfast, Nugget." She sighed, pushed the dark hair from her forehead. Took a sip of coffee. "Don't go far."

Outside the sun hit me so bright it made my eyebrows hurt, really bad. Chance hopped in front of me, karate kicking his way across the lawn. Killing all the bad guys and from the sound of it all their side-kicks too.

"Hey Duff," he shouted back at me, "How 'bout we go see what we can get from the construction site on Marisol?"

"Okay, we can build a fort in the fruit tree."

"Yeah!" he agreed. "An' invite Mama to come and have tea in it with us."

I caught up to him, yelled, "TAG!" and tore off down the hill. He laughed and ran to catch me, his little fist swiping hard and strong at the air. "Roughneck!" he yelled at me; that was Mama's word for when I was beating him at something too boyish, like running. And with all my cut hair off short that's just how I felt.

We were both out of breath after the run down the hill and the chase up the other to the torn-down house on Marisol. I sat down hard on what was left of the old house's concrete steps. "Spell girl," I gasped.

"G-R-R-L," Chance said, certain, leaning against me. He slapped at a bug that landed on my sweaty arm.

"Nope." I shook my arm. "Here's a story to help you remember."

He might not care or even remember the story, but he always let me talk, no matter what I came up with.

"Here's goes." I looked around, then picked up a twig and drew a big 'G' in the dirt at our shoes. "*Girl* always starts with a G," I told him. "Boys will think it's for *goofy*, but girls will know it's for *great*." He made a face, but I kept on. "Once, there was this girl named Iris…"

I started in, making stuff up just for him.

"…Wellll," I finished, "the word-fairie saw this sad situation and she decided that the order these three sisters would stand in would always be Iris first. See the I, Chance? Then Rose to protect her." Here I underlined the big R, "Then L for Lily," I said, "who, in the word *girl* has to be last for the end of time, for punishment. For being so awful." In the dirt the word GIRL lay spelled out with my twig.

Chance jiggled. "Neat!" He said, wiping his nose on the back of his hand. "Hey Duff—"

"Hummm?" I drew lines in the dirt on top of my word till it disappeared.

"Tell me one about the Foster Homes again."

I thought about how all the houses looked back there in that oldest neighborhood when I was so tiny I could barely see over the bushes through the fence in that yard.

I remembered up and down that hill. How the houses climbed along in bright happy colors. The yard was so much better than the dark inside. Outside was warm sun, it scattered between the skinny trees onto the streets and over the roofs, up against the wide sky.

Barbie, in only the bottoms of pajamas, would walk around in that yard saying, "I'm 'Merican, but you're Mex'can." Because of my dark hair. I wondered if she remembered that?

"Happy or Sad?" I asked, squinting into today's sun.

"Happy, make it a happy one, Duff—or funny."

I felt as old as Mama right then. Ready to cry. I always made it funny for Chance when I told it. I came to me that it had never been funny, never at all. I glanced up, then down this sidewalk. This morning's sun nice and bright, like it should be for kids.

No Foster Lady coming to get me here, I reminded myself. No Justine yelling in the darkness of the night… at a Foster Man, *'get away from that crib, she's a baby you—'*

"Well?" Chance asked.

"Why don't we look for wood for the fort instead?" I stood up. Started on climbing the concrete steps, to the stacks of wood, saw-horses, and pipes that were laid out there to build with. Chance frowned but followed behind me. His eyes running like snoopy little dogs all along the ground, looking for stuff to pick up. Nails and tacks disappeared into his pockets.

I'd liked the old house that was here 'till right after we'd moved in on Elliott Street. It stood back, way up off the street, so that you had to walk up the concrete steps with the lawn first up around your ears, then to your waist as you climbed each step.

I told him, "Maybe this new house will be painted some nice pretty color, like the ones on the hills at the Foster Homes."

Chance jumped all over the place, squatting down to pick things up and smiling like it was Christmas. "I love the smell of wood and tools!" he crowed. "I'm gonna be a construction man when I get big."

"Me too," I said, "I'm gonna work in just my undershirt and I'll have dusty jeans and sawdust in my boots."

"And wear a belt with tools!" He added, "I will—but not you."

"Smile when you say that pard'ner."

"No you won't, 'cause Mama's gonna catch you one of these days. Make you wear dresses even when school's out. An' curlers too, just like Barbie and Justine." He was so close to the truth I wanted to hit him. But I thought of Father Rudolph and worked on that. "And the only time you'll get to go out is when you go to the store for groceries."

He was too right to hit. I put my hands in my pockets. Just like that I stopped having fun. Mama already had two girls to dress up, buy curlers and bobby pins for, and all she ever managed to do with them was fight.

I just wanted to be loud in the morning like Chance. Be strong during trouble like Artie. I just wanted to make people smile 'cause I told stories. Even when I just sat still and read by myself, Mama said that was wrong.

The frame of the house stood all around us. It suddenly felt like grownups listening at a doorway without moving, sneaky like. So they'd catch you at something and beat you for it. I felt very creepy all of a sudden. Chance hopped over a board that separated where the rooms would be. He yelled, "TAG! you're it!" Off before I could reach him. Twisting and scooting just away from me. I laughed and chased him 'till things felt right again.

"NONE OF THIS looks like leftovers to me," I said when we slowed down and stopped running.

"So," Chance said, picking up a hunk of wood the size of my shoe. "Let's get some anyway."

"No stealing, Chance. I mean it," I said.

He pleaded, "But what about the fort?"

"No. I already said. Leftovers only." I hated being this way with him; he probably thought I was mean and unfair. I hated that, but more, I hated stealing in front of Chance. Meanness he could think of me, but dishonesty, no.

Ever since that one Saturday, when Mama hurt my hand, it had been coming to me that for everyone in the family maybe that stuff, being mean and unfair, came as easy as yawning and rubbing their eyes in the morning. They didn't even realize they did it most of the time. And that's who I was from.

I was never sure if I hated it because they didn't, or if it was because I really believed it was wrong. I worried over it, because maybe that was what Father Rudolph meant by Pride going before the Fall.

While we played, searching through the trash bin for

scraps of wood, a big dusty blue truck with building tools in the back pulled onto the dirt driveway. The man who got out was young. Real tall. I could tell right away he probably worked here. Suntanned. His clothes real dusty. He smiled at us.

His hair was messy, I didn't like the way his eyes moved. He walked like the Foster Home Men used to, scary in some silent way underneath things. Right away I was feeling guilty and nervous. And not having hair down to my waist made me feel undressed.

"You boys working here?" he joked.

I looked down, but Chance, he spoke right up and asked, "Mister, can we have these little pieces of wood?"

"Lesssee—" the man said.

He came closer, taking the blocks from Chance. I could smell beer-sweat and the smell of cigarettes and toilets all together. I touched Chance's T-shirt; stepping back, I gave it a tug.

"What can you give for 'em?" He asked us and looked right at my chest. He held the wood out of Chance's reach.

"No thanks, Mister," I said real low and quiet, "Never mind, we don't need it for anything."

Still looking down I started backing away for the steps, grabbing at Chance's arm again. But he wrenched away from me. He really wanted that wood bad.

"Let's go, Chance!" I called over my back as I got to the top of the concrete step. I couldn't hear what he asked Chance. Or Chance's answer. I looked back and they were looking over at me. The man handed Chance the wood, real slow so I could see him do it.

He called out, "You kids can come by anytime, hear?"

I RAN DOWN the steps like the devil had my home address and was on the way over. As I ran, all the way back to Elliott Street, all I could think of was how it had been in the Foster Homes. And how much I wanted to kill Chance.

Syllables and Beats

MRS. BETTENCOURT ASKED about my hair. I told her we had to do it 'cause I'd caught lice from someone at the library. She looked at me hard; then I ran out the Market door.

Mama's song was still coming out of our front door, which was open 'cause of the heat. I was kind of liking it now, like a pillow you lean on without even realizing it's there behind you on the sofa.

"Duffy!" Barbie yelled, coming to take the bag, "You got the seasoning salt?" But she didn't wait for my answer. "Man, you're slow, no wonder Mama yells all the time." But I ignored that, pulling out all but three of the coins of change from my pocket. I followed her into the kitchen to hand that to Mama.

JUSTINE WAS IN her bedroom. I came in and flopped on her bed. I could feel the coolness of her sheets on the back on my neck. It was a very nice feeling after running from the Market.

"I think if that song keeps up I'm gonna kill myself," Justine said, pulling her brush through her hair.

"You're just hot," I said. "You need to go to the plunge at the park for a nice long swim."

"Who're you, Ann Landers?" She didn't sound happy. But I didn't take it bad. It was about the song still playing, not me.

"You want some money, Justine? For the plunge? I can spare some," I said, rolling onto my stomach. "What would you like to do today?"

With her brush in the mirror she threatened, "You keep on stealing from Mama's change and someone may do some talking to her, *chica*."

Yeah, I thought. *Who'd do that to me? You?* Sure. "Okay," I said and got up from her bed, "thought I'd help."

Then I went to go play Monsters with Chance in the back yard till dinner.

SOMEONE POUNDED ON the door real fast and important. Mama's eyes went big. We all froze at the table and looked at each other. Then I ran toward the door, and climbed on the arm of the sofa next to it. I moved the curtain just a touch, to make it seem like no one was home looking out.

I yelled, "Artie!" and jumped down to fling the door open.

"Artie!" everyone came running, all of us dog piling on him. Like we use to when we'd play in the yard on Hockert Street. Mama pushed her way through the arms and shouts. She grabbed him to her and just kept repeating, "You little monkey, you. You little monkey," over and over as she dragged him in and onto the sofa.

"Artie look at this!" Chance cried out, "Lookit! *Mira*, lookit what I can do now!" as he climbed onto the back of the sofa and tried to get Barbie into a headlock. "Look how big I am now!" We all wanted him to look, look at us, see how we'd grown, see what we could do now, Mama included.

ARTIE REALLY LOOKED older to us. Everyone kept saying so. After dinner, we all sat out on the porch, while Mama held the hose to water the lawn, and Chance ran back and forth calling, "You can't wet me, Mama. You missed me again! Hey Artie, See how fast I am?"

Artie leaned against the iron rail between the lawn and the porch step; the lowering sun in his eyes. Smiling, watching Chance as he got more and more daring with Mama's hose. It was the old Artie for a moment. Mama most of all saw that.

Then he grabbed me, and for a second I was too heavy for him to lift and tickle. "What're you feeding this one, Mama? Yeast and rocks?"

He stopped talking to Mama and grabbed Barbie over to stand us back to back and measure me. He said, "What do you know—"

Then, as he and Mama got back to talking, Artie kept looking over as I ran with Chance, shaking his head and grinning at me, like I was his prize rose. Like the judges had just given him the award for tallest.

Mama even turned his chin to face her; he was so caught up in watching me. I just stopped in my tracks to yell at Artie. Chance, he ran right into me, bouncing back, falling on his bottom in the damp grass.

"Okay, so I'm growing!" I shouted. And that's when Mama turned the hose on me. Full in the chest—it nearly .

knocked me backwards, over Chance on the grass, from the sudden pressure of it.

A family water fight. With Mama hosing everyone down, all us kids trying our best to crimp the hose and fight our way close enough to try and turn it back on her.

We screeched, squealing and backing up and surging forward. Chance doing his best to be in front of the stream as much as he could. But Mama kept up aiming it at me. Artie paused a bit when he saw what I did—a look in her eyes—I looked down to see my undershirt was showing through my top, and my—*me*—under that.

I stopped dead, cover my chest, but then she was aiming at my face. That hurt too much. Mama had no regard for my wet shirt. Finally I just ran off to the side of the house, to get indoors and dry off.

My teeth were chattering and my knees beginning to knock from the soaking. I could hear everyone still laughing and screaming from the lawn as I stepped in through the back door and sloshed down the hall for a towel.

He didn't stay the night. Even though Mama asked him.

JOANNA AND I were talking about undershirts and skirts made of brown leather. We were in her back yard, looking at a *Seventeen* magazine. She'd seen skirts like the one on the page at a Mode O'Day store on Main Street in Alhambra, in her size. With a big wide belt. It was near her dad's work a few cities over, where her Mom took her to shop every so often.

I leaned in to look at it, but I was saying how I didn't mind undershirts, that I thought maybe a leather skirt would be way too hot in the summer. She nudged me with her shoulder as we sat and just whispered, *Liar* at me. I thought: Cheesh, at least with Becca I could tell her something and she'd just nod along with me.

Joanna was right; I was trying to fool her. Ever since Artie's visit and the water fight I had been worried. About so many things. Like what if, because I was always the youngest one with everyone I hung out with, what if my body wouldn't learn and I never got any bigger?

I was always the smallest in class, always the smallest girl at home, now the smallest at both the Library and Auditorium. I didn't want Joanna thinking I wasn't good enough to hang around with. Her being twelve and a half, near to thirteen, me not yet eleven.

Joanna said, "You'd look real good in the one that's just straight up and down. It's called an A-line. My mom says I'd do better in the pleated ones."

I put my hands on my knees and looking down, concentrated on using my toes to pick up a little rock. I told her, "I don't got any blouses that would go good with a leather skirt." That besides, I only wear tennis shoes to school. "That mix would look real bad, too." But she didn't take the hint, she just kept on talking about prints she'd seen in a fabric shop that would make great tops. Ones with *Fall Florals* on eggshell and cream. Cheesh.

Even Becca wasn't this persistent.

I tried to change the subject by asking her, "So what're you doing this summer after cello?"

And Joanna looked sideways at me, through those nice eyelashes, laughed, saying, "My father won't let me date till next year." *Hah-hah-hah.*

Then she got onto her favorite subject: Joanna wanted

to come to my house. But because I'd lied that day I couldn't let her. 'Lise wasn't my mom. I couldn't explain that away.

She wouldn't stop asking, and I was dead if she found out I'd lied. Maybe she'd stop being my friend. I just didn't know what to do.

"My mom says it's no problem driving me there if I want to spend the night, I mean, if you want to invite me over," she mentioned again, flipping the pages past an article that made me shiver. It was titled "I'm Not Who They Think I Am."

"Keep flipping, I don't want to read that," I said. "Let's find how to paint our knees with the body paint like the cover shows."

But I had to tell her. She needed to know I'd been lying. Part of me hated thinking about confessing, part of me hated that I'd let the quest go so long.

It had to be done. "I have to say something. I hope you won't hate me," I began.

She put her finger to save the page place. "You've found another," she mocked. And I nearly made a joke to back out of things. She kept it up. "No wait—you're allergic to leather."

"Joanna, stop a sec." She lost her place when she pushed her bangs off her forehead and took a long look at me.

"'Kay. Go ahead. It can't be too bad." She smiled, "You're way too little for any serious damage."

I squinted up into the sun, then let out a really big breath.

I started by saying, "Remember driving me home that

one time?" She nodded. "Well, that was Becca's house. Not mine. And Becca's mom, Mrs. Bettencourt. They live upstairs over the Market, not me. I lied to your dad. And you."

Then I just sat there, waiting to be told to get lost. She kept quiet.

"I'll understand if you hate me, Joanna. 'Cause this is a real big lie. And you're someone I don't wanna be lying to." More quite on the lawn, for so long I nearly started to cry.

Finally she said,

"You read *so* much, and yet you're such a little dummy." She let the magazine slip from her fingers and off her lap. "It should matter, I should be really pissed-off. *Don't* tell my dad I said that." She took my hand and tossed it up like it was a balloon. "But, well, it's too late. 'Cause see…I already love you."

She hugged me. I let her. I was crying then, that made her cry, too. Two sissies in the sun. It dawned on me; I was letting someone touch me. It wasn't dangerous at all.

ONE MORNING THERE was another knock at the front door and again no one moved, so I got up to answer it. It was the smelly construction guy, from the Marisol house. Standing at my door, grinning on my front porch, like he was expected. "Chance home?"

Chance bent back from sitting in front of the TV to see who it was. When he saw the guy's boots he popped up and came to stand beside me. "Hey Joel!" he said, "Duff, this's Joel from the house building."

I didn't want Chance talking to this guy or even knowing his name was Joel.

I was ready to tell Joel to drop dead and get off our porch. Like Artie had done that night with Luis, but Chance was so happy and this Joel *was* a grown-up. I had enough things for the Confession on Friday as it was, what with my head talking to my heart all the time about Joanna.

Then Joel reached into his jacket pocket and held out a tape measure, the kind that come from hardware stores, for guys to pull the tape out of its silver box and measure wood, walls, and things.

"Why're you giving him that?" I said, holding Chance's hand down at his side so he wouldn't grab at it.

Joel said, "Chance and I are buddies, right Chance?"

Chance nodded and squirmed away from my grip to get at the shiny square. Once it was in his hands he said, "Sure, Joel." He pulled the yellow metal strip out as far as he could reach. Letting it go, it snapped back inside with a flashy popping noise. You could just see how much Chance liked that sound.

Then Barbie came up behind us and Joel smiled at her and asked, "Well then, is this the Lady of the House?"

Barbie took a look at his present in Chance's hands. She smiled back, saying, "Thanks Mister."

That's when I let go of my grip on the door and just walked away from there, leaving the two of them to be polite to Joel.

I DON'T KNOW how long he stayed there talking to them. I went and stood out in the back yard and looked up to the sky. Sending a prayer up to God and the Minotaurs that my Quest be hard, but not so hard as to have guys like Joel in it. I wasn't sure I was strong enough for that.

When I went back indoors he was gone from the front door and the mail was in. Becca wrote me a letter from her camp and it came right to my house, not to her mom's first. She didn't say so with words but between the lines she wanted to know if Mama and her mom were talking to each other yet. It was kind of like spies and code words. I figured she wrote it like that in case anyone else read the letter. *She must be having so much fun there*, I thought.

ALL THE NEXT day I sat back in my room and daydreamed a bit of being there at Becca's camp myself. The two of us running through the trees, splashing in the lake's cool water. But I got stuck at the best part when Mama yelled, "Duffy!" from the kitchen, and I was off to the Market again.

On the way to the Market I thought about answering Becca's letter with a short story about two best friends, one who couldn't talk and one who couldn't hear. I'd make it have a moral at the end. That would be a good way to let her know what was going on here on Elliott Street.

"READY DUFF?" MR. Delgado asked. We were at Joanna's playing chess with her dad coaching. I looked up to the left for the chess book in my head and said to myself, *Pawns cannot capture while moving forward along the file. Bishop moves to any square on either of the diagonals on which it is placed.*

"Yep, ready."

"Your move, my dear," he said to Joanna, then sat back to watch us go at it.

Music was in the background, *Moonlight Sonata*, it sounded like. And as the album played I let the strings seep into my shoulders to relax me as I moved the pieces, trying to keep a jump ahead of Joanna.

The sun streamed in on our board, it made me feel like these pieces were real because of the sharp shadows they were casting. I said so. Mr. Delgado scolded, "Keep your mind on the game, dearie." But he was saying it as I picked up her second Bishop, so he added, "Or not."

Joanna just smiled, even though I was creaming her. She studied it again, from all sides, the move she was thinking about before she finally lifted her hand from her piece.

"I stopped by your mother's market the other day, Duff." I looked up from the board and met his eyes. He was nodding at me.

"Did you get her to say yes to Duffy coming for more sleep-overs?" Joanna asked, like she didn't know a thing.

"That's one of the things we talked about. JoJo, her Knight, watch that, honey."

"Dad, it's my game, 'kay?"

"So Duffy, you're an MGM? So's Joanna."

I bit my lip and chewed on it. "Yeah, I'm a lion."

He laughed. I reached for the Knight and moved it the three squares closer to her Lady. Though from her side of the board I was hoping it didn't look that way.

"Ever think about moving into the grade you're actually suited to be in?"

"Dad, leave her alone and watch my horrible playing, why don't you?"

I thought about defending myself, but what came out sounded more like defending Mama, 'cause after I said, "Check, Joanna," and knocked her queen down, I let out a big breath and shook my head. "Seventh is good enough this year."

"Eighth is better—as an MGM there's independent study, learn what interests you, no classes to hold you back, if you're at all interested in writing poetry and getting more specific with the English courses and drama classes we talked about."

Joanna looked up from the board, adding, "I'm taking anthropology at Alhambra."

Good, I thought, *take your eyes off the pieces.* But I wasn't gonna budge. "Seventh is plenty good," I said again, kind of really meaning it that time. Then, I added, "Checkmate."

"IS DUFFY HERE?"

It was that *pendejo* Joel. Just hearing his voice from the other side of the front door made me feel guilty and afraid. Mama had already gone off to work. Justine had just left, too. Barbie and Chance and me were the only ones home. I felt trapped. How would I get to writing class if he was out there? I grabbed Chance in from the door and slammed it hard.

"Don't you be talking to him, you hear?" I threatened.

Chance twisted away from me. "Shut up! He's my friend," he squeaked, reaching for the doorknob. "He's gonna get me a puppy!" Barbie came into the living room and kicked at me.

"Leave Chance alone, you ugly stick!" Then she opened the door wide, saying, "Hey, Mister!" All bright and cheerful.

And Joel said, "I'm gonna be driving over to the Library, wondered if Duffy needed a ride?"

I came charging to the door. "Mister, get the fuck off my porch or I'm calling the cops!"

But they all just laughed.

Joel pulled a huge hunk of coins from his pocket, all quarters. You could see Barbie and Chance's eyes get big.

"Well, maybe you guys can use some coins for the pay phone, huh?" He poured the quarters in both Barbie's and Chance's hands before he said, "See *you* later."

I could hear Barbie's counting under her breath as Joel walked away to the curb.

I DIDN'T CRY at all, all the way to the Library. I thought to myself, *I'm keeping a dime in my pocket at all times*. Then, I trudged up the Bike-Killer hill and across the freeway.

But it was a bad day anyway. Miss Patricia put my notebook down, and called me over to walk a ways through the Library to the girls' bathroom with her. She looked—not pleased. She came over to the sink and leaned there, near me, and asked, "Duffy, honey, your poem is a very strong read today. I can see a lot of talent and, mmm ... imagination here. But the topic, you've done a wonderful job, but— Well, where do you get your ideas from, hon?"

I didn't understand. Why was she looking at me like that? *What had I done wrong?* I wondered.

I didn't have an answer for her, because the truth of it was I couldn't remember what I'd written. And I was too proud to ask for it back so I could see it there. I had just gone on counting syllables and beats and trying to rhyme the ending words.

At the end of class she returned the notebook and I acted nonchalant as I reread it. It was titled *A House of Light and Stone*. I thought, *I wrote this? Wow, it's good!* But then I saw what Miss Patricia probably did. I saw why she'd worry about me. It was embarrassing to think she'd think I'd hurt myself, from having to live that life I'd written about right here.

I knew I'd never be able to explain it enough to her—she was a grownup for one. It was Joel I wanted dead—not me. She probably didn't know anything about Foster Homes. About guys like Joel. Or even about how wonderful the small things like golden mornings and purple trees were either. Or how my turning those things into a poem was easy compared to what was in my head. That stuff was too hard to tell.

So, on the walk home I reviewed my Quest. First, embarrassed that she thought I might be writing about myself. More, I'd no idea where that poem came from.

Joel may have to be part of things here, but I didn't want my writing to get trapped and crushed by that. To turn ugly and sad. That's why that poem had been about Light *and* Stone. Not just Stone.

So I decided on a sacrifice. For the quest. And that was the last time I went to the writing class.

THE REST OF the summer I'd take our little hill down to the big Sixth Street hill. Then I'd climb that and go all the way north on Lorena to up where Second Street was. I'd turn left and walk all the way to the Evergreen High School Library to read for a while. My own kind of personal Independent Study.

Poetry to Listen to

FOR SOME REASON Mama's music finally stopped. Mama and 'Lise were suddenly talking, telling us, "Let's do something nice and fun with the families tonight." Becca still wasn't back from camp, but Mama said, "That's okay, families are family even with some of us missing." I knew she meant more than just Becca.

So, from the Market, 'Lise brought fresh peaches and a carton of heavy cream. Mama warmed up her waffle iron and that's what we had for the early dinner.

To drink, she let us make Mexican Hot Chocolate, letting me and Chance grate the sweet chocolate. Barbie just watching, reading out loud from the octagon box: *Autentico Chocolate Mexicano Para Mesa*, over and over. But her blonde bangs were quivering. You could just see her hands were itching to grab the bowl and grater and do it herself.

So, on that first wheel of chocolate I yelled, "Oww, my thumb!" even though I didn't scrape it at all. I handed the grater to her saying, "Damn, you do it!"

So nice to see her happy, with me and my thumb in my mouth, in pain, she probably thought. Experiencing her and her excellent grating expertise.

Mama let us eat picnic style, with blankets on the living

room floor. Waffles, peaches and too much butter, so it slipped out the sides and on to the plate; all that was topped off with the just-made whipped cream. Chance had the two beaters at his plate for licking.

And I brought out the Yahtzee game that Mr. St. John had given the family a while back, but that no one had ever played because the commercials only showed white kids playing it, looking way too goofy for any real fun to be going on.

I figured, maybe with everyone in such a good mood and 'Lise here for Mama, with the wonderful smell of the Hot Chocolate up in the air—well, there might be a chance here.

Frankly, it looked like it might be a fun game, even for us half and full-Mexicans.

The instructions were not easy for us kids. And then Mama saw the five big red dice and she looked at Becca's mom, who raised an eyebrow, retuning that look. They both smiled and asked us all, "Wanna learn how to shoot craps?" And that did sound like more fun.

So that's how we spent the meal: leaning over the plates to keep the butter from the blankets and tossing the big red dice against the wall. Me trying to remember on my turn her instructions about Snake-eyes and Boxcars. Trying not to crap out with the bad 2, 3, or 12 throws. It was a good night after all.

JOEL WAS BACK at the front door. He always managed to be there the days I had to walk to the Library. He wasn't so smelly this time, but that was a small thing to work with. Chance hadn't got to the door first; if he had he'd've opened it wide and stood there and talked. But I got it. When Joel said, "Chance home?" I just slammed it in his face and walked out of the living room.

But there was laughing from the living room. I had to go back and fix that because they just didn't get it about this Joel guy. You'd've thought that Barbie at least would've.

I walked into the living room and set my book bag down on the coffee table. That's when I noticed my shoelace was undone. When I straightened up I saw something wasn't right. Barbie and Chance had their heads together, and that never happened. And they'd stopped because I was there. Something was up.

I PUT MY hands on my hips. "What're you two monkeys up to?" But neither of them answered. Chance avoided my eye. I thought to myself, *"Duff, you gotta let him play with who he wants to. Even Barbie."*

He moved to the front door and stood there with his little hand on the knob, like at a hotel, waiting for me to come through with luggage. "Madam—" he bowed. I laughed and smiled, even thinking about handing him a nickel as I left.

And that's when Barbie snuck up from behind.

SHE GRABBED MY arms and pinned them to my side and shoved me towards the door. Chance had it held open and was crossing his legs and jiggling like he had to go pee. "C'mon, Barbie!" he whined. "Do it!"

"Stoppit you guys!" I yelled. They were both really gonna get it. I thought; *I'm telling for sure.* I didn't want to play "Get Duffy" right now; I had to get going to the Library over at the Evergreen school. Maybe part of me was madder than usual because I was jealous they were playing together.

Barbie kept pushing till I was at the door. "Stoppit Barbie!" I kept yelling, but it was two against one since Chance was in on this.

Though I tried to reach back and grab my bag, they ganged up and shoved me outdoors. Boy, were they gonna get it. *Just wait 'till I tell Mama*, I thought. I heard the click of the lock behind me, and at the same time I saw Joel's shadow. Standing there. Waiting.

It was a trap. I started pounding on my door and screaming like with the doggie that time. So loud you could hear me back on Hockert Street, I bet. He just stood and watched. Smiling, his hands in his pockets, like I was putting a show on for him.

I'd promised Artie, nobody was gonna do us like in the Foster Homes ever again. I kept on pounding and kicking and yelling, "Let me in!" If I would have thought about it, I should have been kicking and screaming at Joel.

The kicking on the door, I think that's what finally got to Chance. Because he had mercy on me and unlocked the door to let me back in.

And that's when I caught Barbie kneeling at the coffee table, her blonde bangs nearly touching the bridge of her nose as she concentrated putting another huge pile of quarters into two stacks.

HE PULLED UP to me at the corner where the Sixth Street Hill started. "Duffy, c'mere a second; I wanna ask you something," But I ignored him. Looking back, I should've crossed over to the other side of the street. But I didn't.

They'd let me back indoors. He wasn't on the porch when I'd started out again. I guess I thought I'd won. Pride probably was going to cancel out my sacrifice about the Library.

He pulled up ahead and waited for me to pass him again, then he put his car in gear and crawled the curb next to me as I kept going.

He said, "I know your mom. She works at the Coffee Shop. I'll tell her I gave you a ride, if that's what's bothering you."

I stopped walking and looked at him. "Or maybe I'll tell her even if you don't." And I knew what he meant. As punishment, what else could Mama think to take from me, but maybe me, my own self.

I wasn't headed anywhere. No one was waiting for me to show up. I only mattered to myself. In my head I apologized to Artie, *mea culpa*.

I got into his car. I guessed the journal and the writing class wasn't enough to give up after all. Not even Chance was on my side anymore.

He pushed the car into gear and pulled away from the curb. We drove for a long time. There was poetry being read in my head. And his voice was just a stupid sound off to my left.

WE PARKED. MOST of what he did to me I just lifted away and ignored from somewhere farther. I kept telling myself it was no worse than being tiny in the Foster Homes. But at least now I had the poetry to listen to. It was too bad that it was only my own.

'LISE WAS OVER at our house one night after dinner. Her and Mama were out sitting on the porch, watching the sun go down. Talking about putting flowers in along the borders on the lawn. "Geraniums?" she suggested. "Iris?" But Mama kept shaking her head no, 'till she burst out with a laugh 'cause 'Lise had lowered her voice and murmured, "Well, hell, Rennie, let's just plant pansies and get it over with." I didn't get it.

They talked about a lot of other neat things. Mama didn't seem to notice me there so I got to listen more, "How about a checking account, Rennie? I hear all the adults are having 'em this year." Mama laughed again.

"Me? No way, 'Lise." She shook her head, taking a long drag on her Chesterfield. "I'd end up in Sybil Brand so fast for kited checks it'd make your head swim. You know that, baby."

I looked up at them because a checking account sounded like an excellent idea, and because of the *baby*; Mama never used that word with her before.

Maybe Mama would let me do the check writing, since I was so good at her signature. She'd taught me. For the monthly money orders. And sometimes Justine used to wake me up mornings to get her notes signed for getting out of gym or out early from her last class.

"I'm saying," 'Lise said very softly, "you wouldn't have to be doing it all alone."

"Yeah, sure, 'Lise," Mama answered, putting her hand on her leg "Like you're gonna come be my knight in white, huh?"

I DREAMT THAT night. Of helping Mama with her checkbook. In the dream I knew exactly how it was done. I drove her to the dream welfare office. I said, *'No more payments for us, Thanks. We're alright on our own now.'* 'Lise was there, proud of me. As she was of Mama. And because I was driving, Joel didn't matter, even though his car still waited at the corner. Even in the dream.

I WAS FEELING so good after spending the day in the Evergreen Library that I ran all the way home the full sixteen blocks, even down the Sixth Street hill, then up our littler one. Becca had sent me another letter from her camp.

'Lise had delivered it first thing that morning to me. There was another picture of Becca, this time with her alone, no arms around anybody. On a picnic bench, looking off to a lake, and the back of the photo read: "Where, oh where, can my little friend be—Miss you, back by August, Love Becca."

MAYBE IT WAS all the extra running. I couldn't tell anybody; that was for sure. When I got home I found everything would be different from then on.

I was in the bathroom, my underwear all red with blood. It must have been from all the running.

Who could I tell—Justine and Barbie? They'd make me wear those awful Kotex pads, like they did. Mama would stand me out on the street and get the neighbors to point and laugh every time she was mad at me. Buying the stuff I needed would just get 'Lise over here to have a talk to Mama. And nobody needed more sad music if that went wrong.

I could just hear Barbie making fun of me, "Shave your legs now, knees together, better carry a purse, Duff. Don't let any of that stuff fall out for the boys to see." It would be the worst.

Then it came to me.

I folded a big length of toilet paper up into my underwear and stood up. Pulling my shorts up and planning.

I came into Barbie's room from the bathroom door and reached for the first thing I saw there on the floor, a brown purse with a zipper on top.

At the Market I raised my voice, calling out, "It's just me Mrs. Bettencourt." And from the storeroom she called back "Hi there, Duff, be right out."

I went down the aisle and opened a bottle of Empirin pills. I emptied the whole thing into Barbie's purse. I squatted down on my heels and added a sanitary belt, like I knew the girls were always washing out in the sink, but I said, *No Way*, to the big blue box of Kotex and shoved a slim box of tampons, the whole thing, in the purse instead.

Further down the aisle I saw the razor blades, and felt up and down my leg, smooth as ever, but Barbie must know stuff I didn't, so thinking about my future armpits and thighs, I said, "Might as well be prepared." And they went in there, too.

Then I stood and doubled back to the ice cream chest, pulled out an orange Dreamsicle, I put down fifteen cents. "Just this."

She looked at the bulgy brown purse. I was clenching my thighs together and just didn't care right now. "Barbie let me borrow it." Her eyebrows went way up at that silly notion.

I hurried back out to the sunshine and on home.

I'D READ EVERYTHING on all of the boxes, and it was then I realized what the sanitary belt was for, so I left it in the brown purse as I tossed it back into Barbie's room.

Then I just sat there in the bathroom. It was cool, still. I laid my head down. Let the realness seep into my bones. Here was too many secrets. Too many responsibilities. And no one to go to with any of them.

I raised my head and looked at my reflection in the bathroom mirror. Really took a long, conceited look. It surprised me to see that there was a really pretty face on me, a touch of Mama along the cheekbone and jaw.

Would anyone ever stand on the tub rim watching how I put make-up on for a night out? If I turned my head just a touch, looking out the corner of my eye, I could see it even more: in the upward tilt of my eyebrows, the high forehead, the reddish hints in my hair now that it was enough fingers long to curl up again.

But it scared me to see all that there. Right there on the surface. 'Cause if I could see that stuff—plain as day, Mama all over, then maybe all the other stuff was there, too, just under the surface.

The meanness. The men like Roy and Joel and even Luis at the porch. All drunk and sobbing. Mama's tirades and her disappointments. Her songs for crying, 'cause without them there were no other ways to feel feelings.

I didn't want that meanness under there, growing and hardening, turning me into another her. I wanted to get all that stuff out. I looked at my face one last time and thought: *Mama was right about one thing, after all.* "You should never spend much time looking at yourself in the mirror, Duffy. Never."

I picked up the package of razor blades and unwrapped one. It was cool and calming in my fingertips. It felt like air, so light. The opposite of me—so heavy. I laid it on the inside of my arm, up high, up under my T-shirt sleeve.

It felt cool there, like maybe it wouldn't hurt. And my breathing slowed to a nice calm pace. I pushed up my sleeve till it stayed on its own and then pulled the razor across the inside of my arm. Making a new line, far from the Life, Heart and the Head line that Mr. St. John had showed me. Far from the line at my appendix, from when I was young.

This was my own personal Sorry line, like an unlucky charm. Right here up high on my arm. I'd never lose it. It would always be there. And no one would come take it away.

"HEY, UGLY!" BARBIE shouted from the hall, "Mama says what's keeping you so long? That mirror's already cracked."

Then I did it again, and again, thin lines going deep but feeling cool: six times in all: One for Artie giving up on us and going. Two for Justine about to follow after him. Three for Barbie laughing on the other side of the door to make Mama happy. Four for Chance, too. Because he couldn't stay sweet baby Chance much longer with all of us around him. Five for being a girl men like Joel would always be reaching for, and Six. For Mama, too.

Each swipe was a penance for each of us. Because I thought I finally had an inkling of what she'd lost keeping this circus going. She'd lost herself.

I STARTED SPENDING a lot of time at Joanna's, or over visiting 'Lise. But mostly at the Evergreen Library; I was glad it was summer. While Mama worked her job and a half no one cared if I was home or not. So I tracked her schedule real well, and then left nearly seconds after she did. Getting back maybe minutes before she did. I stayed off the usual streets, didn't develop a pattern on how I got around. Even Joel didn't find me. Mostly.

I understood Justine now. Always going. I figured: stay away from family. Stay away from danger. That was my motto now. My Quest was shifting—like they do in the books, where the hero finds his true desire is so different from what he thought he wanted after all.

Like my new scabby scar on my upper arm, I kept that discovery to myself.

MR. DELGADO HAD the latest *National Geographic* magazine spread out for us on their library table, even though they called it his office table. We were looking at this month's map: Vacationlands of the USA and Canada.

That's when I started bragging about how far it was to the Robert Louis Stevenson Library from my house, acting like I was still going there; I plucked at my T-shirt sleeve where the scab still was healing and said, "My big brother told me it's, like, twelve blocks to one mile. Approximate. But *my* blocks, over on the other side of Fourth Street, they must be longer than usual—with the Sixth Street Hill. And the long block over the freeway, with the rushing wind all the time. They must equal to at least two miles. If it's an inch," I finished.

Mr. Delgado nodded, saying, "It's not the map, it's the terrain." Which I think meant: *Yeah, farther, alright.*

He rolled his chair to the left and pulled out one of his

desk drawers. Moving stuff around until he came up with a fat fountain pen, he rolled his chair back over to the map and us.

"Let's just put a number on these miles," he said. "Joanna, got a city map there, dear?" He pointed the fat pen to a basket on one of the low bookshelves. I saw it was stuffed full of those fold-out gas stations maps. Joanna flipped through a few of them. That's when I saw his pen wasn't a pen at all but a map-measurer tool—by rolling the pen from my block to the Library he was measuring my walk.

"That's all?" I cried.

"One-point-six, my dear. But like you said, there's the up and down grades and the winds on the freeway overpass to consider. And that hill."

"It's the *Bike-Killer Hill,*" I sulked, looking at the blocks on the fold-out map. Feeling betrayed by numbers and sneaky pens.

"I'm quite sure it is, Duff," he laughed, messing up my curls with his big hand.

"Do from here to your work, Dad."

And he raised his elbows to get a full look of the path to trace with his pen. "Between our two points on the map," he said, "seven-and-a-half miles away." Joanna and I looked at each other with our mouths open; I took the miles and in my head did the math, "That's like ninety blocks!"

Joanna added, "And freeways to get on, too."

I whistled. "Are there signs on the way there saying 'Here Be Dragons'?" But only Mr. Delgado laughed at that.

Joanna said, "During the year I'll be going to high school in Alhambra instead of Evergreen, 'cause that's where he works and he petitioned for it. They said okay."

I thought: *wow, now there's a dispensation.* "You can do that?" I asked.

"Sure, changing schools, skipping grades, if it's for a valid reason. If you know who to contact, anything's possible. Of course, this year it doesn't hurt if the person asking has a Spanish surname and lives in the barrio, get it while you can, hey *linda?*"

He laughed at that, too.

I WOKE UP at 4:23 on Monday, my birthday. I didn't want to miss any of the day. As quietly as I could, so not to wake Chance, I got dressed and decided to make a waffle. Just one. Before anyone was up. Maybe with jam on top, I thought, clicking the bathroom light off and heading down the hall for the kitchen.

I looked into the living room and saw Mama's sofa bed, opened. And flat as the street. She wasn't home. I touched my scar on my arm, under my shirt.

She was out again. And not with 'Lise, or they would have told us. We'd've stayed up late last night. Did she know it was today, my birthday? On her two full-shifts day? I'd spent so much time keeping my mouth shut, being not-conceited, that no one knew that it was today. Not even Joanna.

I put the waffle iron back in the cupboard and started water to boil for coffee. It was my birthday. I was old enough now. Then I walked into the hi-fi and clicked it to start.

I chose my own song from her albums to start my own day. Nancy Wilson. But after the coffee, and only hearing the song five times over, I clicked off the stereo and went back to bed. *Old age must be starting.* I was real tired.

MAMA DIDN'T MENTION Happy Birthday. Neither did Barbie or Justine. And I was too proud to say it myself. Like a morning dream that was lost, the Birthday part of the day just faded away from my grasp. I walked over to the Market and sat and listened to 'Lise's stories about France for most of the morning. My scab itched. It was just another day.

Buildings for Religious Purposes

Joanna's parents invited me to their weekend barbecue and I didn't bother to ask Mama could I go, 'cause it was a Saturday and she'd be working 'till eleven. She'd never even know I was out of the house.

It was the weekend after my birthday, Joanna'd pushed at my ribs as we walked to her house, "C'mon Chavez, live a little." So that's when I decided not to ask. Her folks were very lively people. Even better to watch together than Becca and her mom.

More like people from the movies than her parents, even. I stood indoors, watching Joanna's mother mixing a tray of drinks at their bar with the stools. She called them off as the guests asked for them: "Screwdriver—get yers here" and "Margarita—a fine gal, come and get 'er," and when it was called for, "Tom Collins—Drink 'em while I got 'em." Their sliding glass door stood open to their wide patio, a breeze tugged at the flowered cafe curtains over their kitchen sink.

They had a pool. And a wiener dog that everyone patted and seemed to know. They'd named him Señor Wences, and taught him to walk around underfoot with a cigarette butt in his mouth.

Joanna's father stood outdoors, searing grill marks into thick steaks and hot dogs for us girls. Chlorine was sharp in the air and so was the smell of alcohol, in every glass except my mine and Joanna's. But it wasn't the stinky beer smell I was use to smelling.

The thing that was the best and the worst was in the sounds out on the patio and wide yard. The laughter that came from women. They touched the back of their own necks when they shot back answers to the mean things the men said. Everyone laughed. No big-bellied *chismosas* here.

Joanna seemed not to care about hearing words like *dark meat* and *soul kissing* as we walked around, handing still more drinks to the grownups. Those words made me blush, because not knowing how, I knew I half understood. And a new fear struck me, a fear that I'd one day be the cause of a head toss, a growled laugh. Like Mama. If I ever got out of wearing undershirts.

I tried my best to imitate Joanna's father because I liked him best of everyone who was there, next to Joanna. He smiled like he was more than tickled to be freshening anyone's drink, but I only dared to rest my palm on the small of Joanna's back when offering appetizers around.

Later into the evening when I saw his hand slip down into the back of Mrs. Delgado's low-cut sun dress, all I could think to do was find where Joanna stood, and hope she wasn't looking his way. But I caught her quick glance, down and away, as she picked up a dip bowl.

Twilight had deepened, and their guests began dancing, with the glow of the paper lanterns strung across the lawn, throwing shadows under their plum trees at the far end of their yard, where some of the dancing couples had drifted.

The light of their pool reflected blue waves on the grown-ups' faces, turning everyone into TV stars. I liked it. The sounds of jazz began to melt into the murmurs of the slow dancers.

And it was eleven-thirty before anyone thought to ask, "Why aren't you two in bed, young ladies?" By then the dip bowls stayed empty.

"Joanna," Mrs. Delgado squinted through her cigarette smoke, "Be a good kid and find my bag; I'm outta coffin nails here." She sat back into her chaise and leaned sideways, laying her red-tipped nails on some lady's thigh. "Damn fine evening. No, Syl?"

"Damn fine," Syl said back.

Joanna brought her bag; then I blushed hearing Syl say, "She's going to be a tall drink of water, humm?"

"Yep," her mother agreed. "You know how it is, Syl; legs run in our family."

It was then, that moment, that I felt myself go, before we began to laugh together. I think I fell in love with Joanna right then, when our laughter began, high into the lateness of the night.

It dawned on me that maybe every house on this block, and for blocks all around us and farther out, might have just as different a world going on in it. And all I'd ever seen was mine and Becca's lives so far. One-point-six miles was nothing after all.

It was the sound of ice tinkling in a tall glass, in this world, at the end of a damn fine evening. My hair was already all cut off, and I didn't care that Mama didn't know I was here again.

AFTER VIOLIN, JOANNA and I were in the Library in the 726s – Buildings for Religious Purposes. Because we thought the word *Cathedral* was interesting. Her mom had seen a show on them on the PBS channel, so we were looking things up.

We read: "The builders of old built to the glory of God," and I wondered out loud if, like Father Rudolph said, Jesus wanted our bodies to be temples, did that mean we were all really Jewish?

Bringing that up turned our talk from old buildings to our bodies. Joanna had way more ideas about free exchange on that than Miss Patricia ever came up with over at the other library.

Being taller she tiptoed and shoved the big book back onto the shelf; then she giggled and spun me against the books, whispering, "Well, girlie, I really like your nave." Then verrry softly she touched the back of my neck, where Mama had revealed it with her hair trimmers.

I said to the books, "Man, am I in trouble with Father Rudolph now."

It felt wonderful here in the quiet of the stacks, surrounded, no, protected, by all the books.

And a very stupid thought flashed across my mind: *Does Mama like 'Lise the way I like Joanna?*

ONCE THAT SUMMER Mama asked, "Where the hell do you think you're headed out to again?" I'd just handed her the change from the Market, saying, "Mrs. Bettencourt says hi." But she ignored that. "I asked you a question."

I sat down at the table. What was the best way to say it?

"Mama," I started, "I'm always here when you need

me." She leaned up against the counter, crossed her arms over her chest. "And I always try to do things right." She watched me.

"But here's summer, and most times I feel real stranded, like on a desert island: alone and bereft." She smiled at me. I breathed in, telling her outright—"and I think I've chanced onto a footprint in the sand…"

JOANNA AND ME were in her back yard near the pool getting sun, like her Mother called it. Her parents were out at another function, and Mama had said I could spend the night.

"So, say it again?" I asked. I'd talked her into trying to teach me to cuss in French.

"Why do you want that one?" she said, setting the English-to-French dictionary down on her lap.

"Just, say it again!" I said.

"Okay, but—"

I slapped at her bare leg.

"Owww! Okay, okay…" She started flipping the pages again. "Frankly, I'm not sure I can even pronounce this one right." She sat a bit straighter in the lounge chair and rattled off too many syllables that I still couldn't follow.

"Forget it," I said. And we went on to something that wasn't even cussing. I got that one and went around repeating it the whole rest of the day, *Laissez-moi seul*, Lass-zay-moahh-sool. Saying it with a laugh, then trying it mean and low and nearly spitting it out: *laissez-moi seul*.

Laissez-moi seul. Lass-zay-moahh-sool. Leave me alone.

"You are just too odd," Joanna told me when I said it to guy on a commercial.

"Well," I said, "I'm tired of being nice; I've tried Joanna." She tried to pat my head but I meant it; I pulled away, "—and all I've got was—Jeez, the worst. And from now on I'm doing things my way. So I need a new vocabulary if I'm gonna be different. Be on my own."

"We're barely gonna be teens," she said. "We're not s'posed to be on our own."

She tried her head pat again, and I let her, 'cause she kept her hand there and rubbed my curls. Her finger walking around there in my hair unclenched my shoulders a bit. It felt good and I thought of monkeys grooming each other in a troop. Mentioning that to her to make her laugh.

"If I could dial Sears and place an order for Barbie's school clothes when I was eight years old, I can be on my own any time I want."

"You did that?" she asked, taking her hand back. "You're talking about emancipated minors, then—and you're not one. Not 'till fifteen."

"Still do it," I said about Sears. I reached for her hand and put it back on my head. "Monkey me some more," I said, sliding down on the couch so she wouldn't have to reach. It was a wonderful feeling, and I don't know why— since it was so nice, but one more *laissez-moi seul* slipped out of me. She whacked the top of my head before she took her hand back.

"More," I said, then added, "What's a emansa-thing?"

"Ask my Dad," was all she'd say.

So I did. First chance I got.

HER DAD AND me, we talked about a lot of things that evening. He sat with me out at their pool as the sun went down. Once her mom came toward us in the shade, he waved her back inside—like we were in a meeting. Don't disturb.

We talked about emancipation and the Foster Homes. I mentioned my birthday, but kept quite about my scar. We even talked about how Joanna and I liked each other best. He corrected my French, how I was doing the pronouncing. So I told my heart to take a deep breath, 'cause then I told him about Joel, too.

THE NEXT TIME I saw Joel in his car, Joanna and I were waiting for her Dad after our second–to-the-last violin class for the summer. We were waiting at the Evergreen playground, because Mr. Delgado was driving us downtown to Bunker Hill to see the old houses there.

Joel parked and got out, a little furry black doggie with him. First I froze, then I remembered my newness and the talk I'd had with Joanna's dad.

I said my *laissez-moi seul* to myself and walked right up to him. "You're a sex maniac. And they don't let guys like you on playgrounds, Mister."

That stopped him for a moment; then he leaned down to put the puppy on the ground, stayed squatting there, grinning. He didn't see Mr. Delgado walking up from behind him.

"This little guy is for your brother, like I promised," Joel said, holding the little guy out for me.

I hunched down and took the doggie. That's when I saw Joel had his pants open again, with his ugly thing peeking out like the last time. I just took in a deep breath to keep from kicking him and I stood up, real calm. In a voice loud enough for Joanna's dad to hear I said, in English, "You wind that up or does it run on batteries, Joel?"

I'd thought that up all on my own.

That's when he followed my eyes and saw Mr. Delgado's shadow behind him. A piece of paper in his hand, writing Joel's license number down. While I held onto the puppy, Joanna's dad told him, real kind and informative like, "You know, *Joel*, messing about with little girls this age can offer a fella the opportunity for a nice long jail term. You know? Where you'll get to mess around with men much, much older than our Duffy here."

Funny enough, even though Mr. Delgado and I had role-played it a lot of times, still I felt like crying when it was all over.

THERE ON THE picnic benches, Joanna took her cello from its case. She held it in front of her, between her knees. "Let me lighten your heart, *chica*." She leaned over her instrument, pausing for a second, looking out over the playground. Like she was searching for the song somewheres out there. Then she held her bow in all but her first two fingers and plucked out the opening bars of *I'm So Lonesome I Could Cry*.

I sat listening and hugging my knees to me, I imagined what it would be like to be emancipated and to live at the beach with her, listing to her cello as the sun set over the water, with me cooking like Mama cooked. Joanna's cello's notes floating into our kitchen. To have Mr. Delgado as an almost Dad. Talk about a best life.

IT WAS SATURDAY and Becca was coming back. By now they were probably on the freeway headed to Elliot Street. I waited at the Market, well, actually at their back stairs. With a great big hand-made welcome home card. The outside showing a curly haired girl holding a big sign that said, "You are here…" On the inside a Huge X on a red heart; a heart that jumped like a jack-in-the-box when you opened the card.

It was the best I could think up. I was so proud of the spring-sprong part, I showed it to Mama, and she said "Humm." Chance liked it, though. He kept opening it over and over until I had to say no more, and promise to make one for him later.

When their car rolled up Becca was out of it before her mom had set the brake. We ran to each other. I tripped, banging up the heel of my palm, my knee, too, but I saved the homemade card. "Here, for you," I sobbed, only partly from the pain of my hand.

And Becca, through her happy tears, she read it, and then read it again. Re-opening it like Chance had, to get the heart to pound and pound. We hugged right there on the street. Her Mom standing there with her little suitcase, repeating, "Okay girls, inside with you now, c'mon."

THE FIRST THING that Joanna ever said to Becca was, "You one of her sisters?" And she said it with a sneer in her voice. The first thing Becca ever said to Joanna was, "Who wants to know?" And she said that like a fist. So right from the start I was stepping in between them and saying, "Quit it, guys."

But they still kept at it in small snide ways while we sat at Evergreen Park, under the picnic area in the shade. I got tired of it after a minute and got real bold. Right out loud I said, "If I wanted a fight I'd be with my stinky family, not here. Stop it or I'm going now."

And that calmed them down a bit. It was hard for me because Becca was who I'd come from and Joanna was where I wanted to be. And the guilt that they were against each other was making my stomach hurt.

For a moment I was even willing to tell them about my Quest to get them to stop glaring at each other's neck like they were lions growling at antelope.

"Becca'd probably like those leather skirts you showed me, Joanna," I said, turning to Becca. I added, "We saw 'em in *Seventeen,* May issue."

But Becca snorted, like I'd told her to eat boogers, and that was it.

I stood up and first touched Joanna's shoulder, then ran my hand, light, across Becca's back. And as much as I hate talking that way I said, "Screw it."

Then I just started walking for home.

AT THE LAST violin class, Mr. Simon called us in one at a time to give us the news. He warned us he'd be brief. And he was. Kid after kid came out of the auditorium, with a look of glad on their faces. I asked Joanna what he'd said to her, but she got bossy and just whispered, "Keep going." When it when my turn I figured out why. He called me in and hugged me and said it was nice having me in the class all summer; then he said just two words, *"Stop now."* And I went out smiling.

ME AND JOANNA walked the rest of the way towards her street, and I handed her the poem I'd written her, saying,

"*Don't* read it out loud."

But she did anyway. Smiling about the part where I see her exhale. Then she folded it up and opened her case to put it into the rosin box, laying her cello back over it, like a hand over her heart, saying, "I'm gonna keep that forever, Duff."

On the way back through the neighborhood from Evergreen playground, just before she went up to Dacotah Street and I turned to go down to Fourth Street, she swung her case in a big wide circle and called to me as her steps got farther away. "Have fun in school. Maybe we can sleep over once or twice, sometime. Maybe—with Becca, even."

I waved and turned to go when she called, "Hey, Duff, you look really good in navy blue."

ME AND BECCA were in a dressing stall at Mode O' Day on First Street. Her mom kept going up and down the racks, coming back with her picks. Tossing dresses for us over the swinging door. "Here, Duffy, a few of these, too." I was pulling a pink one over my head and I got stuck. Tugging was making it worse.

"Mom! Help!" Becca called, "Duff's caught!"

So 'Lise stepped in, trying to give the dress a mom's tug. She grabbed my wrists. "Just hold still a second, hon." To Becca, "can you unzip it a bit more?" Then she gasped.

I thought I'd torn it. "Duff! What did you do to your arm!" And I just let my legs go out from under me, sinking to the carpet in a pleated pink-and-green-dotted puddle. My arm—that was all.

I hadn't torn it.

"GETTING IN TROUBLE is not the issue here, girls." Becca's

mom was saying as we sat in front of our dishes of ice cream; acting like they weren't there because she was so serious about stuff. "Why didn't anyone know but Becca? What about Justine? Did she know?" I didn't have an answer to that that wouldn't sound flip. I kept quiet.

So she turned on Becca, "Well?" But Becca didn't say anything either. "And you're perfectly sure your mother didn't do this?"

I was stopped by that. What if I said yes? Would that get me away from her? Could I go live with Joanna or Becca? Or even in a girls' home till emancipation came? But could I do that? *No. Not that way.*

So I told her again: *No. I did it.* To get the pressure off, that's all. Just to get rid of the pressure.

And still we kept away from the ice cream spoons. "I know you're a very advanced girl, Duff. But I have to be assured here. Will this ever happen again? Or do I go to Rennie, *today*?"

And I thought, *Why bother? She'd hate you for it.*

But all I said was, "No Ma'am. It won't. Ever again." I couldn't say the truth out loud to her, with Becca right there next to me, about Mama.

"We'll stop at a drugstore on the way home," she added, sitting back in the booth, giving up. Maybe I didn't have to tell her the truth about how Mama would take this. Maybe she knew it already.

Maybe she knew it and still wanted to have girls' night out. "Vitamin E oil's good for scars." She told me, patting my hand, "Eat some of this, girls, before it's all melt-y."

MAMA NEVER SAID anything about Mrs. Bettencourt buying

me all the new dresses. At least, not to me. And Barbie was the only one who wanted to see them all, so I had to try on each one in the bathroom, then come out to model them for her, like I was the Barbie and she was playing with me and my outfits. We were in Justine's room.

"Justine, does this look good to you?" I asked, holding one of the dresses up to my shoulders, the Navy blue one with the white collar. "Do you think this is my best color?"

She stared from her bed, then reached and turned me left, then right, then made a circle with her finger. So I turned all the way around even though the dress was only up against the front of me.

She smiled. I figured I'd picked the best out. Then she said, "Sure Duff, you look fine, but can I ask?"

"Ask what?" I said, putting the dress back on the hanger.

"Did you hit your head, Muskrat?"

"When?"

"When you fell in love with yourself?"

The Magic of Its Beauty

MAMA DECIDED, *WE need to get out of this damned city for one last time this summer*, even though I thought we hadn't been out once before. So that Monday, the fifth, we were all set to go to the beach for Labor Day.

Mr. St. John and Jeff were coming, too, in the Impala.

Mrs. Bettencourt pulled her car over in front of our house to load us up. Jeff and Mr. St. John were taking Justine and Barbie in their car. Becca, Chance, and me would ride with Mama and 'Lise. Chance was the lucky one to sit up front between them. But even so, it was nice to be in her car and not be sick for once.

We drove for the longest time.

Right when we got into the car I leaned over the front seat. "What mileage are we at right now?"

'Lise told me, 4,424 without asking why. Mama gave her a look. Chance wanted to know, was the number we had to drive to get to the beach? After awhile I gave up trying to explain that that was the number we were starting from. Mama just kept saying, "Sit back or lose it. I mean it this time, Duff."

We were on the freeways from the very start. I'd studied

the map. It was a good thing I wasn't driving. The first freeway was called West Pomona 60, it curved like a pig tail. And right away we had three choices in front of us: West Santa Monica 10, West Hollywood 101, North Sacramento 5.

I thought for sure she'll drive us on the Santa Monica one on the left, like the map said was the way to the beach. But instead she got to the right: North Sacramento 5, you could see the silhouette of City Hall, up straight and tall like a finger in class of someone needing to go real bad.

The next sign read Golden State Freeway. The way it curved, it made the City Hall there, then not there, then there again, off to our left. It made me so surprised to see it was another name for the North Sacramento 5. "Like a pen name," I said.

Mama said, "Sit back." But I didn't. I pointed out the moving City Hall to Chance.

You could see that we'd left Jeff and them pretty far behind already. I kept twisting around, trying to find their Impala, but they drove way slower than Mrs. Bettencourt. Mama called her Leadfoot. I guess that was a compliment 'cause they both chuckled like it was.

Jeff's white car kept peeking in and out of the traffic behind us, sometimes catching up to us and sometimes falling farther behind. I asked about the West Santa Monica 10 and what I'd seen on the map. I was leaning forward again. "Oh, we're going to a much nicer beach than that one," was all Mama said.

Chance asked. "If we're going straight all the time how come City Hall kept moving?"

Mama told us, "Perception, from the sky you'd see we're

curving this way and that."

"It's not the map—it's the terrain," I said, like Mr. Delgado.

And 'Lise, she smiled, "Duff, you've been reading Korzybski!"

It seemed I'd lost track of the others for real after a while. We drove over a tall curve and then the signs still said Golden State Freeway. The street signs were marvelous; I pointed out Los Feliz and Echo Park to Chance.

"Look Chance, that street's called The Happy One; I bet Artie lives on that street."

Chance joined right in, "An' he works at Echo Park, maybe yodeling, huh, Duff?" We giggled.

"Yep," I nodded. "The hills and the houses peeking from the green and the huge trees, that's just like the Foster Homes. Pretty, huh?"

But then that wonderful view changed to West Ventura Freeway 134 and hills so big they could be young mountains. *Then*, the freeway kept its name and changed its number to 101, and I was totally lost. Looking behind me. I hoped Jeff wasn't lost for good.

By then both Chance and Becca were snoozing. Mama got tired of me hanging over the seat, saying the freeway numbers out loud, asking about the mileage over and over. The mileage was up to 4,431 miles now. She reached over her head and grabbed, "*Aplacate!*" Root Yourself.

I froze while the car swayed just a touch. 'Lise reached across to set her hand on Mama's thigh and just left it there, light little pats and rubs, like to comfort a sick baby. "Rennie, she's trying to help, honey."

"Duff, sit back," Mama said, turning me loose. And I

scooted back out of reach. Mama shifted in her seat and told 'Lise, "She's mine and I'll do with her as I please."

I thought they'd start fighting, but 'Lise moved her hand up to the back of Mama's neck and rubbed some more. It was neat the way she could drive so well with just one hand on the wheel.

She told Mama, "Well, like we talked, a bigger house, split it all with me, you can give this one to me to deal with, even. Share the worry."

She said it low, with her eyes front. I wasn't really sure I'd heard it that way till Mama's head leaned towards her; she whispered, "Keep talking, baby, you may well convince me."

Pretty soon even Mama was sleeping too. That left me and 'Lise to do the driving. And still she said we weren't there yet.

She smiled a lot at me in the rear view mirror.

We passed so many new things. And she always looked when I pointed out something else.

"Well would you look at that," I whispered in her ear, 'cause Mama was still sleeping. I pointed to the hay-colored hills up ahead, like I was seeing a new wonder.

"What, dear?"

"That hill over there?"

"Yeah?"

"Don't those trees look like a giant cat used that hill for a litter box then didn't cover up all his poop like he should have?"

'Lise laughed, squinted at the hill, and said, "What a naughty kitty, huh?"

I laughed soft, not to wake up Mama, "Bad, bad kitty." I

shook my head. *"Tsk."*

"There's another one," she nodded with a dip of her head. It was the seventh blue-and-white VW van we'd seen since Mama had fallen asleep.

"They're everywhere." I hung my arms over the seat-back and let my chin set there. I drummed my fingers on the upholstery. "This is nothing like Elliott Street, huh?"

"Nope, quite a change. That's the good thing about trips. No matter the length. Everything changes."

Goosebumps went around the top of my head because looking around at the hills along the road, that's what I was thinking, too. About how us kids had made a trip from Mama's house into Foster Homes and back again. How 'Lise had made a trip from France. And even how much had changed just from Hockert Street to Elliott Street. And how deep in my bones I knew maybe after a time I wouldn't be on Elliott Street anymore, either.

I said a bit of one of my poems to her:

"Everything changes, then fades away."

"Hard to accept, I think." She shook her head.

"I'm used to it," I told her.

"What?"

"People fading away. People stay in my heart, but they never stay around. They're there one day, like Artie; then they're just gone. But it's okay. I'm used to it." I recited the rest of the poem: *"Years I've lost so long ago, I fear they're not as true, as true recites itself to me and I relate to you."* I whispered, soft into her pink ear. "I wrote that."

"That's very good."

"Thank you."

THE MILEAGE WAS up to 4471.5 miles now, we'd come 47.5 miles, a very far way. "Do you think I'd be good at being a real girl, 'Lise?"

"Real? How do you mean? You're real, hon."

"Okay, maybe I'm saying the words wrong. Do you think I'd be good as a girl like my friend Joanna? Or Becca? You know, happy girls with real families?"

"You don't think having all your brothers and sisters and your Mom is a family?"

"Well, no, 'cause we can be split up—taken away at any second. Justine can go at any minute. Barbie could run away like Artie did. Mama could lose us all over again."

"You think so?"

"I know so. It happened once already. Heck, I might grow up to be just like Mama and lose all my kids, too."

"Baby—I—" She shook her head. "Here's how it works Duff, you *could* grow up to be like Rennie. But you might grow up to be someone like me, or like any other lady you know of. Or you could even grow up to be a bit of both. Some of her, but *a lot of you*. Even, and this is the best, you might grow up to be *just* like you, an original. It's your choice." Mama opened her eyes then and stretched, and then she closed them again and burrowed back into her nap.

"Seriously?" I whispered.

"Seriously."

WE TURNED OFF from the freeway at a road called Las Virgenes, and from there her car wove its way farther up into the sandy hills we'd seen from the freeway. I told 'Lise I'd keep a lookout for that giant cat.

It was pretty quiet for a bit. But I wasn't sorry I'd told

her all that. The car twisted and turned on all those curves. And the trees got bigger and taller and more forest looking than I'd ever seen in real true life. It was so beautiful I actually used that word to say so out loud, not afraid of being made fun of at all.

We drove into a deep tunnel that went right into a mountain. In that darkness I felt even braver and told 'Lise about my Quest and how Mr. St. John had promised me the reward.

I said how my Quest, like what I'd done to my arm with the razor, was like this tunnel. It was only dark for a ways. And soon, once I'd made it all the way through, "Well, just watch," I told her.

She was busy concentrating on the twisty road 'cause it took awhile for her to say anything, then she told me, "If I can help, you know I will, Duff."

"Like a Guardian Angel?" I asked as we drove out of the dark.

She glanced over at Mama, sleeping. "I think of myself more as your mom's Guardian Angel." And I nodded. I could see that, too. "How about with us, I'll be like another mom? Someone who *will* stay around."

First, without thinking, it hurt to hear her say that.

I wanted to shove her. To complain, *Don't be making fun of me.* But, then I thought—*Maybe here in this forest place, maybe this is where dreams might come true.*

I worked so hard at trying to accept her offer, of letting things change that much. It stopped me thinking at all and I said what I could let my heart believe, little as it was, "Maybe."

As WE CAME down out of the mountain she looked over at Chance and Mama sound asleep.

"Chacun dort," she said. I was still hanging over the seat back, my head near hers, pretending like it was just us two and she was my only mom.

"Huh?"

"Everyone sleeps."

I whispered, "Becca, too." So we were the only ones awake to see the gleaming slice of ocean ahead of us like a band of silver light.

She said soft, "Make a wish, Hon."

So I leaned closer. "Here's my wish, but keep it a secret. I wanna live somewhere where nobody fights. Where nobody says bad words. Even if it means living with nobody. I wanna be my own Mama. I'd do a real good job. Even better than I been doing so far."

THIS BEACH WAS too good to be real. From the Market, Becca and her mom had packed sodas for all of us and those Hostess cupcakes, too. Barbie'd made up her famous mixed-fruit salad, with the nectarine hunks and the green grapes cut into thin little round slices. Mama'd made us a ton of sandwiches, cut on the triangles, with romaine lettuce and tomato slices in each one. And I'd remembered to pack the salt and pepper shakers and napkins for us all.

The sand was pretty hot so Jeff had to carry Chance to where we decided to put the blankets down, "Not too far or close to the water, 'Lisc," Mama had instructed. Leo Carrillo State Beach. A surfer beach, Jeff said.

We'd brought four blankets ourselves, and Jeff pulled another one out of his trunk when we parked across the highway. So we had a big enough space to keep us all off the hot sand.

Compared to some of the other groups along the beach here, we were nearly mob sized. Four grownups, five kids. Though Justine seemed more teenager than kid. Only Chance's puppy was missing, I thought. Then I froze. I swore in my head, it kept getting harder to remember: And Artie. He was missing, too.

I WALKED OUT of the surf, back towards the blankets. Becca still splashed in the water. The seawater was plastering my T-shirt to my arms and front. But with the sun so hot I didn't feel too cold.

Mama, Chance, and Barbie had walked down the edge of the water towards the big climbing rocks up farther on the beach. I fell right on the blanket, not even wiping off first, I was so tired from the body surfing. I turned and held my hand to my eyes, looking for Becca; then I found her and pointed, "See, she's hopping up and down there."

Her mom followed my finger, then said, "Oh, okay—I see her." Becca still hopped and hopped, trying to catch the next wave that rolled in.

I leaned back on my elbows and let my head drop back to them all on the blanket behind me. I smiled upside down and said, "Thank you, guys. It's been a real great day."

'Lise, she said, "Your mom's idea, hon."

And I said, "But you guys drove. It's been 70.6 miles. I figured a second, then asked, "You guys need gas money?"

She told me, "No, no." And Jeff added, "We're okay, too, Duff."

The sun was headed to the horizon and Justine was

lying off to the side of us on a hunk of blanket all her own. She was snoozing, with a big floppy hat over her face and her fingers laced over her tummy. Her stomach rising and falling showed she was deep asleep.

WITH THE REST of the kids were either back in the water or up on the rocks, it was just me and the adults; Mama sat on the blanket with 'Lise behind her and Mama's back up against 'Lise's bent knees and said, "Duff, another cupcake? There's more here." I thought it might be a trick to make me look bad in front of Mr. St. John and Jeff, but then I looked again at her face. All I saw was happy. Up against 'Lise's leg like that, so I said, "No, thanks, Mama, I'm full."

Jeff reached past me for the cupcake and said, "Your loss, Missy." Just like Artie might have. Then he stood, "Dave?" he asked. But Dave waved him away.

Jeff headed for the rocks as the rest of us leaned back on the blankets, lounging, with our faces to the sun, just feeling good being out in the sand. Mama's dark hair falling into 'Lise's lap.

She was grinning, I was glad I'd done the right thing by being ladylike and not saying yes to the second cupcake. If I could be as good on the ride home, I'd make her even more happy—and it might last into the week.

Mr. St. John put his hand to his eyes, looking for Jeff down the beach. "Where is he?" he said. I looked around then pointed him out over by the rocks where two surfers had just come out of the water with their boards. "Ah."

"Remember that you drove us here, no getting lost now," Justine said from under her hat, sitting up in a sleek, uncurling move, like a girl from a movie. Her hand on her hat and her feet never leaving the blanket. Becca ran up and flopped on the blanket, all dripping and out of breath.

"Man, that was great!"

Justine stretched and said, "Think I'll get wet…." Then she put her chin to her knees and stared out at the waves.

"This year?" Mama asked, and 'Lise swatted the top of her head. The surfers were headed towards us with their boards under their arms. And Jeff and Mr. St. John were now up at the top of one of the bigger rocks, standing shoulder to shoulder. I noticed just then that Jeff was taller.

Because 'Lise had swatted her head, Mama tried reaching around to pinch 'Lise. They started in roughhousing and giggling. Us three girls looked away, like: *they're too old for this.*

But they stopped on their own, 'cause when the surfer boys walked past, one of them said, "First fags, now dykes."

"IT'S NOT THEIR beach, Rennie," 'Lise said to Mama, her hand now on Mama's foot, pink fingernails against red toenails. "They're just stupid boys."

"Just,'cause, just 'cause, you know, they said that stuff doesn't mean—" I started.

"'Lise, I know you're not—" Justine said.

"You do, huh?" Mama looked at me.

"Mom," Becca sighed, shaking her head. "Those guys are crazy. If you two were part of a gang, you'd be like, y'know, wearing way more makeup. Teasing your hair and smoking… and stuff… like gang fights and cussing."

"Part of a *gang?*"

"Yeah," Becca said, "The Dykes."

I WALKED INTO the Market with my three socks of coins

and plunked them down on the counter.

"What's this?" 'Lise asked. And I told her I needed dollars for it. "But where did it all come from?"

I looked her in the eye. "Carrying charges." Her eyebrows came back down, she went, *Ahhhh.*

"There's nearly nine months of coins here," I said, so we both started counting.

"What're you planning on doing with all this?" she asked, as she handed me the all the dollars.

"First," I showed her my fingers, "get Chance a present from the Lorena Drug Store."

"What, this place only sells chickens?" she asked, and I laughed.

"Nah, it has to be from there. Remember Joanna's dad, Mr. Delgado?"

"Sure."

"Well, he says: 'Make your life be the way you want it to be.' Get it?"

"Clear as mud." She asked, "But nothing for you?" leaning on the counter in that way she had, like praying.

"The rest is all for saving. I got plans coming up. But maybe I'll get me something later."

"Like what, hon?" It was nice hearing that. *Hon.*

"I dunno, like maybe I'll replace a book I lost."

I walked up to the Lorena Drug Store and got Chance a really good present. A big book called 365 Bedtime Stories and Poems. It was real colorful. And pretty. And I got a hug when I brought it home.

ON THE FIRST day of seventh grade I was late for homeroom. Because Chance was still at the elementary school and that meant going in the opposite direction before turning around and getting here to the Junior High.

When I stepped into my homeroom class, I found the teacher was Miss Givens. Miss Patricia from the summer writing class. She was writing on the board and just waved her hand without turning, so I took a seat back by the door I'd come in. I scrunched down as far as I could.

"You all can just call me Miss Patricia, if that's any easier," she said as she used her best cursive on the board.

She propped her roll book up on her lectern and started in on the roll. "Andersen? Apodaca? Bettencourt? Chavez? Du Bois? Galante? Garcia? Highland? Montez? Sartori?" All the way to Verdugo. That was crazy Patti, from Catechism.

At my name I just raised my hand so I wouldn't have to say *here*. And it wasn't 'till she said she'd prefer if we'd move the chairs into a circle that she noticed me.

"Pilar!"

She nearly ran to my side of the room. Like an auntie or a little *abuelita,* she stood me up and hugged me, saying, "My, my, look at how tall you got!"

Every one of the kids stared. A few boys laughed. In my heart I heard the echo from the beach: *…now the dykes.*

I felt my face go red. She kept hugging me to her till Tim Garcia said, "That's not Pilar. That's Duffy."

Becca wouldn't even catch my eye; so embarrassing. Miss Patricia just couldn't stop smiling and she didn't even consider letting me go.

She just kept on beaming and hugging.

It wasn't till she finally did let me go that she looked around the room at the others. Then, she came back to normal and realized what she'd been doing. Though she tried to hold her smile at finding me there, as she directed us to push our chairs out into a wider circle, you could see her eagerness was kind of ruined. The class suddenly fidgety and awkward now; just kind of staring at the floor or at the bulletin boards.

She looked so confused. I felt bad.

She started in on correct grammar—that we weren't supposed to say him an' me. That the proper way was he and I. With whoever you were talking about, letting them come first, "As if good manners and good grammar were the same things," she said.

She asked for someone to give an example. Tim raised his hand and in a lady's voice he said, "Pilar and I had an exquisite time together this summer." The whole class cracked up. It was a great big comedy.

It was the worst way to start a new class, especially when I was the youngest one there. Finally the bell rang for the end of Homeroom, and we got to get up and go to our next class. On the way out of the room, Tim made a face and waggled his head. "Pilar," he mouthed. I felt like no good luck at all was gonna come my way this semester.

ONLY A FEW of the Homeroom kids were in my next class because most, but not all, of us were MGM. So at least there was that. But the whole day felt tilted, not what I'd dreamed my first day of seventh grade was going to be like. Like rain in July, the whole day was off for me from then on.

Near the end of the day, when we'd come back to Homeroom from all the other classes, Miss Patricia stopped by my seat and squeezed my shoulder. She leaned to me, whispered, "Smile. This is such good luck. What a year we'll have."

But I wasn't in the mood and I couldn't smile about anything. Not even for her.

After school I didn't even want to walk with Becca.

I'D GOTTEN ALL the way to Chance's school before I realized that Mama said Mondays she'd pick him up from first grade. So that put me in a low mood, too, on top of what had happened in Homeroom.

Walking home up the hill, I punched at my thigh and swore out loud, using all the cuss words I could think of. Right out loud, I was so mad. The kids in class were going to be teasing me forever. I tried thinking about how Mr. Delgado would have some good advice on how to manage this. I tried thinking that it would make a good story some day. How I should save the memory for later, but it was no good. I was just too miserable about it all.

Sad, like it felt I'd never been sad before.

365 Bedtime Stories

MY LEGS DIDN'T even have the strength to move up the hill. I stopped at a house with a stone front and steps leading up to a yard and just sat down there. Was it hurt pride I was feeling? Would I have to sacrifice something to atone for feeling this way? Was God going to make it worse because I'd failed the test of being embarrassed in the first place?

I didn't think I was ready for a daily teasing from Tim if that was what God had in store. Not every day, not first thing in the morning and last thing in the afternoon. Homeroom wasn't supposed to be hell on earth, I thought to myself; I'd had Foster Homes and my now house for that.

And that's when I stopped feeling bad and started to grin, then to giggle, then to laughing out loud as I stood and started walking again. 'Cause then it dawned on me.

This day had been part of the Quest; at least I thought maybe that's what it was. To show me that school might be bad, but still, I'd seen worse. I could remember then about the advice from Mr. Delgado, about saving hard times to write about for later. So still thinking it all over, nothing was as bad right now as my past, even if that was just yesterday.

It was all just part of the labyrinth, and at the end, waiting, was the Best Life. Where I could be a real girl. It was there, I was sure it was. Waiting for me to pass all these small bits. To make the tests into gratitude.

MAMA WAS WAITING for me at the front door. "This better not be a habit," she warned.

I told her that I'd had a real bad day at school and then how I'd forgotten that she'd be picking up Chance today.

"That's a good one," she said, with her hand on her hip.

I thought about that, then said right out loud: "Yeah, it would've been a good one—if I ever needed to lie." Then I kept on down the hall and threw my books on my bed. I got out of my school clothes and came back into the kitchen to see what she wanted from the store.

She didn't say anything about me being fresh. Just handed me money and recited things to get.

After the store and my homework I asked if Chance and me could go for a walk. Mama said, "Just 'till the street lights come on, then be back." And she didn't even put some chore in front of letting us go first. Chance waited, looking back at her from the front door, just in case she was being slow, but then we went.

"IF WE WALK really fast, I'll show you my new school," I told him. I didn't have a bike to ride him on my handlebars like Artie had done for me.

"What if I can't walk fast enough?" Neither of us had even thought to time when the streetlights came on.

"I'll give you a piggyback on the way home if you can make it there on your own." I would've ridden him piggyback both ways if I needed to, but I didn't want him being a baby all the time.

"Okay. Let's do it," he said; so we were off.

LIKE HE WAS reading my mind, Chance asked, "How's your Quest going?" He was walking very fast and trying to miss the cracks in the sidewalk at the same time, his head bent and eyes down.

"It must be going good, 'cause we're on this little adventure," I said.

"Will there be dragons?"

I thought about Mama. "Maybe at the end, but no. Not at my school anyway."

"Am I walking fast enough, Duff?"

"Boy, you sure are." He smiled at that.

"You gotta do this every morning?"

"Well, not this fast, but, yeah, every morning."

"Boy, I'm glad I'm only in First—this's hard!"

AT THE JUNIOR High School, I walked him around to the cafeteria and the Library. I showed him the rack where the boys locked up their bikes and the rows of metal lockers where we kept most of our books between classes. He tried to jump and reach the higher ones but he was way too small. "One day," I promised, "you'll be tall like Artie. You'll be able to see the top of these lockers. Without even getting up on tiptoes."

Chance seemed sad to see we didn't have rings or monkey bars. "What do youse guys do for recess?" he wanted to know.

"There is no recess. Just Homeroom, then class, then another class till lunch, then after that more class, class, and

Homeroom again." It sounded simple and easy to do when I said it like that.

He looked around in pity, taking my hand he petted it, "I'm so sorry about no recess." Then he looked back at the tall rows of lockers, "But I am *really* glad I'm just in First."

We walked across the lawn at the front of the school and I noticed that the streetlights were still off so we felt good about walking slower on the way home. I took a different path to show Chance the Jacaranda trees all along the street that the library was on. Halfway down the Sixth Street hill it dawned on me that this was the first hill we came down when Artie was driving the truck and Chance and me. No, *Chance and I*, had sat in the back and got squished by all the moving boxes. It seemed like hundreds of years ago.

HOMEROOM WAS ALSO English period, so Miss Givens was standing up near the chalkboard and writing out some of the words we *consistently find the need to misspell*. The weirdest one was *people*; it seems a lot of us were spelling it pe-lope. I wondered if we'd all gotten it wrong together from some earlier grade.

But as she put it, *MGM status is no excuse for lax spelling*. She turned to say this to us and stopped, pointed to Tim near the windows and said, "There will be no picking of scabs in *my* classroom, Tim Garcia."

Tim turned red and dropped his hand from his earlobe like it had burned him. And the kids all laughed.

My face got red, for Tim. I looked up to see Miss Givens was laughing, too. Like Mama at home; she was no different than that. Laughing at the weakest someone's expense. I decided then that maybe I wouldn't do very well in this class; maybe I would do really bad. I could even fail.

She was back to tapping the board with her chalk, pointing out other words we needed to relearn. None of them were ones I was getting wrong, so I flipped to a new page in my notebook and started in on a short story instead.

BECCA AND I talked about Miss Givens making fun of Tim as we walked to our next class. I just couldn't stop thinking of her laughing. About how she didn't even consider how Tim must have felt.

Becca said, "Well, it was pretty funny, Duff. And Tim wasn't crying over it or anything, you know?"

But letting it go was hard for me to do. I wondered if Joanna was having this kind of semester at her new school.

We were in class diagramming paragraphs that had antecedents, which was something easier to explain than it was to say out loud. I knew how to do them; I was already finished with my sheet of handout work. But I didn't want to raise my hand or participate because I was still sore about Tim, so I kept quiet and worked on my story in my notebook.

Miss Givens still didn't get it that I didn't want to do any participating.

"Pilar, you know this. I know you do," she said.

But I just shrugged my shoulders and frowned at my sheet of work like it was out of focus. "I dunno." I told her.

"You were the brightest one in summer class—of course you know this." She tapped on the board with her fingertips making little dots of clean on the smeared chalk.

"I missed this one," I lied. "I can't get it."

"I know you can do this—I've got faith in you, c'mon dear …"

One of the boys piped in with, "Just go on and marry her, why don't you?"

It was worse than forgetting and calling her *Mommy* out loud. I'd done that once to a teacher when I was in the second grade.

I RAISED MY hand in third-period Biology class and asked for a hall pass and let myself out of the room and into the cool, dim hallway. I didn't want to be around the other kids. I wanted to run really fast for a very long time.

For a bit I wished I was a boy so I could start a fight with someone and do some kind of damage. I could see why Luis and Artie wanted to fight on our porch that one time.

I thought about going to the principal's office and asking to be allowed to do all my work in the library—away from everyone else. 'Cause I felt like I really needed to punch something. Then I found my feet at Homeroom. And the weird thing was I didn't even realize I'd been heading there.

She looked up when I came in. The room was empty—it was her free period. I told her I forgot something from my desk. I sat and scooched down in the seat to reach into it. Miss Givens went back to writing in her roll book. I watched the way her straight red hair fell into her face when she leaned forward, how she brushed it back, but it fell again, like a curtain. She didn't seem horrible at all like that.

"You may not feel up to this Pilar, but I'll give it to you anyway," she said, holding out a yellow flyer as I walked passed her desk to leave. I couldn't look her in the eye.

A poetry contest. I thought about the last poem I'd given her. A House of Light and Stone. I folded the flyer to slide it into my textbook. I tried to smile. Then I moved to leave quietly; at the door I turned and saw her hair fall back down over her eyes when she leaned into her work again.

BECAUSE I'D MADE her sad, I decided to help out when she asked for poetry submissions for a contest that Scholastic Books was holding. But laying on my bunk, I really couldn't come up with anything worth giving. My head was empty. Like Mama always said.

Chance wanted to hear one of his 365 stories and poems. Since I wasn't getting anywhere, I put down my pen and let him climb up for a read. "You want October seventh or just any old day?" I asked.

And he covered his eyes. "S'prise me."

So I let the big book flop open and it was a poem from April, about someone with no rain boots and a cold.

AT THE END of the day Miss Givens called for me to wait after Homeroom, and someone started in with "here comes the bride" as they all shuffled out.

I still wouldn't let Miss Givens get me to cooperate in class, though I did all my homework and turned it in on time, and I was four chapters ahead of everyone else in the English textbook. So she'd sent home a letter to have a conference with Mama.

I handed the note to Justine when I got home and we both went into the kitchen with Barbie to boil water in the teapot. Richard Montez will say *stick the letter in the freezer*, but Justine and Artie swore by the teapot.

"Duffy, what the hell did you do?" Barbie asked. Because no one had ever sent a note home with me.

I knew it was 'cause of how I was acting in class but I shrugged my shoulders, "I dunno."

Justine shook her head. "What're you gonna do once I'm gone?" But I knew she wasn't looking for an answer to that. If I was lucky the note might be about something else, like back-to-school night or a field trip.

The water came to a boil. "Well, let's see what you're gonna die from," Barbie said. She put on an oven mitt and held the flap of the envelope over the spout of steam, running it back and forth along where it was sealed until the glue loosened and we could slip the note out. "Hold this so the flap doesn't touch anything," she warned, handing me the sticky envelope. Then Justine took the letter to read the note to herself.

"Justine!" Barbie yelled. "Out loud, *por favor!*" Even she was fidgety about what it said.

"*Ay, como chinga!* You're in for it good, sweetie." Justine fanned the limp note against her thigh, like to cool it off. Then she read:

Dear Mrs. Michealson,

Please attend a Parent-Teacher conference this Thursday, at 4:00 p.m. I would like to discuss Defoe's classroom attitude with you. Among other concerns.

Sincerely,
Patricia Givens.

P.S. Duffy may attend with you if you feel she should.

BARBIE REACHED OVER and gave my shoulder a squeeze,

Whoa, I thought: *This was very seriously bad.*

WHEN MAMA CAME home from work she lit a cigarette before she even took her shoes off. Barbie saw that and slipped into her bedroom, closing the door really quietly.

Justine asked if 'Lise was coming over later. Mama brushed the hair from her forehead and closed her eyes. Putting feet up on the coffee table she said, "Probably, why? Duffy, get me a soda from the fridge."

"I dunno, maybe we can play with the Yahtzee dice again. After dinner."

"Sure, we'll see." Then Mama asked us to bring her a pillow 'cause, "I'm beat. I need a nap." She stretched out with her stockings and work dress still on.

While we made dinner on tiptoe, trying not to clang any of the pots, Justine outlined her plan of having 'Lise in the house while showing Mama the letter.

"If Mama goes crazy, it'll be a lot less. And the rest of us kids as witnesses will help, too."

I was willing to try anything, but Barbie said, "Witnesses never helped before."

Justine cooked Chile Verde, with pork, 'Lise's favorite. Barbie made a pot of Spanish rice and the zucchini with tomatoes and jack cheese, Mama's favorite vegetable dish.

I set the table and used all the best serving dishes and the nicest napkins, too. But then Chance forgot and galloped to the door when 'Lise and Becca knocked.

THE BAD MOOD was in her the minute she sat up. I looked around to see what else I could do to but we'd all done our best already. I'd just have to go through it and come out the other end, like Mr. Delgado said last summer about facing Joel.

"MAMA, I'VE GOT a note from school," I said after we'd finished playing our second round of real-Yahtzee. "My Homeroom teacher wants you to come to see her next Thursday, at 4:00. You can bring me if you want, or not."

"You read the note?" 'Lise asked.

"Yep. I mean, Yes. I did."

Becca watched Mama's face as it got more and more mad. The rest of us didn't need to watch for it. We knew.

"I haven't done anything wrong, I just haven't done anything right. And if you want to punish me—"

Justine stood, and said, "Barbie, let's go make coffee. Becca, Chance, c'mon, we can cut up some fruit too…come help." And she lured them all into the kitchen.

Since she started spending time with 'Lise, right after September, she'd hardly ever been really mad at all. But now Mama was furious.

She said, in her lowest, calmest, most dangerous voice, "You're gonna make me lose work time and you're not even sorry for it?"

"Mama, I am sorry. That's why I'm taking responsibility. That's why I'm being brave and telling you instead of hiding it."

"Let me see the note," she said, and I handed it to her, sitting back in my chair, waiting for the hitting, if that was coming.

'Lise leaned in and read it with her, then they both sat back too and stared at me for a moment. 'Lise finally said, "I can drive you from work, Rennie, so you won't have to leave so early and take the bus. Maybe they'll let you make up the time later."

"And the Market?" Mama asked her, while she glared at me.

I wanted not to but I started crying. Mama put her elbow on the table and pointing her finger at me. "I might not get mad—*might not*—if you can tell me what the *hell* you have to cry about, *chica*."

I knew that was a trick—she'd be mad no matter what. So I tried to breathe. I tried to sound okay when I wiped at my nose and told them, "I just, h-h-hate knowing it's cause of me that Miss Givens'll be staying late at school for this. You'll be missing work hours, an 'Lise," I waved my hand, "c-c-closing the Market early just cause of me." I put my hands around my chest, taking real small breaths, trying to hold back the rest of the tears in me.

"SHE'S BECOME MOODY and somewhat solitary this semester, such a change from summer school," Miss Givens said to Mama, her hand on my stack of work in front of her. "No problem with the things she's turned in, she's ahead of everyone in class. She did that on her own initiative. No problem with her attendance."

"These are all 'A' papers then?" Mama asked, touching the edge of the stack herself.

"Mostly 'A+'. She really should be in Eighth this year. Possibly Individual Study, frankly. But I'd like to speak about her moods, and this self-imposed isolation, Pil-uh-Duffy's become such a solitary girl this year."

"What's wrong with solitary?" Mama said, sitting a little taller in the chair. "I'm a solitary person myself—" Mama started.

"But you're not—"

"Yes? I'm not what?" Mama looked from Miss Givens to me. "Someone expected to amount to anything?"

"I was going to say 'someone who was solitary at age eleven'."

I kept my head down.

"Baloney-sauce." Mama snapped as she stood to leave.

"Mrs. Michealson—" But Mama was heading to the door. I just sat and ran my finger over the scar on my hand.

Mama turned and told her, "If you keep hammering at her like this I'm sure you'll be calling me in for something really serious by the end of the school year."

She was gone. And it was just us two there.

Miss Givens reached into her desk and pulled out a typewritten page that she set on my desk, and I began to read—it was the poem I'd turned in for the contest. She'd typed it up on nice paper, and my name was at the bottom—Pilar Chavez. The Poem was one about having a cold and no galoshes. The one I'd taken from Chance's book. From April.

"I AM SO disappointed in you today." I didn't have anything to say. "So disappointed," she added as she moved over to sit in Mama's chair, next to me. "It's a rather well-known poem, Pilar."

"Sorry, Miss Patricia."

"You've read, what? Nearly forty-four books in the last two months? And you go and do this?"

I started to cry. Looking down at my hand. I'd done it to help her. So that she'd be proud that her student could write something good. "Pilar, don't. Don't cry. Just tell me what's going on?" But I couldn't. I couldn't explain *Make your life be the way you want it to be.* 'Cause I'd done it all wrong.

Here was the Fall that came because of my Pride.

She let me calm down and gave me a tissue to wipe my nose. "Hon, your life is—a gift—a gift waiting to be unwrapped. The only question is, will you find a thief and a liar inside, or a damn fine writer? That's what this is all about."

We finished the conference and Miss Givens asked if I needed a ride home. I told her, "No. I'd rather walk."

"No, Pilar," she said. "It's getting too dark for that." And she walked me out to her car for the drive home. But we were surprised 'cause 'Lise and Mama were still there, the motor running. Waiting for me.

"Are you okay?" 'Lise asked on the drive home. She tried putting her hand on Mama's thigh. Mama brushed it off and reached for the radio, switching it to a Spanish station.

"I left my cigarettes at work. My youngest daughter is someone I'll never understand. *And*, that doesn't seem to be a problem for her. I was just lectured to by a fresh-faced twenty-three-year-old lezzie, probably right out of the Peace Corps. I'm in love with the wrong person—maybe even on my way to hell for it. So you tell me how okay I'm supposed to be, Alice."

Nobody talked the rest of the way home.

Sifting for Seashells

ONE DAY 'LISE brought over a card for Mama to sign. And a week later a checkbook with Mama's and her names in it. It was just Mama and me at home. She called it a Joint Account, explaining if one of them wrote a check it had to have both of their names signed on it.

"It'll all be your money, Rennie; I'm just on it so we could open it at the bank, that's all," she promised. 'Lise stopped and asked, "Should we wait for Justine?"

But Mama shook her head, "What for?" She tapped my arm, "She'll do." So she let me stay at the table and listen while 'Lise went on explaining it all.

ALL MAMA SAID was, "The next Big Step," as she nodded and nodded at all the rest of the rules. I listened really hard, and memorized what 'Lise was saying about carrying the balance forward and adding in the fees the bank would charge. I snuck in simple questions that I felt Mama might be embarrassed to ask for herself. It was easy for me to ask; I was supposed to be just a kid.

Mama said, "What if I screw this up?"

And 'Lise asked, "How could you possibly do that?"

BY 6 A.M. Justine and I figured Mama had spent the night out with someone because she hadn't been home to get ready for her morning shift. When she went to the Market, she usually stopped home first to change her work clothes at least. If she was out with someone, she'd probably not left work alone.

So Justine called a no-school day for us and that's why we were all home.

It was my first absence from Junior High school. I hoped Mama'd be home after 3 p.m. and not go back out somewhere because I needed to go over the checkbook and the bills; I didn't want to be like Justine, leaving things to Mama alone, to deal with in all this confusion.

Even if Justine did seem to want just that.

Also Justine was pretty mad about me writing a note for her the week before, when she'd wanted to get out of gym. She'd gotten me up so early, I was grumpy. I thought she'd come back and have me fix it. And it wasn't until they sent her to the office and the girl's principal showed her the note and she read: *Please excuse Justine from gym today – she feels like shit.* That she saw what I'd done. I'd signed it with Mama's name. And Justine really got it for that. There was yelling for days.

THAT MORNING I spent two boring hours in the sun, waiting on our porch with Justine for her paycheck; the mailman was late coming down our block.

Justine was saying, "I can't ask Mama to help move my things out when I go, so Lydia's brother says he'll come by with his van. And I've got two-hundred-and-nine dollars saved so far, and in the time left to go, I'll make it maybe a round three hundred by the time I need it." We were talking so I guess she'd forgiven me about the note.

But my mind wasn't on her list of what she'd do. I was thinking about the floors in the hall and laundry room. Hoping the puppy's wee-wee would be on the papers only, 'cause we were out of cleanser. Once Justine wasn't giving Mama any more money for living here, there'd be even less to buy more cleaning stuff.

"The only things I'm taking when I'm ready to leave is my suitcase of winter clothes and that bowling bag Mom's boyfriend left in the closet." Justine never said Roy's name except by accident. "Don't tell her, but I'm gonna stuff that with shampoo and make-up and her other face junk."

Justine was planning on stealing stuff from our house, and she didn't mind letting me be the one to know about it. For a second, I was nearly glad about the trouble with the gym note. Glad she'd be gone soon. Worrying, thinking how I'd keep things going once she'd run away from us.

I could see that was a sin, thinking like that, but this was too much pressure.

In the laundry room, with the puppy yapping and stepping right into what I was trying to clean up, the more I thought about things the more I had to force myself to just admit that Justine didn't need this either. Hearing her rattle off all her new plans on the porch, I saw I needed to let go and let her get gone without me being mad.

So she'd be freer to go.

She'd found it, the third envelope in the stack, under a second notice bill, two Book-of-the-Month flyers, and a

Sears bill addressed to one of Mama's last names. She'd called me out onto the porch as the mailman walked back to the curb and on to the next house. Justine saw her pay stub and squealed.

"My first raise check from Mr. Solis! I worked eighteen extra hours last month and he said this October he'd do a little something nice." She stared at the check, "Wow."

It must have been real fine, for the first time ever, to see a check made payable to your name alone, one with a raise or overtime must be even better. I was kind of jealous, in a way.

I looked around our yard and then up the street toward the Market. And thought when Mama came home she'd probably take awhile to notice the mail, and my house cleaning.

Maybe a little longer to notice and tell Chance that the puppy needed walking.

First I wished she and Justine were at least talking. Then I wished the same for her and 'Lise.

Then I tried not to think about it.

"After Lydia's, that's just temporary, till I have money to pay a landlady for a room somewheres." I picked at a scab on my knee, as Justine kept on, "I'm gonna ask to use her phone book. I'm gonna look up thrift stores, for one that takes layaways and delivers. And pet stores, for a kitty."

"A kitty, that's so cool," I said, smiling, trying to let all the worry float away, about if Mama just flopped into the sofa bed again, it might be days till she found out we needed more cleanser. "They use a cat box. Lots easier, huh."

SATURDAY NIGHT, IT was pouring rain outside the window, and I was sitting on Mama's sofa bed, up in the corner, against the sofa back and the arm, so that my back was against two solid things. I was thinking about school Monday and how I was gonna sneak two cans of tuna into Chance's lunch bag. I'd promised them for Chance's Thanksgiving collection. And tomorrow was my last chance to get them for him to hand them in.

I listened to Mama in the bathroom, washing off her date makeup. Mama was talking, but I couldn't separate her voice from the water running. I'd decided to stay awake and put the tuna into Chance's bag tonight, after Mama went to sleep. So there wouldn't be a morning fight. I listened again to Mama's muddled voice and raised my own, calling out "What?" just as the water turned off.

She came to the living room though Justine's bedroom doorway, with a shiny scrubbed forehead and her hair twisted in a towel-turban. Wearing the pale rose chenille robe and smelling like a lot of drinks. "I said it's nearly past two, you shouldn't be staying up."

"It's okay, I'm just up, not staying up."

"Still," Mama bent over, rubbing her hair in the towel.

I faked it, "Maybe it's cramps? After you went, I fell asleep here on the sofa. I'm all slept out." Mama looked up from drying her hair, skeptical, so I added, "Does Midol keep you awake?"

As she straightened to take the towel from her hair, a wave of rumpled jet black fell in her face and down around her shoulders. She shook her head, like she was just stepping onto shore somewhere, a Gal Friday I was just finding. "So, What?—You're all slept out now?"

I reached out and turned down her blanket for her. "Yeah, something like that."

"Thinking of a story?"

"No. I have to rewrite a poem I turned in for English a while ago. Now, it's like, for extra credit, kind of."

She dropped the towel on the chair next to the TV and crawled onto the sofa bed. "Well, if you're gonna write trade places with me and turn on the lamp. I can't sleep with the big light on."

I grinned as she scooted over on her bed. We all knew Mama could and had slept on trains, buses, school plays; she'd told us stories of how she'd fallen asleep at our Gra'ma's on weekends, right in the middle of loud family fights. Once I when I was a tiny kid I remembered her fast asleep as she waited at the Welfare office.

But all the same, I crawled out of my corner of her sofa bed to turn out the overhead light. In the span of darkness before I flipped on the small sofa lamp Mama's husky voice quoted, "No light, but rather darkness visible."

"Is that the beginning of a poem?"

Mama thought a moment, yawned, her eyes up to the darkened ceiling.

"Mama?"

"It's from Milton, I think. Paradise something."

I'd slipped back into the corner, sitting. Now Mama slid over and laid her head in my lap.

I let my fingers sink into her hair, "Remember when I dropped all that milk, back on Hockett Street?"

"You did?" she yawned.

"Uh-huh, and you came and picked me up. I cried and you held me on your lap. You kept saying, *No estoy enojada.*

It's okay'."

"I did?"

I pictured Mama's unruly curls as wet sand I was sifting through, for seashells. Like that time at Leo Carillo State Beach.

"Night Mama."

"Night," she answered, "Sweet dreams, sooner or later."

I sat back and thought about the day I'd be gone, too. And wondered if 'Lise would end up being the one who looked after Mama, staying no matter what she did to her.

THAT NOVEMBER MR. Delgado called Mama to ask about inviting me to spend a weekend with Joanna. We had only seen each other on weekends since school started. Sometimes weeks had gone by without seeing each other at all. She'd gotten even taller. Now she was wearing her hair different.

"Because I'm in Eighth, my mother lets me iron it," she told me. And I laughed so much to hear that, I thought milk would come out of my nose, but she was staring me down with those serious eyes, daring me to laugh again, so I just bit into one of her mother's cookies, and said, "Yeah?"

But with her dad it was different. Not that he did something more normal with his hair, but our conversation went smoother. It was easy to tell him about Justine and the gym note and what a mess I'd made with Miss Givens. My stealing the poem from the book.

And that's when I really stopped feeling bad about myself in a whole new way. Like I was confessing to him. Or maybe it was like I was recognizing myself and describing me to someone who finally understood what I was seeing.

At last. I smiled at him and tapped my chest, then said, "Reading between the lines."

"Yes, it takes some of us quite a while to do that—it looks like you have a gift for it."

I asked, "Is this day part of the Quest? The day where I put the last of puzzle together?"

He smiled and ruffled my curls; I never let it grow past my ears now. It was like a badge for me to keep it short.

"Next year you'll be twelve. No one moves backwards in age you know, hon. Twelve's just three years away from Emancipation. If you hold on, anything will be possible. Can you promise me you'll try? Hold on as tight as you possibly can?"

I felt real hearing that. "For Me? For Joanna?" he asked, "She'd hate to lose a real friend like you to a neighborhood like this. I would, too."

I asked him, "There are things out in the real world that I can learn every day of my life, aren't there?"

"If that's want you want."

"And being real's going out and getting what you want. No waiting for what you deserve, right? For making the choice to get what you need? For never saying 'this will do, I don't need anything more?'"

"That about sums it up, hon."

I thought a second more, then asked, "If I wanted to I could go find where Artie was? I could be friends with Justine after she leaves? They wouldn't have to be gone forever?" He nodded again.

I sat back in my chair. "I think I get it."

BECCA CAME OVER with her mom and 'Lise asked us all to come sit down at the dining room table because she had something to say to all us kids. We counted all around, then had to bring an extra chair in from the kitchen. But then neither Mama nor 'Lise would sit down.

Mama stood holding her cigarette and coffee cup like she did that time she let us know we'd have to move. I looked at Justine and started throwing up prayers like a plate juggler on TV. Wondering if we all had our dimes still.

We all sat and watched them do the *You wanna go first?* and *Well, no, you go.*

So I put my elbows on the table and piped in with, "After you, Alphonse." And that kicked things in the rear, 'cause 'Lise stopped moving around the room like some nervous bird and said, "Right."

Mama looked over and warned her, "You'd be giving up something more this Lent than ever before, 'Lise." But 'Lise started talking anyway.

"Your Mom and I think it'll be a good idea if the two of us, with all you kids, moved into a better neighborhood, in a house big enough for all of us. Bigger. Together." She smiled at Becca, "Maybe with a nice yard."

"Living together like sisters?" Becca asked. And her mom smoothed her hair and nodded, *yeah.*

"Maybe in a month or two, but before Easter for sure."

Justine sat back and crossed her arms, asking Mama, "What'd you think?"

But Mama ignored her. Becca's mom said, "Alhambra's nice."

"That's ninety blocks away."

Mama, looked at me. "Is it?"

But Justine still wouldn't let it go. "Well, Mama?"

Mama tried not to get too smiley, but we saw it. She was

gonna joke in that love voice, the backwards one. She spread her hands. "Well…. It's half the rent."

JUSTINE JUST GOT up and walked away from us. So we were back to five again, around the table, just a new five. Although I wasn't, it felt like I was the oldest now. So I did what I could right then: I just breathed.

FEBRUARY. MOVING DAY. And at catechism Father Rudolph was saying, "In these past two months we've covered the last two stations, which will always be the most important ones: Jesus was Buried, and Jesus has Risen." Then he snuck up behind Richard, who was whispering, and thumped him on the head. "And because some of you birds are in need of a little spiritual reinforcement, we will now all recite the Apostle's Creed before we leave today. Twice."

The class grumbled but started in with a droned, "I believe in God, the Father Almighty, creator of heaven and earth—"

I studied my palm, with the little hole Mama had made, and the big promise still there in the lines Mr. St. John gave me; my quest.

Maybe Father Rudolph had it wrong. About the spiritual reinforcement being in prayers we memorize. Maybe getting buried and rising was happening now. In me. Not just a long time ago to Jesus.

The things about me being a thief and a liar or a writer, like Miss Patricia talked about, well, that was for me to choose, not the Gods.

I'd have to pick.

Like 'Lise had said: I could be like Mama or be like me

or even maybe something of both. I just needed to make a choice.

I thought: *If God doesn't have a sense of humor I'll probably roast in hell*, but I knew for sure, with Justine going soon, I'd be doing it mostly unnoticed, on my own. It was my Quest after all.

So when our second prayer came around again, I chose. And then said it, right out loud, *"I believe in me. I will be Pilar, creator of heavens and earths."*